Proper ENGLISH

D1592750

KJ CHARLES

Published by KJC Books
Copyright © 2019 by KJ Charles

Edited by Veronica Vega
Cover by Lexiconic Design
Interior design by eB Format

ISBN: 978-1-912688-11-1

For Talia Hibbert, in lieu of a fruit basket

AUTHOR'S NOTE

This book takes place two years before the events of
Think of England.

In British English the ground floor is at street level,
and the first floor is the next one up.

CHAPTER ONE

Skirmidge House
Stoke St. Milborough
28 August 1902

*D*ear Louisa
Thanks so much for your last. I'm sorry it's taken me so long to reply, but we have been at sixes and sevens with Jonty's wedding for the last two months. You won't be surprised to hear that he took next to no part in the preparations and saw no reason why it should cause him any inconvenience. Brothers are wonderful creatures.

Thanks also for your congratulations on the Championship. Modesty aside, I am pleased with myself even now, and the trophy sits well-polished on my mantel.

It won't be mine for long (the mantel, not the trophy) as I have concluded it is best to set up my own household now that Jonty is married, and I will thus be leaving home. It is rather a wrench, but needs must. I am not quite sure of where I shall settle as yet, but letters to Skirmidge House will find me, once Jonty troubles to forward them.

I have a treat in store first. Do you recall Jimmy Yoxall—the Hon. James, Lord Witton's son? I shall be making one of a shooting party at his family place up in Northumberland for the start of the partridge season. It is to be a very small party: only the Wittons, myself and Bill,

KJ CHARLES

and another friend of Jimmy's. Needless to say, I attend as a gun rather than a lady: you know my views on the practice of leaving women at shooting parties to kick their heels, read novels, and organise jumble sales, but Jimmy is an old friend who respects marksmanship. A few weeks in the fresh air will do me a power of good.

Your sister's teaching work is admirable. Do send her my love and congratulations. I'm so glad that all is well for you and Hugo, and the house sounds beautiful. I must catch the last post now, as I leave for Rodington Court tomorrow. I shall write again from there, and send you both a brace of partridge.

Yours ever,
Pat

Rodington Court, family seat of the earls of Witton, was a very long slog from Stoke St. Milborough. The journey involved several changes of train, a considerable inconvenience since Pat was travelling without a maid or companion for the first part of it, and she wasn't able to sit back and relax until she found herself on the train to Manchester, where she would meet Bill.

She was looking forward to the shooting party intensely, in part because she was, unusually for her, tired. The last couple of months had been consumed with preparations for her oldest brother's wedding, putting the family home in order for his new bride, and working out what she might do with herself when she left. She was annoyingly indecisive about the last of those, which was not her usual state, and she didn't like it. Her path had always been clear in life before, because there had always been responsibilities, duties, tasks to be done, but that was all the new Mrs. Merton's now.

Pat tried not to resent it. Naturally a spinster sister would be uprooted by her brother's marriage. Their childhood home was Jonty's house, not Pat's, for all that she had been its mistress since leaving school, and she could well imagine how uncomfortable it would be for Olivia to have her there, telling her she was doing it all wrong. That was inevitable, since Olivia was without question more decorative than practical. If Pat stayed, she would continue running Skirmidge House, and either she would resent Olivia for treating her as an upper servant, or Olivia would resent her for usurping her rights as head of the household, or both. It was far better that she should leave now while there was still goodwill on all sides.

It was, perhaps, a little hard to find herself in need of a new home and occupation, and that she had to leave the village where she'd spent all her life with nowhere to go and nothing to do. Then again, perhaps her discomfort was a sign that she was overdue a change.

She'd been doing the same thing for too long, that was the problem. If one had enough to do, one could carry on doing it indefinitely without looking up from one's tasks to take a wider view. She'd fallen into that trap, bustling around without ever asking herself what would happen if Jonty married, and now she found herself on an endless plain, with no obvious path in any direction.

She'd find a purpose, of course, with time and application, and she was far from desperate. She had inherited a reasonable sum on their father's death which her brother Bill had invested shrewdly on her behalf. It was a competence rather than a fortune, but if she found a situation as a lady's companion, for example, she would do very well indeed.

Unfortunately, she wasn't terribly well suited to companionship. Pat was neither temperamentally inclined nor trained for most of the occupations that the world presumed women of her class to enjoy: she lacked understanding of fashion, had no perceptible musical or artistic gifts, couldn't make light conversation, felt no interest in the opposite sex, didn't see the point of charity visiting unless it led to swift and meaningful change, and was strongly of the opinion embroidery was

3

best done by those who enjoyed it. It made her an uncomfortable match for those who preferred drawing-rooms to ten-mile walks.

She was, however, an excellent household manager, able to turn her hand to most tasks, and a superb shot—the All-England Ladies' Champion, in fact, as testified by the trophy on her mantelpiece—so all she needed was to find a countrywoman of her own stamp who required a companion and preferred sporting pursuits to social ones. That would be entirely possible. It was just a matter of meeting the right woman. Maybe she could advertise.

But first, she realised as the train pulled into Manchester station, she had to meet Bill. She'd been so preoccupied by her thoughts that she hadn't noticed the passage of minutes or miles.

A porter took her luggage, while Pat attended to her own gun-cases. Bill, who had come up from London, met her on the platform for their next train, and greeted her with a cheery wave, but there was no time to speak in the bustle of supervising the transfer of luggage from one baggage car to another and finding their seats amid the chaos and smoke of the station. Once they were ensconced in the carriage, pleasantly free of other travellers, the train moved off, and Bill sat back with a sigh, fanning himself with his hat against the late August heat.

Pat took the opportunity to look him over. He'd seemed off-colour at Jonty's wedding, hollow-eyed and tight-lipped, withdrawing into silence whenever his attention wasn't demanded. She feared he was overworked. He'd unquestionably been the brightest of her four brothers, taking a First at Cambridge then moving to London to pursue a career in some Whitehall department; she hadn't seen him much since. He came home to Stoke St. Milborough for brief visits at Christmas and gave her lunch when she made her infrequent trips to London for competitions, but this shooting party would be her longest period with him since he'd left university eight years ago.

"How are you?" she asked.

"Oh, very well. You?"

"You look exhausted," Pat said, not bothering with the niceties. "Has work been busy? Or have you been hitting the night-spots?"

"Two-stepping till dawn? No, sadly, it's the former. We've had rather a time of it at the Bureau. I've been burning the midnight oil for weeks."

"Any particular reason?"

"This and that. A tangle which has not become any less tangled through my efforts. I shan't bore you with the details."

"It's a good thing you could get away."

"It was that or a nerve-storm," Bill said, with an effort at cheerfulness that didn't ring true. "I was done in. Three weeks in the fresh air will set me right and with any luck someone else will have unpicked the whole business by the time I get back."

"Here's hoping," Pat said. "So what are you up to other than work?"

"I suppose that's some sort of joke."

"Really, though. You live in London. There must be..." She waved a hand to indicate the delights of the metropolis.

"There's plenty of..." He mimicked the wave. "But I'm not doing any of it. Well, except for helping out in the club—the Hackney Young Men's, it's a gymnasium for poor youth. The aim is to bring them in with boxing and then, when we have them trapped, inflict a spot of literacy on the blighters."

Pat had no trouble interpreting this description of education work. Bill had boxed for his college, and was a skilled and patient teacher with a strong moral streak. They'd all thought he might go into the Church. "Is that a Christian organisation?"

"Non-denominational. We bar preaching and politics. It prevents arguments, and means Jews and Indians come along too, which is important in those parts. And in my view, we're all better off when people have the tools to think for themselves."

"You're all right, Bill," Pat remarked. "I must say, I'd like to do something of that sort."

"Well, I don't think you should learn to box, but I'll happily teach you to read."

"Oh, shut up. I meant to do something useful. I'm uncertain how I'll spend my time when I move out."

"Mph. You're set on leaving?"

"I must. Olivia won't stand on her own feet if I'm treading on her toes, and I'll unquestionably do that. I can't bear watching things done badly."

"At least you know yourself," Bill said. "Are you sure she'll shoulder the load under any circumstances? I struggle to see her as mistress of Skirmidge House, what with the rats and the plumbing. Do you think Jonty's told her about the plumbing?"

"Of course not: she turned up at the altar. I'm sure she'll take charge if I'm not there to do it for her. The question is whether she'll force Jonty to triple the staff and pay for new pipework, or simply move him to London. I wouldn't underestimate her will."

"I wouldn't underestimate Jonty's idleness, but it may be a case of an irresistible force and an immovable object. You're probably best off leaving them to it, I agree. Where are you going to live?"

Pat made a face. "I don't yet know. I'm unsure whether I want a small place of my own or to find someone to share with. I'm going to stay with my old governess—remember Miss Adler?—for a few weeks after the shooting, as a sort of experiment in living with people."

"Isn't Jonty people?"

"Barely."

"Fair," Bill agreed. "It'll be something of a change for you."

"Can't be helped."

Bill looked sympathetic, but didn't press the topic. "Any candidates for companionship?"

"Nothing as yet. I haven't looked awfully hard." She hesitated, then decided to say it. "The other thing is, I was toying with the idea of setting up a shooting school for ladies."

"I say!"

"It's just a thought. You needn't mention it to anyone."

Bill gave her a reproachful look. Alone among her brothers, he had never turned a private confidence into a matter for public ridicule. "Of course not. That *is* a thought. Do you have the funds to set things up, or will you need a loan?"

"I haven't done the sums yet. And it depends on where I might settle."

"Well, call on me if you need a hand. You'd definitely need to be somewhere a bit more central than Stoke St. Milborough. Er, are you thinking of moving to London?"

"Absolutely not," Pat assured him, and noted the tiny relaxation on his face. If she had been metropolis-minded, everyone would have expected her to set up household with her bachelor brother. Bill was sufficiently laconic for her liking, never interfered, and wouldn't expect to be looked after, but sharing his life and affairs with a sibling evidently appealed to him as little as London did to Pat. He had always been reserved to a fault about personal matters. "I'd need somewhere reasonably close to a city, but still with a bit of wildness to it."

"You're an outdoor soul," Bill agreed. "You really ought to marry some landowner with a tumbledown house and acres of land that don't pay. You could spend half the year managing his estate back to health, and the other half striding the moors with a rifle."

That sounded perfect, apart from the marriage. "I think most landowners in that state would rather have an heiress."

"Jimmy certainly would," Bill said, then caught himself. "Sorry. That wasn't charitable."

"Yes, I heard he was engaged. One of those whirlwind affairs, wasn't it? Olivia said his fiancée is a daughter of industry."

"She certainly is. I suppose that sort of fortune covers a multitude of sins."

"Does it need to?"

"Well, she has two broken engagements to her name," Bill said. "And something of a reputation as a jilt, accordingly."

"Goodness. That doesn't sound awfully like Jimmy's sort of girl."

Bill made a face. "The Wittons have fallen on hard times what with one thing and another, and Carruth, the father, is very well off. Self-made man, Birmingham clerk, invented some sort of telephone-exchange device and got himself a fortune and a knighthood to go with it. One might not call it the best match for an earldom that dates back to the Normans, but I suppose if it wasn't an industrialist it would be an American. The estate will doubtless do very well out of it, assuming Jimmy gets the girl to the altar this time around."

Pat frowned. "The Wittons can't be so hard up that they'd marry him off to any old heiress for ready cash."

"They really are in a bit of a hole. I'm afraid the Earl was dabbling in finance, which went as well as you might expect considering he has no more brains than Jimmy."

"Oh dear."

"Quite. Miss Carruth must have seemed a godsend, and you know Jimmy: he hits on an idea and then thunders along like a juggernaut instead of giving the slightest thought— Anyway, it's not my business. For all I know, she may be as delightful as she is rich. I hope they'll be very happy."

"Will Miss Carruth be at the party?" Pat asked.

"No, it's just you, me, Jimmy, and Preston Keynes. I don't recall if you've met him? Good sportsman."

"Thank goodness for that. These sorts of things are miserable for ladies."

"Technically, you're a lady," Bill pointed out.

"Not for the purposes of a shooting party I'm not, and Jimmy had better remember that."

"He will," Bill assured her. "Nobody would invite the All-England Ladies' Champion to a shooting party and ask her to crochet doilies."

"Oh yes they would."

"Well, Jimmy has more sense than that, at least," Bill said, though he didn't sound wholly convinced.

CHAPTER TWO

Stonebridge station, where they alighted for Rodington Court, was a tiny place, no more than a pair of platforms and a shed. It was four o'clock when they reached it, but the sunlight was noon-bright, the air clear and fresh except for the railway smoke. Bill and the single porter between them got the bags to the front of the station, where a man in shabby tweeds stood waiting with a sooty contraption Pat identified as a Daimler.

"Jimmy!" Bill called.

The Honourable James Yoxall raised a hand in greeting. "Bill!" He came over, smiling at Pat. "And the champion herself. Hello, old thing. Belated congratulations on your triumph." He shook hands with Bill, and they all spent a couple of moments in mutual assurances that they looked well and the weather was good. It felt oddly awkward, considering that the two men were friends of long standing. She hoped Bill hadn't disapproved too obviously of Jimmy's forthcoming marriage. That would put anyone's back up.

Pat had once wondered, in an academic sort of way, if she and Jimmy might make a match of it. Jimmy was a countryman who she'd assumed would want a solid, sensible wife. He'd never been known as a womaniser, they rubbed along very happily, and she would have loved to run an estate up here, in partridge country. It had seemed to her the perfect basis for marriage: a friendship combined with a job opening.

The idea hadn't struck Jimmy, which caused Pat slight regret but no heartache. She hoped he'd be happy with his choice, and that his motivations were more than financial despite Bill's gloomy outlook. He might well have fallen head over heels in love with his flighty heiress: one could never predict the human heart. After all, they lived in a world where a sane woman had voluntarily chosen to marry Jonty.

"Right, well, shall we go? You two are the last to arrive and I'm jolly glad to see you. Hop in the bus. Pat?" Jimmy opened the passenger door for her.

"No, no, you two catch up," she said, gesturing Bill to take the front seat.

"No, no," both men said together. Pat rolled her eyes at the display of chivalry, and opened the door of the back seat for herself. Bill shrugged and took his seat by Jimmy, and the car moved off.

Pat looked around at the landscape as they drove, letting herself soak up the atmosphere. They'd clearly had the same dry, cold summer up here as down in Shropshire; the vegetation around was sparse but not scorched. It would be good shooting weather if it held, and she felt a tickle of anticipation. Tomorrow was the thirty-first so there would be a day free before the season began; she wondered if Jimmy would give her a lesson in the motor-car. Jonty hadn't yet bought one so she hadn't had a chance to get behind a wheel, and was itching to try. Thank goodness this was a Scots-style party, with no nonsense about socialising.

"I'm sorry, *what?*" Bill demanded from the front seat, loud enough for her to hear over the wind and engine noise. "What do you mean, she's here?"

"She's my fiancée, dammit. She said she wanted to come. I could hardly refuse."

"So you'll be dancing attendance on her for the duration," Bill said, with clear resentment. "Fine."

Pat turned to look out over the moorland again, angling her head so the wind prevented her from overhearing anything more. She wasn't happy to hear Bill being like this. His disappointment was understandable if he had been looking forward to a dedicated shooting holiday, but one had to respect the sanctity of marriage, it was Jimmy's affair, and mostly, she would prefer Bill met Miss Carruth before coming to conclusions about her. This wasn't worthy of the brother she respected. Maybe she ought to take his airy remarks about a nerve-storm seriously; he sounded as though he were fraying around the edges.

A forty-minute drive brought them to Rodington Court. This was a large, aggressively defensive sixteenth-century building in solid yellow-tinted stone, squat and square. It was clearly built to protect against marauding Scots, the weather, or both. Jimmy brought the car up the drive with panache, and leapt out to open the door for Pat. "It's almost six. Come on in. I'll show you around the grounds tomorrow once you're settled."

Pat stood for a moment, absorbing her surroundings. Rodington Court stood on high ground, and the land stretched grey-green-gold around them, empty for miles barring shepherds' huts and the odd stone fence, rising to faint mountains in the distance. "It's lovely here."

"It is, isn't it." Jimmy was at her shoulder. "Come on, old thing, no roaming off into the blue yonder quite yet. It's not long till dinner."

The house was dark inside, its thick walls pierced by narrow and insufficient windows. They'd conserve heat in winter, no doubt, but the effect in high summer was rather gloomy. Pat was allotted a bedroom along a first-floor corridor in the West Wing.

"We're all in the West Wing," Jimmy explained as he escorted her there, carrying her case. Evidently the footmen were busy. "Easier for the staff if they don't have to run all over the house. If I had my way we'd shut the East Wing altogether, but there. Ladies and family are on the first floor, gentlemen on the second."

"Ladies?" Pat asked. "Your fiancée?"

"And the rest." Jimmy rolled his eyes. "We've an absolute houseful. My sister and her husband have come for the summer, bringing a guest, Mother's goddaughter has extended her stay, and yes, my fiancée is here. It's like Piccadilly Circus."

That was deeply unwelcome news. Pat would have thought twice about accepting the invitation if she'd known it would involve intimacy with so many strangers, and the presence of other ladies might make it awkward for her to be a gun. Not that she cared particularly, but open disapproval would make everyone else uncomfortable. "The more the merrier?" she offered, trying to hide her disappointment.

"I dare say." Jimmy didn't sound enthusiastic himself. "Here's your room. There will be a maid up in a moment. We're a little short-handed what with five unexpected people, so my apologies for that."

"I could send for someone from home, if you need?"

"Not at all. We'll manage."

Her allotted bedroom was panelled in old wood, dark and heavy, with a carved bedframe. Light was flooding in through the small window now, but it would be gloomy in the mornings. There wasn't even a gas-mantel, merely candlesticks and an oil lamp. No doubt bringing gas up here would be prohibitively expensive. Perhaps they could go straight to electricity, if Miss Carruth's father was generous enough.

As promised, a maid knocked at the door after a few moments, bringing hot water and offering help with dressing. Pat didn't need much assistance: she had no intention of lacing herself into an S-shaped silhouette with a pigeon-chest, her waist squeezed to nothing, and her bottom jutting out in the name of health. Her evening gowns were not fashionably low-cut, since she had no glittering jewels to display, and not a great deal of bosom to display them on. She put on her mother's turquoise necklace with a simple blue-grey gown that the maid clearly found disappointing, allowed the enthusiastic girl to pin her hair into loops, and went downstairs as a huge clock boomed seven.

The drawing-room was an improvement on the hall in terms of light, offering a good-sized window with a view across the landscape. Bill was already there, talking to an attractive Indian woman. She had black hair and dark brown eyes, and wore a striking dark red gown with a necklace that looked like amber across a modest décolletage.

"Ah, Pat," Bill said. "Miss Singh, please let me introduce my sister, Patricia Merton. Pat, Miss Singh, Lady Witton's god-daughter."

They exchanged the usual politenesses. Miss Singh had an oval face, strong features, and marks on her nose that suggested a spectacle-wearer.

"Are you come up from London?" Pat asked.

"Yes, I live in Knightsbridge. And you?"

"Outside Ludlow, quite in the countryside."

They made conversation about that. Miss Singh was somewhat abrupt in her answers, in the way shy people often were, but seemed pleasant enough in their brief chat until the next pair entered: a tall man in his late thirties with sleek chestnut hair and a well-clipped moustache, and a very thin woman with fair hair and prominent facial bones, tightly corseted in the most fashionable style. They were introduced as Lady Anna Haworth, Jimmy's sister, and her husband, Mr. Maurice Haworth. The latter greeted the other guests with great bonhomie, including Pat.

"Ah, Miss Merton, the lady shooter! Do I understand you'll be making one of the guns on Monday?"

"I will, yes."

"You shoot?" Miss Singh asked, sounding startled.

"Pat is the All-England Ladies' Champion," Bill said. "That's target shooting, of course."

"As the competition demands," Pat put in for avoidance of doubt. "I'm here for partridge."

"You'll be shooting to kill?" Mr. Haworth asked.

"That...is the idea, yes."

"I ask because some ladies have a horror of the sight of blood," the gentleman observed. "Poor little bunny rabbits, you know, poor persecuted foxes."

"I'm not squeamish."

"I must say, that shows rare nerve for a lady," Mr. Haworth replied with a smile. "Anna never picks up a gun; she prefers to hunt other game. And you, Miss Singh? Are you an aspiring shot? Tigers back home, perhaps?"

"I don't kill animals, for sport or any other reason," Miss Singh said, voice tight. "I am a member of the Society for Prevention of Cruelty to Animals."

Oh Lord, a fanatic. Pat cast about for something to say, but Mr. Haworth got in first. "So you oppose hunting. How very interesting. Is that on religious grounds?"

"It is a moral stance based on my views of how animals should be treated."

"But your convictions nevertheless allow you to attend a shooting party?" Mr. Haworth raised a brow. "How very flexible."

"I should hope we can visit one another without sharing every one of our beliefs with our hosts," Bill said. "Look, here's Preston."

Maurice Haworth's mouth tightened slightly, but he turned with the rest of them to greet the two men who entered. The elder, who looked to be in his early thirties, was impeccably dressed and strikingly good-looking; the younger was a rugged sort with a face that suggested he'd done a lot of boxing and mostly lost. They were introduced as Jack Bouvier-Lynes, the handsome one, who kissed each lady's hand with great style, and Preston Keynes, the pleasantly ugly one, who offered inarticulate but enthusiastic congratulations on Pat's sporting triumph.

"Marvellous stuff, awfully good. Heard all about you. Looking forward to seeing you handle a gun, if I may say so."

"Thanks," Pat said. "What do you shoot for partridge?"

That topic, about which any shooter could talk for days, instantly removed all constraint. She and Mr. Keynes talked animatedly for several minutes about Holland and Holland shotguns, Farquharson sporting rifles, and the best ammunition to use in each. Around them Mr. Bouvier-Lynes and Mr. Haworth stood with Lady Anna, while Bill chatted to Miss Singh, and the odd feeling of tension in the room ebbed away. Pat was just in the middle of describing a particularly tricky shot with which she'd taken a rocketing pheasant last season when the sound of approaching feet echoed on stone, and the final members of the party entered.

The Earl and Countess of Witton were a pleasant if not greatly distinguished pair, he an elderly man with a slightly harried look and an expansive moustache, she a comfortably-built woman in her late fifties. Jimmy was with them, looking as if he'd been squeezed into his evening dress, and on his arm was the loveliest girl Pat had ever seen.

Miss Fenella Carruth was irresistible. She had brown hair that the candlelight picked out in glints of copper, bronze, and gold, and big sparkling pansy-brown eyes in a heart-shaped face made for laughter. She wore a gown that even Pat could tell was desperately fashionable and which had obviously been tailored to display a delightfully plump figure to its best advantage without squeezing her into a wasp waist, a task to which no whalebone could have been equal. The gown, of a soft pink, was adorned with a profusion of bows and lace that would have looked absurd on Pat and suited Miss Carruth to perfection. She had plenty of bosom on display, and plenty of jewellery on it, a three-stringed necklace of rose-coloured stones that glittered over her fair skin. Her hair was beautifully dressed in artful ringlets, her rounded arms were adorned by bracelets; she looked like the kind of woman that angular, plain Pat could never have been, and had never particularly wanted to be. She'd never aspired to turn heads; she truly didn't think she was jealous of those who did.

But oh, she ached at the sight of Fenella Carruth, lovely in the candlelight.

Pat evidently wasn't the only one struck. Mr. Keynes' ears had gone red and his gaze was fixed on Miss Carruth's bosom. Bill's face was set. Mr. Haworth was smiling, not entirely pleasantly, and so was Mr. Bouvier-Lynes with open admiration, and Pat saw Lady Anna's nostrils flare slightly as she looked from one to the other.

Miss Carruth didn't seem to notice being the cynosure of all eyes, or perhaps she was used to it. She dimpled as the various introductions were made, and hung on Jimmy's arm looking delightfully happy to be there. That was marvellous because Jimmy deserved a laughing young lady with sparkling brown eyes and glorious curves. Pat was thrilled for them both.

She said as much when she was introduced to Miss Carruth, who gave a little trill of excitement. "Mr. Merton's sister? How wonderful! Jimmy's talked so much about you both, I feel as though I know you already. Jimmy went to university with your brother, didn't he? And he tells me that you're a champion shot!" She looked around to Jimmy for confirmation, and seemed slightly startled to realised he'd slipped away to speak to Bill.

"That's right. I won a competition."

"And you'll really be shooting with the men on Monday?" Miss Carruth's eyes rounded dramatically.

"Yes. That's why I'm here. For shooting. I like it." Pat felt ludicrously wooden next to this bundle of excitability.

"But isn't it terribly loud? All the bangs, and walking for miles, and the mud—not that you need to worry about mud in this weather of course—but the poor *birds*. To think of those treetops full of empty nests, the babies cheeping for their mothers—"

"Partridges nest on the ground," Pat felt compelled to observe. "And it's illegal to shoot in breeding season. And the chicks leave the nest within hours of hatching anyway."

"Oh. Oh, well, that's better, isn't it?"

"Uh, probably." Miss Carruth seemed to have a great deal of enthusiasm, but less behind the sparkling eyes than one might have hoped. Pat, who liked silence, couldn't help a sinking feeling at the idea of three weeks of social fluttering. "If you're asking about the morality of shooting animals, Miss Singh might be the right woman for the conversation. I'm very happy to hunt, and to eat what I kill."

"Oh, I adore partridge," Miss Carruth assured her. "Daddy's cook does the breasts with a delicious cream and mushroom sauce."

"Well, someone has to shoot those partridges before the sauce goes on, and I see no reason it shouldn't be me." Pat sounded a little aggressive in her own ears, but Miss Carruth let out a chirp of laughter.

"But imagine if they didn't. Partridges strutting all over the plate while the cook chases them with a ladle of cream sauce!"

"'I said I wanted it served rare, but this is ridiculous,'" Pat offered in a tone of dowager's complaint. Miss Carruth shrieked.

Jimmy came over, smiling, though he looked tense. "I'm glad you two are getting on. Since we're an informal gathering, I thought we'd mix up precedence at dinner. Pat, I wonder if I can entrust you to Preston."

Pat duly took Mr. Keynes' arm and they went in to dinner. The dining room was a very large, echoing space amid imposing wood-panelled walls hung with faded and motheaten tapestries. It caught some of the golden evening light now; it would be dark and cold at dinner for perhaps eight months of the year. It did not look like the future home of frothy, giggling Fenella Carruth at all.

They took their seats. The table was inevitably unbalanced, due to the odd number and informal make-up of the party, with two sets of brothers and sisters to be separated plus the married couple. The Earl had his place at one end of the table and the Countess at the other. Pat sat between Preston Keynes and Jimmy; Miss Singh was opposite her, seated between Maurice Haworth and the handsome

Jack Bouvier-Lynes. Pat felt, on the whole, that she preferred her own seatmates.

The dinner started pleasantly enough. Jimmy was talking to Miss Carruth, on his right, so Pat could happily carry on her conversation about shooting with Mr. Keynes. The Earl, at the head of the table, took advantage of the party's informality to join in their argument over the comparative difficulty of partridge, pheasant, and grouse, and did so with gusto. Pat was thoroughly enjoying herself by the time the meat course was brought in, a hearty dish of beef. Her attention was entirely on the Earl's hunting anecdote, until Maurice Haworth's voice cut through the general buzz of conversation.

"Hey there. You've forgotten Miss Singh's beef."

The servant looked round. Miss Singh said, calmly, "No, he has not. Thank you." That was to the footman, not Mr. Haworth. "I am a vegetarian. I don't eat meat."

"Of course you don't. I must have forgotten." Mr. Haworth wore a tiny smile. "We are blessed by our considerate hosts, aren't we? Nothing is too much trouble when it comes to their guests' little idiosyncrasies."

Pat heard an intake of breath from somewhere from down the table, and Miss Singh's cheeks darkened at that suggestion she was causing unnecessary trouble. The Earl's face was tense, but he didn't say anything, and nor did the Countess.

Well. It was an informal gathering; one could surely speak across the table. Pat said, "My father would have called that the highest possible praise for any host. His sole rule for hospitality was that every guest should feel comfortable in behaving as though they were at home. Of course, if we did *that*, Bill and I would be rendering the table hideous with constant bickering."

That got a general laugh. Bill said, "Sadly true. You're very brave to invite a brother and sister, Lord Witton."

"You're all most welcome," the Earl said. "Every one."

Maurice Haworth was still smiling. Pat found she didn't much like his smiles. "No matter how unconventional. It is delightful to see so many young ladies unconcerned with following the old-fashioned rules of behaviour. Alarming for we men, but I suppose it's terribly outdated to be concerned with a husband now. At least Miss Carruth prefers to follow my wife's example, not that of Misses Merton and Singh." He leaned forward to look across the table at Miss Carruth. "*You're* a maid meant to marry, eh? Or so Jimmy must hope."

"I suppose that's Shakespeare? You're terribly clever, Mr. Haworth." Pat was on the same side of the table as Miss Carruth, so couldn't see her without craning, but her voice rang with ingenuous admiration. Apparently the little simpleton didn't realise she was being insulted. "But I don't think I am old-fashioned."

"I've heard that about you," Haworth said with a smile. "They say you're very dashing. Always looking for the newest thing."

Miss Carruth giggled, a musical peal, as though he'd uttered a joke rather than a flagrant piece of spite. Pat flashed a look up and down the table. The Earl was scarlet, the Countess frozen, both silent. Lady Anna looked like a marble statue, as though she couldn't hear a word; Jack Bouvier-Lynes's expression was fixed in a slight smile; Jimmy to her right was rigid and silent. None of them spoke.

What on *earth*?

She took a breath, but Miss Singh spoke first, quite calm. "I should call Miss Merton the most modern of us all, as a sporting champion. Tell me, Miss Merton, are you allowed to compete on equal terms with the men?"

"We're not," Pat said. "An absurdity, since there can be no question of physical inequality in target shooting. I should very much like to see mixed competitions."

"Allow us our delusions," Bill said. "You'd trounce us all."

"What a loyal brother," Mr. Haworth said. "But I suspect Miss Merton is not among the usual run of womankind."

His eyes ran over her as he spoke. Pat felt her mouth drop open, the blood rushing to her face. Bill said, "I beg your pardon?"

"In her talents, I mean. I very much doubt most ladies could acquire any skill with a gun."

"I disagree entirely," Miss Singh said. "Why should we not?"

"Quite," Pat agreed. "I dare say any lady here could become a satisfactory shot with practice."

"Perhaps we should make it a wager," Mr. Haworth said. "Miss Merton to instruct Miss Singh in the art of shooting, the test to be if the lady can bring down, shall we say, a brace of partridge. Will you take the bet?"

"I will not," Miss Singh said composedly. "I do not hunt."

"You won't put your convictions to the test?" Mr. Haworth spoke as though he'd scored a point. "What a shame."

"Ooh!" said Miss Carruth, an excitable squeal. "Then may I?"

The expressions around the table suggested Pat wasn't the only one startled by this. Jimmy said, "May you what, Fen?"

"Be Miss Merton's student, of course."

"That would be an awfully good idea, but I don't think you should wager on it," Jimmy said carefully. "It is a skill that takes some work, you know."

"I could work," Miss Carruth said, with just a fraction less bright enthusiasm in her tone.

"Of course you can," Pat said. "I'd be delighted to give you a few lessons. Unless Jimmy would rather do it."

"Oh, I'll probably be an awful duffer, and I'd hate to make him impatient," Miss Carruth said, with a giggle. "I'm sure you're a wonderful teacher, Miss Merton. I doubt I could ever shoot birds, though, poor little cheeping things, even if they don't have much of a family life."

Mr. Haworth's mouth twisted with incredulous mockery. Miss Singh's face was so blank that the blankness was an expression in itself. Pat couldn't help glancing round at Jimmy, who had shut his eyes.

"I'm sure I can help," she said. "I'd be delighted to show you the ropes tomorrow."

Mr. Keynes cleared his throat. "Speaking of grouse," he began, and launched into an unstoppable hunting monologue that kept everyone including Maurice Haworth silent for the next five minutes, allowing the atmosphere to settle. Pat addressed herself to her plate with some relief, and wondered what on earth was going on.

The ladies decamped to the drawing room after the meal was over. Pat had rarely been happier to leave a room. Jimmy hadn't turned to speak to her once, and she'd had Maurice Haworth's nasty little smile opposite her for the duration of the meal, which was enough to put anyone off her food. No wonder Lady Anna was thin.

It was a cosy room, wood-panelled and adorned with numerous gilt-framed pictures, ornaments, and whatnots, from a pair of china King Charles spaniels to a glass bell filled with dusty stuffed birds, a ship in a bottle, and a curved knife with an intricately patterned steel handle in a beautifully carved sheath. The decidedly Victorian trappings of an old-fashioned family home. Pat wondered what Miss Carruth might do with it. Would she sweep it all away for a modern look?

The Countess seemed somewhat strained as she sat down and waved at the maid to serve tea or coffee. Lady Anna was tense and silent; Miss Carruth wore her apparently permanent bright smile. Miss Singh sat up straight with her cup of tea. She did not look happy at all.

"Well, how nice," Miss Carruth trilled, seemingly oblivious to the atmosphere. "It's always a relief to let the men have their drinks and cigars, isn't it? Did you mean it about teaching me to shoot, Miss Merton? Do say you will."

"I'll do my best," Pat said. "I'm not promising anything. Do you jump at loud noises?"

"I *might*," Miss Carruth said with a comical expression.

And squeal, Pat was prepared to bet. She'd had her ears boxed to nip that habit in the bud. "That's something you'll have to get used to. But I dare say Jimmy will be happy for us to set up a target. Do you shoot, Lady Anna?"

"No." One word, icy.

"How about you, Miss Singh?" Pat asked, mostly to be polite. "Would you care to have a crack after all? Only target shooting, of course."

"I practice archery," Miss Singh said, unexpectedly.

"Really? I used to handle a bow myself. That was a long time ago."

"Oooh! Perhaps you could have a match," Miss Carruth suggested.

"We could certainly take one another's measure," Miss Singh said. "I insist on that before any formal competition. I have grave suspicions that Miss Merton is being modest about her accomplishments."

"I did win a county championship," Pat admitted.

"Ha! I knew it." Miss Singh smiled then. She had a remarkably lovely smile, one that lit her dark liquid eyes.

"It was at school!" Pat protested. "And I haven't picked up a bow in years."

"In that case, a match it shall be," the Countess said. "Anna shot at school as well. Anna, perhaps you will organise the ladies' shooting and we'll have a tournament."

Lady Anna did not acknowledge that with so much as a blink. Miss Carruth said, clapping, "What a good idea! I shall keep score for you."

"Maybe Miss Singh could teach you to shoot a bow," Pat suggested.

"If Miss Carruth is interested. Although it can be more difficult for ladies with substantial embonpoint."

"Oh, *I* know," Miss Carruth said. "Amazons used to cut off their bosoms, didn't they? I shan't be doing that." She glanced down at her impressive bust. Pat couldn't help following her gaze. "No, it would get in the way, wouldn't it? I'll stick to guns, I think."

"It might be best," Miss Singh agreed. "Miss Merton, I wanted to say that I hope I didn't offend you earlier."

"Me? Not at all. How would you have done so?"

"When we first discussed shooting. I feel strongly on the subject, so I express myself strongly."

"I had four older brothers," Pat said. "I'm used to people expressing themselves strongly and really, I see no reason why you shouldn't. We can still be friends if we don't share all our beliefs, can't we?"

"I should think it depends on the belief," Lady Anna remarked. "If Miss Singh believes that you are a murderer for shooting—"

"I did not say that," Miss Singh said levelly. "But since you raise it, I do think the mass slaughter of two or three thousand birds at a time is an unfit pursuit for gentlemen. Or anyone."

"I couldn't agree more," Pat said. "Firing into a cloud of birds in the hope that some fall down isn't sport. That's what did for the passenger pigeon and in my opinion it is a criminal waste."

"The passenger pigeon?" Miss Carruth asked. "What is that?"

"A bird that used to fly in such numbers that it blotted out the sun," Miss Singh said. "Fifty years ago there were flocks of millions and the noise of their approach was like thunder. The last of them in the wild was shot last year, though I believe some pairs remain in zoological gardens."

"The last? But what happened to them?"

"People killed them. Firing into a cloud of birds and watching them fall, as Miss Merton says."

"Well, it was more than just unchecked shooting, though that played its part," Pat added. "The American West is being civilised, towns built where the birds once bred. I suppose it's the march of progress, but it marched over the passenger pigeon."

"But they can't have killed *all* of them." Miss Carruth's pretty mouth was round with shock. "Not *millions*."

"We observe game seasons and hire gamekeepers for good reason," Pat said. "And yes, millions. There are certain sorts who like to go out and pull the trigger till the birds lie in heaps that are left to rot. I don't, myself, consider those people guns."

"One might think you were describing the Prince of Wales and his set in those disparaging terms," Lady Anna observed coolly.

"I am." That had clearly been intended as a snub, and Pat had no great desire to pick a fight with her hosts' daughter, but this was not a subject on which she was prepared to equivocate. "And I'll repeat it to anyone's face. It displays gross self-indulgence, and no respect."

"Is there respect in killing single birds?" Miss Singh asked.

"Someone killed every bird, fish or animal I've ever eaten," Pat said. "And at least the partridge I shoot has a chance to dodge, unlike the chicken whose neck I wring. Of course, you don't eat chicken either. Do you know, Miss Singh, I have far more respect for that stance than I do for those who eat meat but shudder at killing. In fact, I think you're quite right." Miss Singh's brows went up. Pat opened her hands. "Not right, as such, but your position is entirely consistent. If I condemned shooting wild birds, I could hardly approve of eating domesticated beasts."

"And conversely, if I believed that eating animals was right, it would be foolish to balk at shooting them. In other words, we hold the same view, but from opposite perspectives."

"It sounds like it." Pat offered her a smile. Miss Singh smiled back.

Miss Carruth clapped her hands. "*That* is agreeing to disagree. Goodness me, ladies are civilised. Now tell me, if I eat meat but am terribly squeamish about hunting, where do I come on your spectrum of opinion?"

"You fall off it, because you don't have a leg to stand on," Pat said. It came out a little drily. Miss Singh laughed aloud, and Miss Carruth gave the most delightful gurgle, just as if she were in on the joke too.

CHAPTER THREE

The next day dawned bright and extremely early, since the sun rose at around five o'clock this far north. Pat was woken by the dawn chorus, made a perfunctory effort to get back to sleep, then lay in bed, thinking about the previous night.

The men had joined the ladies after half an hour or so, and instantly ruined the comfortable atmosphere they'd developed. Jimmy had given every impression of being made of wood, barely speaking either to his fiancée or to his old friend. Bill had seemed preoccupied to the point of rudeness; Pat hoped he wasn't thinking about work. Miss Singh had relapsed into silence as soon as the men were present; by contrast Lady Anna had dropped her cold, brittle anger in favour of smiling flirtation with Jack Bouvier-Lynes as her husband looked on, smiling too. It had been a relief when Mr. Bouvier-Lynes had proposed a round of cards and taken himself, Haworth, Jimmy, and Mr. Keynes off. Bill had gone to bed.

This ill-assorted gathering was not at all what Pat had expected or wanted and she gave some serious thought to making her excuses and leaving. It would be rude to Jimmy, but frankly, he deserved it after his inexplicable silence at Haworth's astonishing behaviour. The man might be his brother-in-law but that was no excuse for tolerating such poor manners.

Especially to Miss Carruth. Pat could quite understand that Jimmy had found her irresistible: the laughing eyes, the generous mouth, the soft and very lush curves. Not an intellectual, perhaps, but very pleasant, and Jimmy was hardly over-burdened with brains himself.

Only, Jimmy did not seem to find her irresistible. He'd barely spoken to her, and he'd apparently given no thought to her entertainment. Pat wondered how long her sparkling humour would last if she were left with Miss Singh and Lady Anna for three endless weeks of thumb-twiddling. It seemed a rash way to treat a fiancée upon whom one was depending for financial rescue, especially one with a history of bolting.

Maybe Jimmy was hoping she'd bolt, since he didn't seem charmed by her chatter. Pat wasn't a lover of empty nonsense either, but it was hardly the worst characteristic one could expect in an advantageous marriage. It seemed greedy to demand perfect compatibility if one's prospective spouse also had a kind heart, overflowing coffers, and that bosom. Not that it was any of Pat's business, because the woman was marrying Jimmy. Lucky bloody Jimmy.

She stared up at the ceiling, slightly startled at herself. She ought to be thinking *Lucky Miss Carruth*. Jimmy was a decent fellow who would one day be an earl, and whose estates might be suffering financially—there were notably fewer staff on view than Pat would expect for a house this size—but were not to be sneezed at. He was steady, too, the sort of man who would probably be a good father and a faithful, or at least discreet, husband. In fact, he was an excellent match, and Pat couldn't for the life of her see why Miss Carruth would want any of it. The thrice-engaged Miss Carruth who jilted men ought to have a husband who danced with her at balls, or covered her in jewels, or...or took her to Monte Carlo, possibly? This was outside Pat's experience. In any case, a man who'd kiss her hand and adore her, much as Jonty adored Olivia, patting her hand and telling her, inaccurately, that he'd take care of everything.

Pat would have loathed that, but she wasn't soft or helpless or delicious. She was plain in looks and manner, and had never regretted that because she had never particularly wanted to attract a husband. And yet, Miss Carruth undeniably made her think about soft curves and lushness and pretty, frivolous primping, and why those things were so very desirable to see, or to have.

Pat been looking forward to the shooting party precisely because she could be as mannish as she pleased with Jimmy and Bill. She hadn't expected to feel undermined by her lack of feminine graces because another woman was there, being different. And it wasn't just "another woman", either, because she was unconcerned by the sylphlike, fashionable Lady Anna or the poised, elegant Miss Singh. It was Miss Carruth's presence that bothered her, and Pat's irrational nonsense was hardly the girl's fault.

The longer she lay in bed and thought, the worse she was making herself feel, so she got up and dressed. Pat did not corset. She had had no mother to train her waist to a span of eighteen inches or so; her father thought wasp-waists were for insects and preferred his daughter able to walk, climb trees, shoot, and run around the house. She had never learned to be laced, although she had eventually and reluctantly obtained a loose pair of stays for evening wear. It was one of many things about which she had rarely thought in her life at Stoke St. Milborough, and might have to consider when she moved to live elsewhere; she didn't wish to be perceived as an eccentric. Or perhaps that would happen anyway, so she'd do as she pleased.

As an adherent of Rational Dress, she was able to clothe herself without a maid's assistance. She simply donned combinations, drawers, camisole, stockings, undershirt, petticoat, walking dress, and boots, and was ready to face the day.

It was not yet seven o'clock; breakfast would doubtless not be served for an hour or more since they weren't shooting today. She came downstairs anyway, deciding to find a servant who would point her to a quiet back door, and came across Jimmy Yoxall sipping a cup of coffee.

"Goodness, you're up early."

"You too," Jimmy returned. "Sleep well?"

"Very. You?"

Jimmy shrugged. "Up rather late."

"Playing cards with your chums."

"Well, with Maurice, Jack, and Preston," Jimmy said. "Bill was wise to go to bed. Jack's a devil with a pack of cards; he cleaned Preston out. Are you off for a walk?"

"I thought I would. How do I get out without waking the house?"

"Give me a moment to put on my things and I'll come with you. There's a pot of coffee here. I usually wake early these days."

Pat gulped down the coffee—from the temperature it seemed that Jimmy had been up a while—and strode out with him into a very pleasant day. It was bright, sunny, and breezy, the wind rolling over the long open curves of the land.

"It's lovely here," Pat remarked.

"It is. Would you find it too remote? If you were called upon to live here, I mean?"

"*I* wouldn't," Pat said cautiously, "but I'm not much of one for society, or cities. Or towns, even. I'd be perfectly happy not seeing other people for days on end, going to dinner three times a year and visiting a tailor twice, but that wouldn't suit everyone."

"No," Jimmy said. "It is rather a way to the nearest town, and that's not awfully big. Fen remarked on it when she arrived."

"Presumably Miss Carruth has been here before?"

"No. No. Our engagement was a—what do they call it when one proposes in a spur-of-the-moment sort of way? Not to say I didn't consider matters, of course, just that it was terribly quick. All in London. This is the first time she's seen the house, or the area."

"Does she like it?"

"She's awfully enthusiastic. Marvellous girl. I'm not sure she's grasped what the winters are like up here."

"Shan't you live in London when you're married?"

Jimmy made a face. "We have a house there, but it's a terrible expense and I wanted to persuade the parents to get rid of it. But Anna and Maurice live there, you know, and it's not as though one can ask them to move."

"Do they not have a place of their own?"

"Not any more. Maurice lost his job and their money in the crash."

"What crash was that?"

"Stockbroker's firm. Overextended, fell to pieces. They're living in the family house now."

"I see. But he and Lady Anna surely won't carry on living there when you and Miss Carruth move in."

"Oh yes they blasted will," Jimmy said, with suppressed vehemence. "Maurice hasn't anything of his own, and he's spent every penny of Anna's that he can get his hands on. That pair live entirely off the Aged Parents. If it wasn't for him— Well. And of course one couldn't ask Anna to move to some ghastly hovel while Fen and I take the London house, but you've met Maurice. Would you want to live with him?"

"No," Pat said frankly.

"No. And if he can't live in London, he and Anna will come here, and you've already seen how he is when he can't get his cocktails, or his cocktail waitresses. I don't know if my parents could put up with it."

"I'm awfully sorry."

Jimmy exhaled. "It's a sorry business. Anna won't leave him, I don't know why the devil not. Well, there's the child."

"Is there a child?" Pat hadn't seen or heard any evidence of one.

"My nephew. He's three years old. They've left him with a nanny for the entire summer because Maurice doesn't like the noise. Mother asked them to bring him, since she hasn't seen him since February, but

Maurice prefers to grant her the sight of her grandson strictly on his own terms, and when he can take the boy away at any time."

"Good heavens," Pat said. "Oh, Jimmy. This is rotten."

"Anna made her own bed when she insisted on marrying the blighter, and now we all have to lie in it. It wouldn't be so bad if they weren't both so determined to make everyone around them miserable, but you've seen how he is, and Anna is just making it worse with her extraordinary behaviour with Jack. I don't know what she's playing at."

"It doesn't sound like Haworth is much of a husband," Pat pointed out. "What's sauce for the goose is surely sauce for the gander."

"I dare say, but the sauce gets ladled out on the rest of us with a lavish hand. You heard how he spoke to Victoria, and to Fen."

"I heard the deafening ring of your silence as he insulted your fiancée, yes. What was that about?"

"Oh, Lord, don't." Jimmy took off his hat, swiping it through the air at insects Pat couldn't see. "You don't understand."

"I understand what I'd think in her shoes."

"Yes, well, you might, but the fact is— Look, it's complicated. And I can't go into it, but you can take my word for it that one day, when I have a chance, I'm going to break his bloody neck. I wouldn't have sat there listening to him speak like that to my father's guests at my father's table if I didn't have to."

"That doesn't sound awfully good, Jimmy."

"Don't I know it."

"Why on earth did you invite a houseful of people under these circumstances?"

"I *didn't*," Jimmy said explosively. "I wanted a bit of peace and quiet with a few decent human beings—you, Preston, Bill—while I still could. Fen invited herself, Victoria was meant to have left before Maurice arrived, and Jack Bouvier bloody Lynes wasn't invited at all except that Anna asked him to pop along without telling anyone until it was too late!" He made a strangled noise of frustration. "Sorry, Pat. You came here for partridge and I'm piling my family troubles on you."

"That's all right." Pat hesitated, but Jimmy was clearly in need. "This engagement of yours—"

"Fen is a lovely girl. Any man would be lucky to have her."

"She is lovely."

"Beautiful, rich, awfully jolly. I'm terribly fortunate she accepted me, though I can't imagine why she did."

"Er—"

"Well, you've met her. She's quite the butterfly, and I'm not interested in Society parties and so on. Her last two fiancés were both men-about-town."

"Maybe that's why she's picked a countryman," Pat said. "If the modern man-about-town is anything like Mr. Haworth, I don't blame her."

"He's a thoroughly nasty piece of work and I'm sorry to bring you into his orbit but, frankly, we had no choice but to shut the London house over summer. Couldn't afford to keep it running, couldn't afford to send Maurice and Anna off to Brighton or Bath or Baden-Baden, and since Maurice has run out of hosts willing to tolerate him, here they are."

"Are the finances that bad?"

Jimmy made a face. "The agricultural depression has hit rents hard across the board, of course, but on top of that Father was the biggest investor in Maurice's firm and we lost rather a lot in the crash. We need to take drastic action to repair matters, sell some land and invest in other industries, but the old man is set in his ways. He won't accept that things have to change, or hand the reins to me. It's not marvellous, honestly."

"But when you marry…"

"Oh, yes, my future father-in-law has proposed a very generous settlement." Jimmy looked less excited about this than one might have expected. "Which means Father won't have to make any decisions like selling land, or asking Maurice to get a blasted job."

"Some people would call you lucky," Pat observed.

"Yes," Jimmy said. "I am lucky. Jolly lucky. Fen's a very nice girl, and I dare say it's about time I was married. Let's not bore on about me."

"All right then." Pat watched the heat haze over the grass as they walked, the great sweep of the land. "What about Miss Singh?"

"What about her?"

"Only that she doesn't seem entirely the right fit for a shooting party. Very pleasant, but, well—a vegetarian?"

"Oh, Victoria's not one of those cranks. She's Mother's goddaughter, you know. She came up for a week's stay, and then asked if it would be possible to extend her visit for another week—I believe she was going on to people who found they had scarlet fever in the house, though frankly if I were her I should have risked the contagion rather than Maurice. He's a racialist, of course. She knew what she was letting herself in for, but I cannot imagine why she would."

"I expect she knows what she's about. She seemed a very intelligent woman to me."

"I thought you'd like her," Jimmy said. "She's serious, but I don't see why women shouldn't be serious. It's all very well to talk nonsense and do nothing all day, constantly dressing for breakfast and lunch and afternoon tea and dinner and going out and meeting people in order to talk about other people one met yesterday, but what is the *point*? Why do women want to waste their time on that? Are you really going to teach Fen to use a gun?"

"If she wants me to."

"I wish you would. I dare say it might take some time, if you don't mind that. You'll have to be awfully patient, I warn you. She's not the, uh, the brightest—she's not like you, old thing. Not *competent*."

"Perhaps not, but men don't tend to marry for competence, do they?"

She meant it lightly, but Jimmy pulled a face. "I don't know why not. It's all very well being bubbly and charming in drawing rooms but unless one has the wherewithal to live without shouldering responsibilities—"

"Now hold on," Pat said, suddenly roused on Miss Carruth's behalf. "If a woman is brought up to do nothing except get married and mix in society, it's hardly fair to blame her for carrying out the job she was given. If you didn't want that sort of woman you shouldn't have proposed to one, and having done so, it's hardly fair to criticise her for it."

Jimmy's mouth dropped open. "How—that is, I'm not doing that. I don't blame her. I just— Well, it would be a lot easier if about half the people at this accursed party weren't here, that's all."

"I dare say."

"Ugh. I'm sorry, Pat, I sound like an ungrateful cad. Look, you'd really do me a service if you'd give Fen a few lessons. She's going to be desperately bored for the next couple of weeks and I have certain things to do. I'm not asking you to miss out on the shooting, of course, but if you found yourself at a loose end, I would appreciate it."

Pat knew she should encourage him to put some effort into his engagement. She didn't. "I'll have a crack. Shall we get back for breakfast?"

"Yes," Jimmy said. "Yes, I suppose we should."

CHAPTER FOUR

Breakfast at Rodington Court was an informal affair. Bill and Miss Singh were down when Jimmy and Pat returned, the Earl and Countess had been and gone, and there was no sign of the more fashionable members of the party.

"Pat's going to teach Fenella to shoot this morning," Jimmy announced. "I wish her luck. I'm at everyone else's disposal if you'd like to take a stroll around the grounds."

"That would be lovely," Miss Singh agreed. "Won't Miss Carruth want to join us?"

"She's not much of a walker," Jimmy said. "I don't intend the guns to spend all day in the field, by the way. Those who like can, but we have so many guests who aren't shots that everyone should feel free to do as you please. Liberty Hall and all that."

"That suits me," Bill said. Pat, who had been hoping to spend all day every day under the sky, suppressed a sigh. She very much hoped that she wouldn't be expected to nursemaid Miss Carruth throughout the party. She didn't think Jimmy would serve her such a trick, but he was a man, so her expectations were low.

Miss Carruth hadn't appeared by the time Pat had finished her breakfast, nor had she emerged an hour later, by which time Pat had finished her book and was trawling the well-stocked library for works on field sports. Jimmy, neither surprised nor daunted, produced a pair of small-bore rifles suitable for target-shooting and informed Pat that the South Lawn would be an excellent place to practice, "once Fen gets up."

Pat rolled her eyes, but set off in that direction. It was a beautiful day, and she thought it would be more pleasant to be out of the house now the rest of the party was stirring.

Rodington Court's grounds were extensive, though perhaps a little unkempt, as if they needed one more gardener than they had. The South Lawn rolled down a gentle slope to an ornamental lake surrounded by greenery. It was a lovely prospect in the sun and nobody could walk into even the most wildly misdirected shot; it would do very well if Miss Carruth wanted to practice, and if she didn't, it made a very pleasant spot for Pat to settle down with the latest *Wildfowler's Shooting Times*.

She chose a bench that stood in a hollow cut out from a large juniper bush, which gave her a view of the lake. It also obscured her from casual view, she realised as the next hour passed, because her attention was attracted from the pages every now and again by movement, but nobody seemed to see her.

Bill passed first, striding down to the lake in a way that suggested a man chafing for exercise. He disappeared into the wood, presumably to take a wider circuit round the grounds, since he did not reemerge. Mr. Keynes and Miss Singh crossed the South Lawn some time afterwards, heads together in earnest talk. Pat wondered what on earth they found to discuss, given her entire conversation with Mr. Keynes had revolved around hunting and shooting. Still, he had good manners, and they seemed happy enough. Ten minutes after that, she saw Lady Anna walking with Jack Bouvier-Lynes, and sent up a mental malediction. She couldn't blame Lady Anna, since her companion seemed to be very personable from the little Pat had seen of him, but if Maurice Haworth came out after his wife, she didn't want to be in earshot.

Fortunately, the next person she saw was Fenella Carruth.

Miss Carruth wore a very dashing green day dress of flattering cut and a broad-brimmed hat against the sun. She was walking alone, with slow, heavy tread, and as she passed in front of the juniper, her expression was so sombre that Pat would almost not have recognised her. Her lips were pressed together, eyes distant, and Pat found herself blurting, "Miss Carruth!"

Miss Carruth recoiled in shock, then turned, and the usual sparkling smile spread over her face as though the look of misery had never been. "Miss Merton, there you are. I was looking for you."

"Here I am," Pat agreed. She wondered if she could say, *Are you all right?* but was drowned in determined cheerfulness before she had a chance.

"Wonderful. I *am* looking forward to learning to shoot. Not to kill things because whatever you say I prefer to let other people do that for me and one would hardly slaughter one's own cows, would one? Unless one was a farmer, and I am *not*, even if I shall be married to a country landowner, but in any case, no. But I ought at least to understand what you get up to on these excursions, and muzzles and bullets and the difference between a fowling-piece and a revolver and everything else Mr. Keynes talks about. Oughtn't I?"

Pat hadn't followed the flood of verbiage closely enough to pick out what the question was. She was preoccupied with Miss Carruth's velvet-brown eyes, and the shimmer of moisture over their surface.

She had no right, or no standing, to pry and Miss Carruth couldn't have made her desire to keep up appearances clearer.

"Yes, of course," she said, more or less at random. "Shall we go down to the end of the lawn?"

She picked up the gun case and set off. Miss Carruth hurried to match her stride. "Goodness, you walk quickly."

Pat slowed. "Sorry. I had four older brothers who were always on at me to keep up."

"Four! Good heavens. Is Mr. Merton the oldest?"

"Third. Jonty is the oldest. He's on his honeymoon now."

"And what do your other brothers do?"

Not much. The words rose to Pat's lips; she bit them back. The twisted humour that helped one through grief could not be shared outside the family. "I'm afraid they're no longer with us. Ladysmith."

Miss Carruth looked round sharply. "You lost *two* brothers there?"

"The same day. We had the telegrams together."

"That's dreadful. Oh, Miss Merton. I'm so sorry to be so clumsy."

"You weren't to know. Really it's nothing—the mention, I mean. I'd rather people talked about them than pretended they never existed. Please don't think anything of it."

Miss Carruth's brows drew together. "It's very kind of you to make me feel better about a faux pas but really, in these circumstances, I wish you wouldn't. Were you very fond of them?"

"Moderately," Pat said, and saw the other woman's startled look. "I dare say that sounded odd. Do you have siblings?"

"No. My mother died when I was very young, and my father never remarried."

"Mine too," Pat said. "Only I was the youngest of five." They'd reached the end of the lawn. She put the case down and dug out one of the old tin tea-canisters she'd hunted up, then balanced it on a fence post. "Frank and Donald were as noisy and boisterous as poorly trained dogs. They called me names and broke my toys and did all the horrible things brothers do—except Bill, he was always decent—and we were really only just starting to get along in a civilised way when they went to South Africa. I can't honestly say I missed them when they were gone. It was a lot more peaceful and a lot less work, and I was perfectly content until I learned they wouldn't be coming back."

She stopped there because she couldn't think of anything else to say. Miss Carruth's eyes were impossibly huge, fixed on her face. "I'm so sorry. That's wholly inadequate but I don't know if there's anything else one can say."

"Not really. Certainly not, 'At least you still have two left.'"

"Please don't tell me people say that to you."

"Of course they do," Pat said. "As if mathematics apply to families. And particularly when one of the remaining brothers is Jonty."

Miss Carruth gave a squeak of laughter. "Oh dear."

"He's not bad really, so long as one doesn't live with him," Pat said. "Or at least, I hope he won't be when I don't. Shall we begin? Rifle or revolver?"

"*Revolver?*" Miss Carruth echoed. "Does one shoot with a revolver?"

"They're not much use for anything else," Pat pointed out, and felt a tingle of pleasure at the smile that lit Miss Carruth's eyes.

"What a pity. I thought I could use one to dress a hat. But surely grouse and pheasants and so on involve rifles?"

"They do, but you said you'd prefer not to shoot game. There's always target shooting, for which you'd use a small bore rifle. But if you just wanted the experience of handling a gun, you might find a revolver easier to use, and I do think it's a valuable skill to acquire. You never know when you might need it."

Miss Carruth looked somewhat startled. "Why would I ever need to use a revolver?"

"Well, I have. Our house is isolated, a mile from the village, and we've had intruders, including a group of men who broke in during the day when only Father and I were at home. He was very elderly then, and I was fifteen. I heard them in the hall and came down to confront them. It was really quite frightening."

"Good heavens, I expect it was. What happened?"

"I told them to get out, and they wouldn't go." That single sentence covered an exchange that couldn't have lasted much more than a minute, but in which time had seemed as slow as treacle. She still dreamed of it, very occasionally. "They laughed at me, and one of them made some rather unpleasant threats. So I shot him."

"You—"

"In the shoulder," Pat clarified. "And then Father wheeled himself out in his bath chair with the shotgun across his lap, and they left in a hurry. But you may imagine that I was glad to have the means to defend myself."

Fen's mouth was an O. "Good *heavens*. Is that the sort of adventure one might expect in an isolated house? Daddy has taken a place in King's Norton now, outside Birmingham, but I've always lived in Birmingham or London."

"Oh, goodness, no." Pat felt a stab of guilt for raising the prospect. "I shouldn't think you'd have any trouble up here. It's as well to know how to defend oneself, all the same. Better to have the ability and not need it than need it and not have it."

"Yes, I suppose so. Do you know, nobody has ever before suggested that I might defend myself, rather than having someone do it for me."

"I dare say it depends a great deal on your upbringing," Pat said. "My father found it easiest to behave as though he had five sons. I think he sometimes forgot he didn't."

"Mine does try to remember he has a daughter." Miss Carruth gave a bright smile. "Very well, then, a revolver it shall be. They do ones for ladies, don't they?"

"They do." Pat opened the small walnut-wood case and showed Miss Carruth. "This is a Harrington top-break revolver."

Miss Carruth took the proffered weapon with extreme reluctance. "Will it go off?"

"It's not loaded. We never leave guns loaded. Nothing bad will happen."

"The handle is very pretty." Miss Carruth turned the gun cautiously. "Mother of pearl. Ooh, it says PM. That's you. How nice."

"My brothers had it done for my twenty-first birthday."

"That's very... I suppose that was what you wanted? A monogrammed gun?"

"I'd given up hoping for ear-rings by then." It was a joke, but Miss Carruth's brows twitched as though she wasn't happy with what she'd heard. "It's a lovely piece," Pat added, feeling as though she should defend the gift. "Handles beautifully, light, with a nice sensitive trigger. Let me show you."

She loaded the gun under Miss Carruth's alarmed eye, took a few steps away—she was merely demonstrating the operation, certainly not trying to impress anyone with her skills—and fired. Miss Carruth, inevitably, jumped and shrieked as the tin span off the post.

"You'll need to stop that," Pat informed her, going to retrieve the target. "The squealing, I mean. Here, you have a try."

She handed the gun over. Miss Carruth took it in a cautious fashion that suggested she thought it might explode. Pat sighed. "Hold it firmly. No, like this." She wrapped Miss Carruth's fingers around the inlaid handle. "Don't put your finger on the trigger yet. Just feel the weight and get used to it."

"It's awfully heavy."

"Not really. Extend your arm and sight down the barrel. No, straighter." She took hold of Miss Carruth's plump arm, feeling a slight tremor—that would be the unaccustomed muscular effort, nothing else—and adjusted her stance. If that meant a certain amount of standing very close to Miss Carruth's warmth, inhaling her scent, it couldn't be helped.

She did her best to focus on explaining aim and warning her pupil about recoil, and stepped away when she could. "All right. Eyes on the tin and squeeze the trigger gently."

Miss Carruth's finger moved, her whole arm jerked, and she let out another piercing squeal as the gun went off. The tin stood unmoved, which was no surprise; Pat almost expected a bird to fall from the sky.

"You can't make a fuss like that. Try again. Properly."

"Oh, but it was such a shock! The way it jumped in my hands—and so loud!"

"Guns make a loud noise," Pat said. "You knew that would happen. Screaming about guns going off is like saying you want to drive a motor-car and shrieking when it moves. It's what the machine *does*, it's quite predictable, and it's silly to pull the trigger and then be shocked that it fires."

Miss Carruth's eyes were wide. "Are you telling me off?"

"I wouldn't say—" Pat began, and then, "Yes, I am. If you want to acquire a skill you need to set your mind to do it. You won't learn anything if you're busy being helpless and—and cherishable."

"And what?"

"You know. Having other people look after you. Being too silly and frivolous to do anything. It may be what men want of you, but you're not going to learn that way."

Miss Carruth's mouth was open, not in the pretty O of mannered surprise, but actually slack. She looked genuinely shocked. Pat went over her own words in her head again and realised they had been somewhat rude. She fought down the urge to apologise. She'd been asked to teach, not to pander to a display of winsome uselessness; Miss Carruth would have dozens of people to do that for her.

Miss Carruth's lips moved slightly and Pat realised that there was a sheen in her eyes again. Oh God, was the girl going to cry? Had Pat made her cry? She wanted to walk away in exasperation just slightly less than she wanted to comfort her until the sunny smile returned to Miss Carruth's face, and she was damned if she'd do either.

"I," Miss Carruth began, and swallowed. "I dare say I'm very silly."

"*You're* not silly. Screaming when you pull a trigger is silly, and more importantly it's dangerous because you aren't controlling the gun. Stop doing that and I expect you'll do very well. But you can't hit a target when you jump and shriek. It's like trying to shoot from a trampoline."

That got a gurgle of laughter, as Pat had hoped. Miss Carruth loved her absurdities.

"Yes, of course. I didn't mean— May I try again?"

"Of course. As many times as you like. Anticipate the noise, and watch for the recoil this time—that is, the gun jumping in your hands when you fire. You need to be firm in your grip, but not frantic. You're in control."

"Control." Miss Carruth took a deep breath and set her very pretty chin at an obstinate tilt, which Pat would have been delighted to observe at any other time.

"Put your head down a little. Relax your shoulders. You're in charge of the gun, not the other way around. It's your tool to use. Deep breath now, and exhale as you squeeze the trigger."

Miss Carruth fired again. She missed, but she kept her arm level this time, and there was no squeal.

"Better," Pat said. "Try again."

On the fifth shot, the tin span into the air with a clang, and Miss Carruth let out a shriek that had absolutely nothing coquettish about it. "I did it!"

"Yes, you did," Pat said, with equal pleasure. "A damn fine shot— Sorry. I'm used to shooting with men."

"Please don't apologise. It was a *damn* fine shot." She spoke with delightful relish. "Oh, that was satisfying. Do you think I can do it again?"

"I don't see any reason why not."

Miss Carruth proceeded to pepper away at the tin for the next ten minutes, until Pat's ears were ringing, she'd added ten yards to her distance, and she was hitting the target four times out of six. Pat stood back and watched, offering the odd comment about breathing, stance, or technique, mostly observing the way Miss Carruth's eyes narrowed and the set of her jaw.

She wanted this, it was abundantly clear. She wanted to master the skill and she wasn't backing down. Miss Carruth clearly had reserves of determination she didn't show. Maybe she wouldn't be the ornament Jimmy seemed to expect.

She stopped only when they ran out of ammunition, and looked up at Pat with a laugh in her sparking eyes and a comical expression of embarrassment. "Oh, goodness. I have shot you out of house and home."

"That's all right," Pat said. "You did tremendously. Next time we'll use a proper target. Er, if you want a next time, that is."

"I should love a next time," Miss Carruth assured her. "I might cry if you denied it to me. I actually think I might be able to do this and I cannot tell you how good that feels. Thank you so much for giving me your kindness and your time, Miss Merton— Oh, but that sounds so formal when you've told me off and taught me to use a gun. May I call you Patricia?"

"Nobody is permitted to do that, but please do call me Pat."

Miss Carruth positively glowed. "And I'm Fenella. Fen. Don't we sound brusque? Pat and Fen."

"Efficient, rather than brusque," Pat suggested, packing away the pistol. "Will you pick up the tins please? Er, I should probably apologise for telling you off."

"Oh, no you shouldn't," Fen said. "You took me seriously. You thought I could do it if I tried, and I *could*. I'd prefer that to any amount of cherishing."

She smiled then—not the blinding beam full of merriment, but a smaller, quieter expression. It was a serious smile, if such a thing were possible, and Pat stared at her and found no breath in her lungs and nothing to say. Fen's smile faded into something else, an intent look with her eyes fixed on Pat's, and Pat would have—done *something*, she couldn't say what, except that her name came to her ears in a masculine cry that was perhaps the last thing she wanted to hear in the world, because the caller was Jimmy.

"Hello there, ladies. Been practising?"

Fen didn't react at all for a second, and then she turned, the bright laughing look appearing on her face again as though by magic. "Jimmy, darling. How lovely."

45

"Lovely. Yes. Lovely weather. Lake looks lovely. Why don't I take you for a turn? I'm sure Pat's discharged her duty as a teacher; I heard you blasting away."

Fen's eyes flicked to Pat's and away, so quickly it was almost impossible to read the expression. "It wasn't a duty," Pat said, a little too loudly. "It was a pleasure. Fen's done enormously well."

"Oh, really, Pat, you're too kind." Fen tilted her head flirtatiously at Jimmy. "I'm an awful duffer, of course, but she's been terribly patient."

"Don't let it worry you," Jimmy said, extending his arm. "It's not as though you need to learn, and we can't all be All-England champions, can we? Thanks, Pat. I hope it wasn't too much trouble."

"It was a pleasure," Pat repeated. "Shall we have another go—" The shooting started tomorrow. Pat wasn't going to miss the first day for anyone's bright eyes, but the day after tomorrow suddenly seemed a dreadfully long way away.

"That would be lovely," Fen said, apparently not noticing that Pat hadn't specified when. "Thank you. Won't you come for a walk with us?"

"I'm sure she'd like some time to herself, and I'd like some time with you," Jimmy said. "I've barely seen you, let alone given you a proper tour of the grounds. One day this will be yours, and all that. Thanks, old thing." He tipped his hat to Pat and steered Fen off without further ado.

Pat stood, watching them in some bafflement. She had no idea why Fen hadn't trumpeted her achievement, and even less what was wrong with Jimmy, why he sounded so brittle and was speaking with such forced bonhomie.

She got her bits and pieces together, including the tins, and set off back across the lawn alone.

It was still only around twelve when Pat returned to the house. She had no great desire to speak to anyone, so she looked for a convenient place to clean her weapon. It was not a job she left to anyone else, and working with her hands might clear her thoughts.

She headed for the gun room, but heard conversation—it sounded like Preston Keynes and Bill—coming from it and veered off. Mr. Keynes was very pleasant, but she'd had enough of people for the moment. She decided to lurk in the East Wing instead. It was mostly unused, Jimmy had said, so she ought to be able to have a bit of peace.

She crossed the main hall, turned into the East Wing's ground floor corridor, and tried a door. It opened on a room that didn't look as though it was particularly used or useful. It had rows of dusty books on the shelves, a plain old table, a couple of chairs that had evidently been sat on by dogs. It seemed like a room with no purpose, which was hardly surprising. Rodington Court had been built to house a far greater number of people than the current family, and that always gave a house a hollow feel. Pat and Jonty had been rattling around Skirmidge House ever since the other brothers had left and Father had died, and that was a far smaller building than this great barrack.

On the bright side, unused rooms meant she wasn't invading anyone's privacy. Pat settled at the desk, spread out a cloth from the case, took out her tools and bottle of oil, and set to work. The smell of gun oil was a pungent comfort.

She wasn't even sure why she wanted comfort. It had been a delightful morning, with a perfectly pleasant companion. No, it was more than that: Pat had made a new friend. Fen was a thoroughly nice girl, with reserves of character under the frivolous exterior, and it was marvellous that there was more to Jimmy's future wife than had first met the eye. It was also marvellous that Fen had enjoyed their lesson. It bade well for her new life as a countryman's wife, and perhaps Pat could come and visit them in future years when Fenella's obvious love of colour and comfort, and her father's money, had turned the great bare house into a fashionable destination, and she and Jimmy were terribly happy and probably had a brood of children—

47

Pat jammed the cleaning rod down the barrel slightly too hard, and swore under her breath at the impact.

That would be a happy outcome indeed, and she would not begrudge Jimmy his stroke of luck in securing himself such a wife. Her old friend deserved to be happy. He surely would be, if he appreciated his own good fortune and didn't, for example, stay silent when his obnoxious brother-in-law abused his fiancée, or casually assume she must be as foolish or prettily helpless as she chose to seem.

Why did she choose to seem so?

Pat had no idea what was going on with whatever games they were all playing. She'd never been very good at allusive conversations; couldn't really see the point, since it was a great deal easier if one said what one wanted, rather than expecting other people to guess. She hadn't grown up in that sort of milieu: her brothers had been barely capable of hearing the plainest demands, let alone delicate hints. And she didn't like the idea of suggesting and requesting and laying inviting openings for others to generously offer things, instead of just asking. It seemed a waste of time and, worse, supplicant, as though one were playing the beggar maid to King Cophetua.

Why would Fen wheedle her future husband with coy words and self-deprecation? Surely that couldn't be what Jimmy wanted? Then again, Fen had been proposed to on at least three occasions, whereas Pat had never once walked out with a young man, or even held hands with a boy. She *had* received a proposal, technically—a request relayed by a hysterically laughing Jonty from a fifty-year-old widowed neighbour who admired her housekeeping—but she was fairly sure that didn't qualify her to judge. Perhaps Fen knew what men liked, although Jimmy hardly seemed enthusiastic.

Jimmy had never treated Pat in that dismissive way, but perhaps that was because, like most of the friends she had through her brothers, he didn't really see her as a woman. That seemed a bad omen, and Fen deserved better. She was funny, and brighter than she let on, and she obviously took care to make people around her happy. And she was lovely, too, with those bright eyes and soft, generous curves, which wasn't relevant to her moral character but undeniably occupied quite a lot of Pat's attention. She couldn't help but recall a poem about corsets that had appeared in *Tit-Bits* a few years ago, and which Frank and Donald had quoted endlessly at her. The author bemoaned the fashion for tight lacing and wasp-waists and felt that the ideal female waist was "strong and solid, plump and sound, and hard to get one arm around." Pat's didn't qualify, being straight and bony; Fenella's absolutely did.

And she was engaged to Jimmy, for good or ill, so Pat put aside thoughts of what it might feel like to slip an arm around her waist, which meant she finally noticed the talking.

It was coming from a dark panelled door in the dark panelled wall to her left, which presumably led into the next room as part of a connected set. She hadn't observed the other door when she sat down to clean her gun, and had been lost in thought since. Now she realised that people were speaking in the next room, and possibly had been for some time. Something about their talk had finally snagged her attention. It might have been a raised voice.

Pat had no interest in discovering anyone's private business, and was, at best, indifferent to most of her fellow guests. But in that moment's sudden awareness of a sound she'd missed, she did listen consciously, and she heard Maurice Haworth speak just on the other side of the door.

"There's no point whining. If you want me to keep quiet, you'll have to make it worth my while. That's all."

Pat's hand stilled on the cleaning cloth. Someone else spoke—a male voice, further away and pitched low—and Haworth gave a sneering laugh. "I know what it's called. Do you want me to dress it up—ask you for a loan on indefinite terms, while we both pretend to be decent English gentlemen? I know what you did. Pay up, or so will the world."

The other voice spoke urgently, still very quiet. Haworth laughed again but replied at less volume, moving away from the door. Pat sat, back very straight, staring ahead.

This was not a conversation she wanted to overhear, still less one she wanted to be caught overhearing. It would be impossible to claim one hadn't heard a word, even if it were true. Haworth would assume she'd been eavesdropping, and for all she knew his conversational partner might believe she'd overheard his secret.

Not conversational partner. Victim. That was the word for someone subjected to extortion, wasn't it? And that was what Haworth was doing, no two ways about it. She'd overheard blackmail, and she had to...

She had to what?

Well, for one thing she had to ensure she heard nothing else. This was bad enough without knowing which of her fellow guests harboured a shameful secret, let alone what it was. She'd have liked to get up and slip silently away, but she had all her bits and pieces on the desk, including the monogrammed gun and case. If she left it all there, Haworth might see it and realise she'd overheard, and if she tried to pack up she'd make a noise. In fact, she could do nothing. She would just have to sit and concentrate, hope they went out the other way, and deny hearing anything if she was discovered.

So she focussed fiercely on her work as the seconds dragged by and the murmurs from the next room went on, mentally damning Haworth's culpable carelessness. Really, what sort of extortioner didn't even choose a suitably private location?

At last the luncheon gong boomed. Pat stiffened in alarm, but it appeared that the next room had another exit, because the men didn't come through. She sagged with relief in her chair, then carefully packed up her case, giving them plenty of time to mingle with the rest of the party.

She'd assumed she'd be the last for luncheon after that. In fact, Lady Anna didn't appear at all and nor did the Countess or Miss Singh, leaving Pat and Fen the only two ladies present. The Earl made no excuses; he simply launched into a monologue about what they could expect from the shooting tomorrow, apparently forgetting that Fen might not find this the most scintillating topic of conversation.

Mr. Keynes joined in with some good observations, and Jack Bouvier-Lynes, though cheerfully admitting himself to be a city sort of fellow, asked enough questions to keep the conversation going. Jimmy was notably silent, contributing a few terse remarks when directly addressed by his father. Bill and Mr. Haworth were both content to listen, the last with a nasty little smirk on his lips, as though some unkind remark hovered on the tip of his tongue.

Pat and Fen ate in silence. Fen presumably did so because she had nothing to contribute to the discussion of what bore rifle to use for different types of game, and because her fiancé, sitting next to her, did not manage a word on a subject that might interest her. Pat didn't speak because she was confused, disturbed, and, she realised as the meal proceeded, furious.

She moved swiftly as soon as they rose from the table. "Do you know, I haven't been around the lake. Fen, would you show me, if you aren't busy?"

"I dare say I can find an unoccupied hour." Fen spoke with a smile, and addressed the words only to Pat, but behind her Jimmy winced. It served him right.

CHAPTER FIVE

They strolled down to the lake together in silence. It was full sun now, a glorious day, though the sky had a hint of yellow to it that suggested storms might not be out of the question.

"Are you all right?" Pat asked at last.

Fen turned her head, looking startled. "Me? Yes, of course. My arms are a little tired, but nothing terrible."

"I don't mean that. I mean…" She tailed off, wondering if this was too much of an intrusion. It was none of her business, but the whole thing was becoming unbearable to witness. "How long have you and Jimmy known one another?"

"Oh, about three months."

"And you said you haven't visited him here before."

"No. This is my first time in this part of the world."

"Mmm."

Fen shot a glance under the brim of her bonnet. "You seem to want to say something. It probably isn't anything I haven't heard before."

"How do you mean?" Pat asked, though she knew very well what Fen meant.

Fen confirmed that in the next breath. "Oh, let me see. *Haven't I been engaged before?* Yes, twice. *Isn't this something of a whirlwind romance too?* Yes, it is. *Am I going to jilt him as I did the last two?* Ooh, I simply don't know yet." Her voice was as sweet as ever, but there was a definite edge to it. "*Have I thought about it sensibly?*—"

"I'm sure you did," Pat said over her. "And Jimmy is—or I always thought he was—a very decent man. I wouldn't have thought a girl could do better than a sensible, pleasant fellow like him."

"Well, then, that's all right isn't it?"

"No," Pat said. "That's why I wanted to know how you are. Because if I'd been asked to guess how Jimmy would treat the woman he'd just got engaged to, in his own home, where she was visiting for the first time—"

Fen held her hand up. It was a sudden, sharp gesture, almost jerky, and Pat stopped talking. They walked on, skirts rustling, feet crunching on the gravel path that ran around the lake.

"Is it terribly obvious?" Fen said at last. "Or is this just because you know him well?"

"I'd call it obvious," Pat said. "Sorry."

"Don't be sorry. I knew it, really. It certainly seems obvious to Maurice Haworth, judging by the way he smiles."

"He's a piece of work, isn't he? Look, I'm a friend of Jimmy's but in a, well, a mannish sort of way. I've never known him with a girl. I don't really know if he's used to being a fiancé, or if he understands that he's not paying as much attention as he ought."

"Are you making excuses for him?" Fen asked. "That is, do you think I ought to disregard the fact that he barely listens to me, had nothing to say to Mr. Haworth when he insulted me last night, and very obviously finds my presence an inconvenience at his party?"

That was a deal blunter than Pat had expected; in fact, blunt enough to make one reflect that this deliciously frothy young lady's father, at least, must be both fiercely intelligent and fiercely determined. She took a moment to adjust her expectations before replying. "I'm not making excuses, no. And I've no idea what you ought to do. But I'm fairly sure that if he's disregarding you now, before your father—" She clamped her lips shut, too late.

"Before my father has made over the large sum of money that's his reason for wanting to marry me. You might as well say it. Everyone knows it. *I* know it."

"If that was his reason—or his only reason—for proposing, he's stupider than I realised," Pat said. "Any man ought to think himself lucky to have you, leaving the money out of the question. But, yes, it is in question, and—" Loyalty to Jimmy and liking for Fen warred for a moment, along with a weaselly awareness that she wouldn't mind at all knowing that the engagement was off. That was unworthy, but Fen was alone and distressed and needed a friend. Pat salved her conscience with determination to be that friend. "Look, since you ask, he isn't showing himself to advantage in the slightest, and I think you'd be advised to have it out with him before you take an irreversible step. I do think he's capable of better," she made herself add. "I have the impression he's under a lot of stress at the moment. But he might need reminding of his responsibilities."

"You're contorting yourself to be fair to him," Fen observed. "I don't suppose you'd tolerate a fiancé treating you with disinterest."

"To be honest, if I had to marry, I'd far prefer a husband who was mostly unaware of my existence."

Fen gave a yelp of laughter. "Pat!"

"Well, I don't see the appeal," Pat said, grinning. "Men are dreadfully self-centred in my experience. One is expected to listen to everything they want to say while making their lives pleasant and all without a word of thanks. I may be biased," she added fairly. "I mostly know brothers, not husbands, and I've never felt any urge to marry, so you probably shouldn't ask my opinion. But I do feel that if you are to marry, if you *want* to, then—well, the other party ought to want to just as much."

"And Jimmy's not giving that impression," Fen said. "Is he?"

"Men do get cold feet, I understand," Pat said, before remembering she was talking to a double jilt. "Er..."

"And so do women, yes, yes. I didn't actually *want* to get cold feet again, you know. If I end a third engagement, people will say the most ghastly things about me, and Daddy will be quite exasperated. I've been telling myself that it's my fault for inviting myself here, trying to believe there's nothing at all to worry about and I'm just being silly. But there is something wrong. Isn't there?"

"Sorry," Pat said wretchedly. "Though I really don't know if—well, if it's anything to do with you."

"Who else would it be to do with?"

"Has Jimmy told you he's been having some sort of trouble with Haworth?"

"No," Fen said. "He hasn't told me anything. He hasn't said anything of any significance to me at all."

"Oh. Well, he did mention it, and…" Oh God. Was Haworth's victim Jimmy? He'd told her he couldn't retaliate against the man as he'd have liked. Suppose Jimmy was under his brother-in-law's thumb in some way?

She couldn't say so. To stain Jimmy with the suspicion that he'd done something worthy of blackmail would be utterly unfair. "I don't know. I have the impression there's more wrong with Haworth than just being a remarkably unpleasant man."

"Well, yes," Fen said. "For one thing, he's all but bankrupt. He was a junior partner in Threppel and Swing, the stockbroker business that collapsed six months ago and took a number of fortunes with it, including much of the Earl's. And for another—well, have you ever seen a more obvious drug fiend?"

"I *beg* your pardon?"

"Do you not think so?"

"I have absolutely no idea what a drug fiend might look like," Pat said. "Do you?"

"One meets them in London often enough—oh yes, in Society. The nervous tension and irritability are common signs. The thinness as well, in Lady Anna's case. I am pleased to know *I* shall never be suspected," she added, with a saucy look. "I should guess both Lady Anna and Mr. Haworth are habitual users of cocaine or some such, and if he is deprived of his supply here, or finding it hard to indulge freely, that will no doubt contribute to his dreadful ill temper."

"Well," Pat said, impressed. "Goodness. Lady Anna, really?"

"She's in with an awfully fast set. But, you know, none of that has changed from how it was when Jimmy proposed to me. I can't see what difference it makes."

"Having Haworth under his eyes, I suppose. Or maybe something did change that we don't know about. Or perhaps he's just an idiot. What are you going to do?"

"I really don't know," Fen said. "I thought that this would be a sensible choice. I didn't expect him to be terribly romantic, although he did propose awfully nicely, but I thought he would be *solid*. Do you know what I mean? I'm so tired of faces."

"Of what?"

"Faces. One meets someone, a man, and he has his society face for a stranger, and then a face for women, and another for his family, and one with his friends which is different from all the rest. That was why I ended my first engagement, you know. I heard him speaking of me to his friends. But I thought Jimmy was straightforward."

"I think that's a great deal to ask of anyone," Pat said. "Saying what one means and not doing the pretty leads to one being considered eccentric, or mannerless, and that's not awfully enjoyable. It's a great deal easier for everyone if we behave as expected in the circumstances."

"You don't."

That didn't come as a surprise, but it was still a blow. "I do try to. I wish I could do it more easily."

"I didn't mean it as a criticism," Fen said swiftly. "The opposite. I think it's marvellous. You say what you mean."

"Yes, and people think I'm dreadfully odd for it. But if one has four older brothers, the choice is to be uncompromising or a hopeless doormat. I chose to be uncompromising, and when one has acquired the habit of that, it's hard to stop. It feels like giving in, and I don't have any great urge to pander to others."

Fen stopped and swung around to face her. "No," she said forcefully. "Nor do I, at all, not inside, and yet I *do* it, all the time. Because that's what one is supposed to do. One is meant to be pleasing, and—and *cherishable*, as you said, and all those other things, and I've tried not to be like that, but it just doesn't work!"

"But I can't see why it would." Pat was hopelessly out of her depth. "That is, if you want Jimmy to be straightforward with you, why are you putting on an act with him?"

Fen's lips parted. Pat pressed on, recklessly. "Take the shooting. You did awfully well, you worked so hard, but as soon as Jimmy arrived, you started the fluffy business again. And he'd love to know you could shoot. He'd be thrilled. Why didn't you tell him?"

Fen didn't reply. Her eyes were huge.

"Why didn't you say?" Pat asked again. "Because I'm sure you don't need to put on a difference face for Jimmy. You're lovely as you are, and if he saw you as you are, surely—"

"But he didn't," Fen said. "He didn't see me; he didn't even propose to me. He proposed to rich Sir Peter Carruth's daughter. And I do understand he needs the money—but if he liked me, wouldn't he have looked at me properly?"

"But if you liked him, why wouldn't you show yourself properly, instead of pretending?"

"Because one can't," Fen said. "That's the whole point of different faces, that's why we have them. Because if you let people know who you really are and still all they see is a stupid trollop with delusions of being a New Woman—"

"Fen!"

"Look at me. I don't *look* serious. I've got a big bosom and a giggle. Nobody ever takes me seriously. Daddy has never explained telephones to me, not once, and when I set myself to learn he looked at me as though I were a dog that had set itself to turn head over heels, and laughed, and then two days later he sent me to finishing school. So that was that. I am *pretty* and *sweet*." She enunciated the words. "I have been brought up to be pretty and sweet just as you've been brought up to be uncompromising and I *want* to be uncompromising. I want to absolutely smash Maurice Haworth when he says vile things instead of turning it away and pretending not to be offended in order to smooth things over. You wouldn't giggle if he insinuated something horrible about you."

Pat wasn't entirely sure he hadn't. "I don't know what I'd do if he was openly rude to my face, though we may well find out before this party is over. But there's nothing wrong with trying to keep the peace. Guests at the Earl's table can't get into brawls with his son-in-law."

"Yes, but I bet you won't just giggle." Fen sounded furious, possibly with herself. "Whereas I always react with—with *fluff*."

"That's not a virtue of mine, it's an incapacity. I'm no good at smoothing over situations and making things easy for people, and I couldn't be fluffy to save my life. May I make an observation?"

"Go on."

"You're awfully down on yourself, and I don't see why," Pat said. "There's nothing in the world wrong with you, including your laugh." She didn't mention the bosom, with which there was absolutely nothing wrong at all. Quite the opposite. "And really, it seems to me that you'd have less trouble getting people to treat you with respect if you gave yourself a little more. People are awfully lazy, and ready to take other people at the value they put on themselves without thinking twice. You can't expect someone like Jimmy to, to—"

"Have any insight into his future wife's character?"

"I don't know how you get away with the fluffy business for a minute," Pat said with feeling. "All right, yes. But that's in your hands as well as his. If you want to marry him and be happy, perhaps you need to have a frank conversation about what you're both hoping for before you find yourselves stuck with one another for good under a lot of misapprehensions."

"Yes," Fen said. "We should. Only, I have been here for three days now, and every time I have asked Jimmy to explain how something works, or to talk about the future, he's changed the subject. That walk around the lake we had earlier—I hoped he might talk to me, and I thought he might make love to me, but do you know what he actually did?"

"No," Pat said, with foreboding.

"Talked about you."

"What?"

"He talked about all your shooting achievements," Fen said with precision, "and then he talked about how he'd met you, which led him on to a number of reminiscences of your brother at Oxford and visits to your family and how marvellously you ran the house and what a wonderfully quiet, soothing person you are—"

"Fen! Listen. If you are afraid Jimmy harbours any sort of—of feelings for me, you couldn't be more wrong. We've known one another for years. He could have proposed at any time if he wanted to, and he didn't."

"Did you want him to?" Fen asked, then caught herself. "I beg your pardon. I shouldn't have asked that."

"It's all right," Pat said. "I considered it as a possibility, in a theoretical sort of way, but not because of any feelings I have for Jimmy. I'd love to live somewhere like this, to run this estate, and I think I'd do it well, but the husband would be the means to an end. I did wonder if Jimmy might want that sort of business partnership because he's never seemed terribly interested in love affairs, but it seems he just hadn't met the right woman."

Fen gave her a look. Pat winced. "Sorry, that was trite. But you must agree, if he hardly seemed interested in women before and then fell in love with you more or less at first sight, that says something."

"It could say a number of things. Such as that the woman he really wanted simply wasn't interested, so he might as well make an advantageous match—"

"No, I am not having this," Pat said, setting off walking again. "It's honestly not right. I may not be one for romance but I'm sure I'd have known if Jimmy thought of me that way. And he's Bill's best pal; he would have said something. You're wrong there."

Fen sighed. "I'm not sure if I'm pleased to hear you say so."

"Why not?"

"I was preparing to renounce him nobly. Nobody could blame me for breaking an engagement to a man who promptly married someone else."

"You're thinking seriously of breaking the engagement?" *Do. He's all wrong for you. He won't appreciate you. You ought not be weighted down by men and marriage and motherhood.* Pat bit all that back. "Should you not talk to him first, have that frank conversation?"

Fen didn't answer for a while. They paced on together, rounding the end of the lake and heading back up the other side, towards the house.

"The thing is..." Fen said at last. "This will probably sound terribly self-centred, but I am so tired of not being seen. I want someone to be interested in what I want, and who I am. Not all the time, but just a little. Just to *notice*. Just to talk to me instead of flirting with rich Peter Carruth's daughter, or expecting me to sit and listen while they speak. It's why I got engaged the first time. He paid me so much attention and it felt like nothing I'd ever experienced. It was an awfully good technique, if he'd been more careful about being overheard. And Jimmy...well, he's terribly nice, but he isn't looking at me. He hasn't since I arrived. And if he isn't interested in doing that, I don't want to ask him to. I oughtn't *have* to ask for the most basic acknowledgement of my existence."

"I don't understand," Pat said. "I'm sorry, but I don't. How would anyone not notice you?"

"I don't mean being looked at or being the centre of attention at a party because I have jewels and dresses and the bosom. Well, in fact, that's the point. Everyone looks at those. Everyone thinks silly, frothy Miss Carruth with the—" She made a hand gesture indicating a chest twice the size of her own that made Pat's stomach flutter. "Nobody looks past it."

"But you— Oh. That's the fluffy business, isn't it?" Pat said. "You're daring people not to see."

"Not daring. It's just, if they aren't going to see me anyway, I'd rather they ignored me for an act than for the real thing."

Pat stopped again and turned. Fen was flushed, eyes wide, seeking understanding, and Pat didn't even realise she'd reached for her hand before she felt the soft, warm fingers grip hers. Neither of them was wearing gloves, and Fen's skin on Pat's—

It was only the touch of hands, for all the pressure of Fen's fingers. It didn't mean anything.

"I don't understand how anyone could not see you," Pat said again. "I don't see how they couldn't look. I don't see how they could stop."

Fen's lips parted slightly. They were adorable lips, plump and dark pink, which was an awful thing to notice when someone was upset. She didn't speak, and Pat couldn't think of anything else to say. They just looked at one another, fingers clasped, and something fluttered in Pat's chest like a partridge flushed out of cover.

Fen was engaged to Jimmy. He didn't even appreciate her. It wasn't *fair*.

The moment stretched. Pat didn't want to break it, had no idea what else to do. Then Fen gave her a sudden, quick smile, and turned to continue walking, and Pat had a fraction of a second to feel the devastating wash of disappointment before a tug made her realise that Fen hadn't let go of her hand. She hurried to catch up before Fen had to let go and they kept walking under the afternoon sun, in silence, up to the top of the lake nearest the house and then, in unspoken agreement, back around for a second circuit.

It was a lovely lake.

It felt awkward at first to be quiet. Pat was very happy to sit or walk in silent companionship, but many people found that uncomfortable and were desperate to fill the void with noise. She had assumed the voluble Fen would prefer speech to silence, but they sauntered on, and the minutes passed filled with nothing but birdsong and the striation of insects.

"I've been rather silly, haven't I?" Fen said at last.

"Possibly," Pat said with caution. "About what?"

"Oh, I don't know. Men. Marriage. Myself, mostly. Goodness, that was alliterative. You're quite right. If I took myself seriously, I wouldn't have plunged headlong into one engagement, let alone three. And I shouldn't stand here—walk here—hoping that Jimmy will realise he isn't behaving well. He *ought* to, but since he isn't, I shouldn't wait for him to do so, or tolerate it if he doesn't. Do you think I ought to talk to Jimmy, really, to try and make it work? I shan't say *if you were me*, because you wouldn't be in this position in the first place, but—should I?"

I think you should break it off because he's too pig-headed to understand what he's got. I think you should stay here with me, walking in the sun, and come back to a house that isn't Jimmy's to sit over tea and cakes, and in the evening...

In the evening, nothing. Pat stepped hard on the thought. Fen couldn't escape her engagement without consequences: even a wealthy heiress could expect the invitations to dry up if she jilted a third fiancé. Jimmy was a decent man, and if he was a little self-absorbed, that made him no different from anyone else. Pat had no doubt he could become a good husband, if matters were clearly explained to him. Fen would be a countess, a marvellous one who would turn Rodington Court into a fashionable destination, and Jimmy could keep up the estate and the hundreds of people whose livelihoods sprang from it. It was the best outcome for everyone.

"You should talk to him," she said. "You should tell him what you want and expect. And if he listens, then—then I imagine you'll be very happy."

"And if he doesn't listen?"

"Talk louder until he hears you, I suppose." She couldn't resist adding, "And if he doesn't like what he hears, you'll have information on which to base a decision."

Fen glanced at her, eyes glimmering bright. "That sounds terribly sensible."

"I am sensible," Pat said. "That's exactly what I am. I wear Rational Dress and sensible shoes and run a household and make carefully thought-out decisions. I do all those things because they have to be done, but I think people ought to have some frivolity too. Circuses as well as bread. And if Jimmy, or anyone else, tells you that you ought to become serious and competent and sensible, they're wrong. Lots of us can do that. Very few people make others happy, or care to, and that's clearly something you do."

Fen's hand tightened convulsively. She swallowed, and Pat had a terrible moment wondering if she'd been too much, too outspoken, before Fen replied.

"That is the loveliest thing anyone has ever said to me. Thank you, Pat."

"Well, it's true. And why ought you or anyone conform to a particular idea of how you should be? There's no shortage of any kind of people, so we might as well let each other be ourselves."

"*Yes*," Fen said intensely. "That is absolutely right. Why should one woman not be a serious vegetarian, and another a champion shooter, and a third a fluffy sort of—"

"—delightful person to be with," Pat put in.

Fen dimpled. "And the fourth a drug fiend, I suppose, but one must take the rough with the smooth."

"Maybe Lady Anna wouldn't be a drug fiend if Haworth wasn't such a dreadful specimen."

"It just goes to show, one must marry with care," Fen concluded. "I can't tell you how much better I feel for talking it out. Thank you for talking to me, Pat. Thank you for noticing."

"Of course," Pat mumbled. She was trying hard *not* to notice the increased pressure of Fen's fingers on hers. "Any time."

"Oh," Fen said after a few quiet moments. "Have you been to the gazebo?"

"I haven't."

"It's lovely. This way." Fen tugged her off the lake path through a stand of trees. After a few moments in the dappled shade of the woods, they came out under the sky, and Pat caught her breath at the vista as the land opened up in front of them.

"Glorious."

"Isn't it? And one can sit and appreciate the view out of the sun. Jimmy showed me."

Pat preferred walking and sunshine to sitting and preserving her complexion, but Fen's company trumped the rest. She followed her to the indicated summerhouse, which her housekeeping eye noted as needing a lick of paint, and they seated themselves on wrought iron chairs.

"That's better," Fen said. "I don't envy you the prospect of spending all day marching over the moors."

"I love it. I do a lot of walking at home. Or, I did."

"Do you have to stop?"

"I have to leave. It's my brother's house, of course, and now he's married—"

"They're throwing you out?" Miss Carruth sat very straight, eyes sparkling with indignation. "That's horrible!"

"Of course they're not. They both asked me to stay. But I've been running the house on Jonty's behalf since I was a girl, which was all very well when I was mistress of the place, but that's Olivia, his wife, now. If I stay I'll end up acting as housekeeper, because I'm an awfully managing person. That wouldn't be fair to Olivia in her new home, and it wouldn't be fair to me."

"Oh, I see. So what will you do?"

"I don't know. Good heavens, I am tired of those three words," she added with feeling. "Bill and Jonty keep asking me, but I simply don't know. I have to find some sort of purpose, though; I'm not ready to fill my idle hours with trivia. I want something to *do*."

"What sort of something?"

"I thought I might teach shooting," Pat said. "If one had a school, just ladies, so they could practice without men offering comment… It's just an idea. I've some money of my own, I wouldn't need to make a fortune, but it would be an occupation. I've had an occupation all my life and I don't know what to do with myself now it's gone."

Fen's face was such a picture of sympathy that Pat had to look away. "That seems dreadfully unfair."

"It can't be helped. Jonty is entitled to marry and I hope they'll be very happy. But it did remind me that I have no place in the world. It's an odd feeling to find myself uprooted."

"You don't *seem* rootless," Fen said. "We're rootless, Daddy and I, because he's risen out of his sphere. His family are embarrassed to mix with a very rich man and the people we *do* mix with tend to look down because of where he came from. I'm betwixt and between. Whereas you seem to know exactly who you are."

"I did. I've a family line that goes back to the Plantagenets. I had a house to run and a lot of brothers to look after. And now Jonty has Olivia, and I barely see Bill any more, and it's not my house, and the Plantagenets aren't much of a comfort under the circumstances. I need to find a life of my own, only I don't really know what that ought to look like, and I don't want to end up a put-upon companion, or one of those unwanted elderly spinsters always in people's way. Sorry," Pat added. "I'm pouring all my troubles into your lap and they're really very insignificant."

"Nonsense." Fen leaned forward in a rustle of cloth, putting a hand on her knee. "Of course they're significant. It must be horribly difficult and disconcerting—and I know what you mean about wanting to find something to do. *I* do, except all I'm fit to do is marry somebody and I haven't even done very well at that. Whereas you're wonderfully capable and you have *ideas*. I think the shooting school is a marvellous plan. I shall be your first pupil and give a testimonial." She squeezed Pat's knee. Pat's thigh tensed in instinctive response; she prayed Fen didn't notice. "I am sure you'll find your place once you decide what you want it to be. And I dare say that seems awfully daunting when you've always *had* a place and never had to think about it, but you aren't in a rush, are you? You can take a few months to learn how not to live your old life, before you decide what the new one ought to look like. And once you've had some time to *not* be Pat who looks after her brothers, that might make space for Pat who's going to do something else. Does that make sense?"

She was positively clutching Pat's knee with her earnestness now, and Pat had to pause for a moment to take in the sensation, and the meaning of the words, and the fierce interest. "It makes the most sense I think I've ever heard," she said at last. "Really, it does. I'm not fond of putting off decisions, but you're exactly right."

"Maybe you should *decide* not to do anything, then. Set yourself to actively not do things. Wake up in the morning and make a list of idlenesses, all of which must be strictly ignored before dinner-time."

"I might have to do that," Pat admitted. "Thank you, Fen. That really does help. You're very acute, I think."

Fen positively glowed. Her eyes were bright, her mouth was a perfect curve of satisfaction, her hand was warm on Pat's knee, and if Jimmy Yoxall had appeared at that moment, Pat might have been tempted to shove him into the lake.

CHAPTER SIX

A fter such a day, Pat could not muster any enthusiasm about going down for dinner. She had had more intense conversation over the course of a few hours than she usually had in a month, not to mention the extraordinary one she'd overheard. She would have liked to retire to bed with a plate of sandwiches and a chance to think: to cherish that time with Fen around the lake, to consider both of their predicaments in the light of their talk, and mostly to recover her moral strength. She found people far more exhausting than any bodily exercise, and the prospect of two hours of conversation over a meal with Maurice Haworth followed by tea with the ladies felt like a burden she had no desire to lift. She just hoped the evening would be less unpleasant than the previous night.

But Fen would be at dinner, so Pat dressed as best she could. If she'd owned a gown that could be called frivolous she might have selected it to demonstrate solidarity, but she did not. She donned her best necklace, a seed pearl choker that had been a gift from Louisa, and toyed with the idea of asking the maid to arrange her hair into something more elaborate, but lost her nerve. It was only an informal party. Bill would think she'd run mad.

Her reluctance delayed her to the point that she was the last into the drawing-room. Everyone else was there, everyone was silent, and the atmosphere as she walked in had all the joie de vivre of a thunderstorm.

Preston Keynes even looked thunderous. He was standing in a corner with Miss Singh, shoulders hunched aggressively. Miss Singh's face was blank in the sort of way that made Pat think she was trying very hard not to let her feelings be seen. Lady Anna's eyes were bright, her facial muscles tight, and she spoke to Jack Bouvier-Lynes in a rapid, high-pitched tone that would doubtless have sounded natural at a Chelsea cocktail party. Bill and Jimmy stood with Fen and the Countess. Jimmy looked strained; their hostess had spots of red on her cheekbones; Fen was smiling, but her cheeks were scarlet, and not in a pretty way.

Maurice Haworth and the Earl were together in the centre of the room, angled as if speaking but too far apart from one another. The Earl's face was tense. Haworth was smiling.

Pat straightened her back as she came in. "I'm terribly sorry; am I late?"

"Not at all, Miss Merton," the Earl said with hollow heartiness.

"Ah, Diana, the huntress," Mr. Haworth said with his curling, nasty smile. Pat gave him a rapid once-over. She knew nothing about the drug habit, but anyone could see there was something wrong with the man. She put it down to a twist in the head, herself. Maurice Haworth liked to make other people unhappy, and that wasn't a symptom of any drug she'd ever heard of.

"My name is Patricia, Mr. Haworth," she said briskly. "How's the weather looking for tomorrow, sir?"

"Windy," the Earl returned. "I fear we must expect storms later in the week."

"Oh, what a shame!" Pat exclaimed. "At the very start of the season. Rotten luck."

"The consequences of our location. We're as prone to bad weather as any Scottish house—more, perhaps. It's not unknown for us to be cut off by flash floods."

"Really?"

"There are two rivers coming down from the high ground to the north, you see, and when there has been a dry spell followed by torrential rain, the results tend to be spectacular. We plan for it, of course; we shan't run out of supplies."

"Thank goodness," Pat said. "One wouldn't want to be reduced to eating one's fellow guests."

The Earl gave a hearty laugh, but Maurice Haworth's eyes lit up. "What an idea, Miss Merton. I wonder who we should cook first? You and my dear wife have too little meat on you for a satisfactory meal, I think, whereas Miss Carruth would be rather a *rich* feast under any circumstances. And the flavour of Miss Singh's flesh—"

"What a very peculiar subject for a drawing room." Pat spoke with all the ice at her command, and Haworth actually stopped in his tracks, probably reminded of his old nurse. She didn't give him any time to recover, but turned to the Earl. "We must take advantage of the good weather as it lasts, then. May I ask what ground we'll cover tomorrow?"

The Earl's eyes had flickered to Haworth, a tiny fearful movement, but he made an effort at joviality as he replied. "We'll go in the direction of Trinder Wood first. I think we can promise you some good coverts."

"Oh, excellent," Bill said at her shoulder. "I had some marvellous shooting there two years ago, I don't know if you recall, sir?"

His cheerfulness sounded forced to Pat's sisterly ear. He was probably angry, as well he might be, and she felt a little glow. Perhaps everyone else in this house was intimidated by the loathsome Haworth, but if the man chose to tangle with the united Mertons he'd find out his mistake.

The Earl sounded distracted as he set out their route for the next day. Pat kept her eyes fixed on his face, attempting to demonstrate her absorption in shooting to the exclusion of all else. She could feel Haworth's gaze on her skin and knew a decided sinking sensation when it was time to go into dinner.

Buck up, girl, she told herself as she seated herself opposite him. *If nobody else is going to put him in his place, you can show Fen how it's done.*

The meal began, if not well, at least adequately, with a manful effort by Preston Keynes to start a conversation by offering, apropos of nothing at all, an anecdote about a visit to a theatre he'd made earlier in the year where a man had had to be removed for shouting Irish Nationalist slogans.

"Oh, we saw that show," Bill said. "Jimmy and I. No Irish nationalists then, though. It was a good piece, I thought."

"Jolly good," Jimmy said, so flatly that it caused an embarrassed silence. This time Mr. Bouvier-Lynes leapt in with a story about a well-known actress that got a few laughs, although it caused the Countess to purse her lips. Miss Singh restored decorum by speaking with knowledge and surprising animation about the work of George Bernard Shaw, a playwright whose intellectual pretensions were over the heads of most of the party.

"I saw *Captain Brassbound's Conversion*," Fen offered unexpectedly. "That's Mr. Shaw, isn't it?"

"One of his comedies. Did you like it?" Miss Singh asked.

"It was very…" Fen hesitated. "Thoughtful. It had more talking than I expected for a play about lady explorers and smugglers and Moorish castles."

"Were you hoping for melodrama?" Miss Singh's smile robbed the words of offence.

"Yes, honestly, I was," Fen said. "I like spectacles and adventures and excitement and sweeping passions. And chariot races! Jimmy took me to see *Ben-Hur* at the Savoy, you know, with the race and the horses, and it was desperately thrilling, wasn't it?"

There was a pause. Pat couldn't see Fen, on Jimmy's other side, without leaning forward in an ill-mannered way, but she could well imagine her smile faltering. She wondered if she ought to kick his ankle, even as Bill said, "Was it, Jimmy?"

"What?"

"Miss Carruth was just saying how you took her to *Ben-Hur* and that it was thrilling." Bill's voice had a decided edge. "Did you enjoy yourself?"

Jimmy's lips parted. He didn't reply.

"For heaven's sake, are you mute?" Lady Anna said, with contempt that sounded to Pat more than just sisterly. "We saw it, didn't we, Jack? A ridiculous noisy farrago only fit for the feeble-minded."

Pat heard Fen's intake of breath; saw the tiny smile curve Haworth's thin lips. The Countess said, *"Anna."*

"I saw it as well," Bill said loudly. "Marvellous stuff. Enjoyed every minute. In fact, I want to see it again. Pat, old thing, would you care to come with me when we're back down south? My treat."

"I'd love to," Pat said. "It sounds precisely my sort of thing." She caught Miss Singh's tiny approving nod, and added, "Would you care to join us, Miss Singh?"

"Oh, surely—" Maurice Haworth began.

Miss Singh said over him, "I would be delighted. Thank you. I am sure I shall find it entertaining."

Lady Anna's cheeks were heavily powdered for Pat's taste; it didn't hide the flare of red over her cheeks. Mr. Haworth drawled, "Such unity. And what did you think, Jack? Do you share my wife's opinion, or will you side with the majority?"

"I found it absurd yet greatly enjoyable," Mr. Bouvier-Lynes said with a smile. "So I agree with all parties."

"Of course you do." Lady Anna sounded icy but her nostrils were flared. Apparently she hadn't expected to be slapped down quite so comprehensively. "How strange. I had thought you said something completely different to me. A man for all seasons, aren't you, Jack?"

"Mr. Bouvier-Lynes is behaving with decorum at the dinner-table," the Countess said. "Something that I should not have to tell my daughter to emulate."

Lady Anna inhaled sharply. "My dear," the Earl mumbled.

"This is my table," the Countess said. Her voice was edged with something like defiance. "I think I may speak to my daughter as I choose. Now, let—"

"But she isn't your daughter," Haworth said silkily. "She's my wife. I think some of you around this table are in danger of forgetting that, aren't you? Anna certainly does, and I think it slips Jack's mind too."

The Countess's mouth was a rigid line. She was looking ahead, not at Haworth. Jimmy stared at his plate. Pat tried to catch Bill's eye. She couldn't tell what was happening, but the atmosphere was thick as stew.

"Granted she is your wife," the Earl said, with audible reluctance. "But she was our daughter first and my wife is entitled to speak to her—"

"No, she is not," Haworth said. His tone was light, even pleasant, except for a coil of malice that hung around the words like cigarette smoke. "I don't choose to have *my wife* insulted. Do I, Anna?"

"For God's sake," Jimmy said through his teeth, as though the words were forced out. "A few words in the heat of the moment. Let's just forget it, shall we? We're starting at seven tomorrow, gentlemen—which includes you, Pat; does everyone have things ready?"

Pat thought for a moment that Haworth was going to take umbrage. He stared at Jimmy with an unpleasant smile, then sat back and returned his attention to his food as Preston Keynes, conversational martyr, launched into a description of his shooting gear which had the sole merit of papering over everyone else's silence.

Pat didn't think she could bear retiring with the ladies. It took a strong moral effort and a mental reminder that she'd otherwise be leaving Fen with her future sister-in-law to force her to the drawing room, where she was rewarded with the announcement that Lady Anna had gone to bed with a headache.

"What a shame," said Miss Singh, in a tone so flat that Pat had to turn away and examine a vase to recover her composure. "Are you all right, Aunt Mattie?"

"Of course," the Countess said, and then, "No, not really. Perhaps you will all excuse me. I have the headache too. Victoria, please order tea."

"I'll come up with you," Miss Singh said. "Miss Carruth can do the honours, I'm sure."

Fen assured her she could, gave the Countess good wishes, rang the bell once they had gone, turned to Pat, and said, "Do you need something other than tea?"

"Definitely."

"So do I. What does one drink after dinner that isn't champagne? Or should we just have that?"

"It must be marvellous to be rich," Pat said. "I don't know if the Wittons keep champagne on ice at all times. To be honest, I usually have brandy with my brothers. Sherry?"

"Brandy sounds like a good idea. It's medicinal, isn't it?"

"Yes, but it's hardly—"

A footman entered. Fen said, "Oh, thank you," with her usual smile: she was, Pat had noticed, always warmly polite to staff. "Could we have the brandy decanter and two glasses, please?"

"The...brandy, miss?"

"The brandy, yes."

The man opened his mouth. Fen gave him a sparkling smile. He blinked, bowed, departed, and returned shortly with a tray.

"Thank you so much. That will be all, please shut the door," Fen said, with decision, and sloshed brandy into a balloon glass as he left. "Here you are."

Pat took the half-full glass she was handed, with some trepidation. "Good heavens, this is enough to stun a horse. Have you ever drunk this before?"

"No." Fen took a sip, and made a gargoyle face. "Gah. I can see why not. Ack. Do you *like* this?"

"Yes, but one does have to get used to it. It is definitely medicinal, though."

"Like chloroform." Fen flopped onto the settle, very much to one side, despite her skirts. Pat took up the unspoken invitation and seated herself, a little self-consciously, by her. "My goodness. *What* an evening."

"Wasn't it just."

"That might have been the worst meal since…the previous one. Good heavens."

"What is going *on* here?" Pat demanded. "You must have some idea. I could swear Haworth was threatening the Countess. Why on earth is everyone tolerating him?"

"I have no idea. How could Jimmy let him speak to his mother like that?"

"How could he let Lady Anna speak to you like that?" Pat returned.

"Oh, but Mr. Merton was awfully nice," Fen said with a glimmer of a smile. "I felt quite rescued."

"He's all right, but he oughtn't have had to do it. For heaven's sake. If this is how Haworth behaves with guests there, what on earth is he like en famille?"

"Actually, it would probably be better, or at least no worse," Fen said. "He seems to like humiliating people, and I dare say that's even jollier done in front of witnesses."

"Good Lord. That *is* an observation." Pat thought it through, with a decided and growing revulsion. "Yes, I think you're right. No wonder Jimmy can't stick the idea of him moving in for good. I still don't understand why the Wittons put up with it."

"I wonder if they know something will get worse if they argue with him."

"That he'd take it out on Lady Anna, you mean?"

"Or their child."

They both contemplated that for a moment, then Fen took a very deliberate sip of brandy, hardly wincing at all. "Do you think Miss Singh knows what's going on?"

"She may. Let's ask." Fen snorted; Pat grinned. "Well, be dam— that is, let's not bother with subtlety. This is the family you're meant to be marrying into. Which—"

"Oh, don't."

"I'm sorry, but I think I have to." *No, you don't!* friendship shouted. She ignored it. "There's something badly wrong here, and Jimmy isn't dealing with it, and nor is the Earl. It seems to me Haworth has licence to be as malevolent as he chooses to his extended family. I think at the very least you ought to know why before you sign up to be his sister-in-law."

"I know," Fen said. "Only, I did try to catch Jimmy earlier and he said he was busy and tomorrow the shooting starts—"

"You can't just drift into marriage because your fiancé doesn't have time to talk to you."

"I *know.*" Fen spoke more sharply than was her habit. "I have no intention of ignoring this. And whatever sort of brute Haworth is, tonight started because of Lady Anna being appallingly rude to me, if you recall, so even if there was nothing wrong with him, I'd want to know what on earth is wrong with *her*—"

Her eyes were glistening wet. "Don't cry," Pat said hopelessly.

"I'm not." Fen pressed her lips together. A single tear overspilled her eye and slid down her cheek; she batted it away. "But the fact is when someone is so rude and hateful— I have never done anything to her! I've always tried to be polite even though nobody would receive her if she wasn't an earl's daughter. Why do they both hate me so much?"

It was a cry of real pain, and Pat grasped her hand without even thinking. "Oh, Fen, don't let them worry you. He hates everyone. Like Iago, you know, who hates Othello because *He hath a daily beauty in his life That makes me ugly.* That's Haworth all over, if you ask me. And as for Lady Anna—"

"Don't tell me she's jealous. I hate it when people say that about bullies, especially when it's clearly not true."

"I was going to say she's probably very unhappy and taking it out on other people. I have no idea if she's jealous of you, but if she isn't, she ought to be. You're ten times prettier, a hundred times nicer, and not married to that dreadful man."

"I am not at all prettier," Fen said, perking up. "She has a wonderful figure."

"That's in the eye of the beholder. And if the beholder likes good eyes and a lovely smile and the spirit of a delightful, happy person infusing them, not to mention a quite outstanding bosom—"

Pat stopped herself there, suddenly aware that the strong spirits on top of two glasses of wine had led her into indiscretion. Hard on the heels of that came the realisation that Fen had almost certainly thought of her words as a purely aesthetic compliment, the sort of thing ladies always said to one another, and wouldn't have seen anything in it if Pat hadn't cut herself off like that...

Fen was looking at her, eyes wide, lips quivering on the verge of a smile. Pat very much did not want her to laugh.

"Outstanding?" Fen shifted round, facing Pat, and moved her hands to cup the sides of her spectacular décolletage, giving it all a gentle, slightly jiggly boost upwards. "Would you say so?"

Pat couldn't look away. Nobody could, from that expanse of creamy skin. "I... well, it's certainly standing out. In that dress, I mean. Yes. Not— it's not just the dress," she added hastily. "It's definitely the bosom."

She tore her gaze away and up. Fen's eyes were brimming with mischief and glee and something else, which looked almost like excitement, and Pat thought, *I could kiss her. I could lean forward and—*

She's engaged to Jimmy. Your friend.

He doesn't deserve her.

That's not up to you.

No, it's up to her.

The thoughts arrived in Pat's head on one another's heels. She wanted to kiss Fen more than anything in the world and couldn't make herself do it. An engaged woman; a new friend she might repel, which would be worse than anything; and even if Fen wasn't repelled in principle, why would someone like her even *think* about angular, mannish Pat with her straight figure in a plain dress?

Fen's brows angled in a little frown. "Pat?"

"Yes?" Her voice sounded rather feeble.

"You say such awfully lovely things to me." Fen's eyes were on hers, searching her face. "And I don't think I've ever said anything complimentary to you."

"That doesn't matter. I'm not fishing." Were they, after all, merely engaging in girlish chatter of the sort Pat had never mastered but other women seemed to do by instinct?

"Of course you're not," Fen said. "You've never fished in your life except for trout, I expect. And I don't think you think much of yourself, do you?"

Pat felt her face heat, with embarrassment or disappointment, she wasn't sure which. "There's not much to think of," she muttered, gruffly.

Fen leaned forward, studying her face, then raised a brow. "Eye of the beholder," she said, and kissed her.

It was a swift brush of lips on lips, which could conceivably have been a kiss between friends, because Fen didn't repeat it, but she didn't move her face back either. Pat froze, hopelessly wanting and locked in uncertainty, and then Fen kissed her again, still lightly but with much more deliberation, and Pat thought, with overwhelming relief, *Right. Yes. This.*

She lifted a hand, touching her fingertips to the soft, powdered skin of Fen's rounded cheek. Fen gave a little whimpering noise that tingled through all sorts of places, and then they were kissing again, both of them this time, Pat's lips moving by instinct, Fen's warm and soft and tasting of brandy. Pat slid her hand down, meaning only to drop it to Fen's hip, and discovered she'd miscalculated Fen's bosom when she felt bare skin and a hard frill of lace under her fingers. Fen squeaked; Pat froze, ready to begin an apology, but Fen pressed her own hand over Pat's, keeping it there, and she might in fact be dead now, or hallucinating, because this was heaven. She, plain Pat Merton, kissing the loveliest girl in the world, hand on her breast—

There were footsteps and male voices, outside the door.

Pat jerked away, too violently. Fen's eyes widened in distress; then the footsteps approached, the door handle rattled, and within a fraction of a second her face slid into the mask of Delightful Young Lady, even as she swiped at Pat's mouth with a firm thumb to remove powder or paint. She turned smoothly as the door opened, reaching for her brandy glass. "Oh, Mr. Merton, how nice! And Mr. Keynes. We were wondering if we'd be alone all evening."

"Is Miss Singh not with you?" Mr. Keynes asked.

"She went upstairs with the Countess, who has the headache, as does Lady Anna."

"I'm sure," Bill said. "Are you drinking brandy?"

"Yes," Pat said. She couldn't recover with anything like Fen's lightning speed—her lips still felt swollen, her body oddly sensitive considering Fen hadn't even touched her—but she had her self-control more or less in place, plus a faith born of experience in her brother's lack of observational skills. "Aren't you?"

"I already had a post-prandial glass with the gentlemen." Bill didn't sound as though that had been the most enjoyable of evenings. "I'd ask what has brought on this debauchery, but…"

"Indeed. Where are our fellow guests?"

"Jack volunteered for a game of billiards with Haworth," said Mr. Keynes. "Good fellow. Jimmy is with the Earl, I believe. Something to discuss."

"I imagine he'll be some time," Bill said, with a bite in his voice. "Miss Carruth, I hope you're all right?"

"I'm very well indeed," Fen assured him. "Did you really go to see *Ben-Hur*?"

"I did, yes. The first week of June. When did you see it?" He fired the question at her like a prosecutor.

"Er...the week after that, I suppose?" Fen said, sounding not unreasonably startled. "It was early June, I—"

"And that was when you got engaged?"

"Jimmy proposed a few days later. That weekend. Why do you ask, Mr. Merton?"

"Oh, nothing. Wondering if *Ben-Hur* is the route to a woman's heart, I suppose. I'd have thought he might have picked something a bit more romantic."

"You'd have to ask Jimmy about his thought processes, I'm afraid." Fen spoke with a smile, and Pat couldn't hear any tension in her voice, but she was positive it was there. She wished Bill would shut up, or pick any other topic. She didn't want to talk about Jimmy herself, so she couldn't imagine what Fen felt, and the nerve-scraping atmosphere that seemed to attend every gathering in this atrocious party was back again.

Or perhaps that was just her. Perhaps that was how one felt, and deserved to feel, when one kissed a good friend's fiancée.

"Well, it's the first tomorrow," Mr. Keynes said into the silence. "Start of the season, eh? I might turn in, get a good night's sleep."

"Good idea," Bill said. "I imagine we'll make a long day of it, if the weather holds. Best to take advantage, if there are storms coming."

"Storms?" Fen repeated. "You mean, you might not be able to go out shooting?"

"Yes, we might all be confined to the house together," Pat said. "That will be jolly."

"Won't it," Fen said faintly. "Mr. Keynes is right: I shall go to bed. I need to gather my strength."

CHAPTER SEVEN

The day started magnificently, in large part because Maurice Haworth wasn't there.

Pat had lain awake for a couple of very uncomfortable hours the previous night, torn between guilt and desire, with the memory of Fen a palpable presence on her lips and a tempting ache between her legs.

It wasn't the first time she'd kissed, or been kissed. She and Louisa Maitland had been inseparable at school, a passionate friendship that had meant significantly more to Pat than to Louisa, because the latter had married her Hugo eighteen months ago. It was the way of things, she knew. Schoolgirl passions happened and were forgotten, everyone said so. Perhaps Pat should have grown out of them by now.

But she hadn't, because Fen was taking up a very large space in her thoughts. It was desperately sweet, badly tempting, and wrong. Fen was engaged, for heaven's sake, and Pat ought to keep her admiration to herself. Girls crushed on other girls; grown women left that sort of thing behind in favour of men. Or, at least, that was what she'd been told at school, though the headmistress's speech had been so vague and allusive as to be near-incomprehensible. The gist of it all had seemed to be that she would discover an interest in men along with interests in all the other adult things that seemed so tedious, like painting, or playing the piano, or embroidery.

The throb at her core was a reminder that she hadn't. She wondered uncomfortably if Maurice Haworth had somehow sensed that, in that comment about not being like other women; she wondered again why Fen had kissed her. If she'd had passionate friendships at school too; if she'd outgrown them; if she would soon marry, just like Louisa. If, if, if.

Pat felt somewhat frowsty in the morning, but her crochets were quickly blown away by the breeze. The day was bright, early September sun giving the world a golden glow, and it was possible for a while to think of nothing but the hunt.

The party consisted of the Earl, Jimmy, Mr. Keynes, Mr. Bouvier-Lynes, Bill, and Pat, plus three well-trained dogs and the beaters with the game-cart and hampers. They started at a cover on the edge of a spinney. The wind was fairly stiff and the birds wary, making for tricky shooting. The Earl, used to the weather, bagged four birds; Jimmy and Mr. Keynes both took three. Bill, who was sadly out of practice, only winged a single partridge and cursed himself for an incompetent; Mr. Bouvier-Lynes wasted his shot entirely; and Pat brought down seven.

"Magnificent, old girl," Bill told her, with a clap to the shoulder. "By God, you get better and better."

"I'm awestruck," Mr. Bouvier-Lynes said. "When you've finished instructing Miss Carruth, will you accept a new pupil?"

"Superb," Jimmy agreed. "I did tell you, sir."

"He said you'd outshoot the best of us, Miss Merton, and he was right." Lord Witton seemed himself out here, in his weatherbeaten shooting garb, walking his lands with a countryman's leisurely stride. He looked decent, dignified, happy, not the silenced old man of last night.

By the time they'd had their late breakfast from the picnic basket, Pat was on first-name terms with Jack and Preston, it being a great deal easier for gentlemen to relax if they could treat her as an honorary man. She took a fervent part in the analysis of weather, terrain, cartridge, and distribution of game, then sat back as the conversation became more general.

Jimmy didn't seem as able to forget his troubles as his father. He had the miserable, strained look that he'd been wearing for much of the visit. Bill too had a set look to his face, and spoke as though his mind wasn't really on what he was saying. Jack and Preston were both cheerful enough, though Pat doubted they'd be seeing the former for many more shoots. Still, one could not think poorly of a man who took failure in such good part.

The morning's shooting was excellent, but by noon the wind was decidedly getting up, and there were clouds scudding over the sky. They ate luncheon under a spreading oak tree and discussed the likelihood of storms.

"There's weather on the way. It'll come by nightfall, I should think," the Earl said.

"So we'll take advantage now?" Jimmy asked. "Suits me."

Everyone agreed with that, although Jack's nod wasn't wildly enthusiastic. They set off to their next location, walking along a path that ran by a small, brisk river and was only wide enough for pairs. Bill and the Earl were leading, followed by Jack and Preston, which left Pat to bring up the rear with Jimmy.

"I think he's got blisters," she said with a nod to Jack where he walked ahead.

"I'm sure he does. Those are new togs, aren't they?" Jimmy's own shooting clothes, like those of any self-respecting gun, could have belonged to a tramp. "Fellow's a lounge lizard. Has he hit a thing all day?"

"Count your blessings; he hasn't hit me, you, or a beater. At least he's good-humoured about it."

"Very true," Jimmy admitted. "He isn't a bad fellow, or at least he wouldn't be if he wasn't hanging around my sister."

"I'd rather have him than Haworth too," Pat said. "Can I take it your brother-in-law isn't a gun?"

"Thank God, no. I don't know if I could bear him all day as well as in the evenings."

"But if he came out, we could shoot him and blame Jack. Jimmy, why on earth—"

"Don't ask."

"I really think I must. It's one thing that he's vile; it's another to see it tolerated in this extraordinary way. As a friend, I have to ask, are you afraid of something?"

The colour drained from Jimmy's face. Pat had seen that before, when her father had received the telegrams about Frank and Donald, healthy ruddiness turning a nasty sallow colour. "What do you mean?" he managed.

"I don't know," Pat said, somewhat alarmed. "That's why I'm asking. Is he liable to be violent if crossed? To Lady Anna or—" Good heavens, she didn't even know the child's name. "—your nephew?"

"Is he a wife-beater? Not as far as I know. I wouldn't put it past him, but his tongue is weapon enough. They have the most awful rows, although any man might if his wife—" He nodded at Jack up ahead to complete that thought.

"Then if you're not afraid of what Haworth might do, why don't you send him to the devil?"

Jimmy scowled, much as a man might on realising he'd just failed to grasp a convenient excuse. "It's not that easy. He's Anna's husband."

"And you're Fen's fiancé," Pat said. "And if you were my fiancé, Jimmy, after last evening I should be returning your ring to you, and you'd be lucky if it came back by post rather than thrown at your head. Do you *want* to marry her?"

"Of course I do."

"There isn't any 'of course' about it. Nobody would think you gave two hoots for her."

"I don't know what business it is of yours," Jimmy said, attempting dignity. "My relations with my fiancée—"

"Oh, come off it," Pat snapped. "I've spent more time with her than you have here, and Bill's made three times the effort to stand up for her." He winced. She pressed her advantage. "Really, Jimmy, if you don't care for her you should do the decent thing and talk to her. And if you do, you should make some sort of show of it."

"Has she said anything to you? About the engagement?"

"If she had I shouldn't repeat it, any more than I should repeat your words to her."

"No, of course not. But— Oh, God, Pat, I've made a bloody awful mess of this."

"You have, yes."

"No, you've no idea. Really, you don't. This business with Fen is only the start."

"What on earth is wrong?" Pat demanded. She was beginning to feel seriously worried.

Jimmy kicked a stone into the river. "I don't know where I'd begin. Suffice to say, we're in a dreadful hole, I need money, and this seemed the best way to go about it. Fen gets a coronet, I get the funds, everyone's happy."

"You don't look happy. And nor does she. And I haven't seen anything to suggest she's on the hunt for a title."

"Well, she accepted me."

"Possibly she was under the impression you were a decent sort of chap," Pat said icily. "I used to think that too."

"Oh, don't," Jimmy said. "I *know*. I thought I was doing the practical thing. I thought I could be a good husband, I truly did, but everything's gone wrong, and of course blasted Maurice is setting out to sabotage the engagement for the hell of it, and there's damn all I can do about it."

"You could talk honestly to Fen. She doesn't know what's going on, does she?" Jimmy shook his head. Pat clenched her fists, feeling an upswell of anger. "It won't do, Jimmy. You can't marry her for her money and foist your debts and troubles and Maurice Haworth on her without warning. You don't have to tell me your secrets, but you have to tell her, and give her a fair choice. If she understood, perhaps she could help you. Stand by you. At least know not to be hurt when you throw her to the wolves."

"Not all women are like you, old thing. I have no doubt you'd stand by your man and fight his battles. Fen's more the taken-care-of sort."

"Rubbish," Pat said. "You have no idea what she's like, because you've never bothered to find out. You haven't even been bowled over by her pretty face; I'd think more of you if you had. She isn't a featherbrain in the slightest, I think she'd fight tooth and nail if she had to, and even if she were a frippery sort of person she'd still deserve a great deal better than a man who only cares for her father's wallet."

"I do care for her." Jimmy was entirely scarlet now. "She's a great girl. Good fun. It's just, this is absolutely the worst possible time for her to be here."

"But she is here. And if she is fool enough to marry you, she will continue to be here. So you'd better get used to it, and start behaving as if you *want* her here. Hadn't you?"

Pat didn't give him a chance to reply but lengthened her stride and speed, stalking away. She was shaking with anger and, she realised a few moments later, she was also deeply and profoundly miserable.

The fact was, she didn't want Jimmy to be a decent fiancé. She wanted him to be terrible so that Fen would end the engagement, and it would be nothing to do with her own behaviour when Jimmy lost the industrial wealth on which he was depending to pull Rodington Court and the Earl and Countess and himself out of that hole of theirs.

It was a shameful hope. If Fen broke things off, no matter how justified she might be, it would be her third jilting. The whispers about her would turn to sneers; she'd be branded fast, unreliable, foolish, a joke. Not at all the sort of woman that a good, steady man should pick. Her father's wealth might mean she was still received but it would attract the kind of predators who liked nothing better than a wealthy woman with limited marriage prospects. Whereas if she married Jimmy, she would one day be Countess of Witton. Women married far worse men than Jimmy could ever be for the sake of a title.

Not to mention Jimmy. Whatever was going on, he'd sounded desperate, and he wasn't given to histrionics. Pat was a practical woman, and saw nothing wrong with a practical marriage so long as both parties were happy with the arrangement. It didn't matter if he didn't love Fen as long as he was kind and she was happy; she suspected that he would fall in love with her after the marriage anyway. Who could not?

Fen and Jimmy both needed this marriage, and a friend who cared for either of them would help them to make it work. Pat had done the right thing in giving him a talking-to. It was exactly what she'd have done if she and Fen had never shared that dizzying kiss, which meant it was the right thing to do because, in the end, what did a single kiss between women count for?

She told herself all that as she walked on. None of it made her feel better.

The afternoon's shooting was trickier. The weather was moving in on them faster than expected, and the partridges kept low to the ground, a sure sign of approaching storms. The Earl called a halt around four o'clock.

"We've a long tramp back and we'll be doing well to beat the rain," he told the party with a glance to the darkening sky. "Let's go."

Pat moved towards Bill as they set off, but he had attached himself to the Earl once more. Preston and Jack paired up again, leaving her to walk with Jimmy, somewhat to her annoyance. He was Bill's friend; why the blazes couldn't they talk to each other?

"Think we'll make it home without getting soaked?" he asked after a few awkwardly silent moments.

"Possibly," Pat said. "It's going to be a big blow. Listen, the birds are quiet already."

"Mmm. Looks like a day indoors tomorrow."

"I'm sure we can occupy ourselves."

"Thank God it's a big house," Jimmy said. "Look, Pat, I want to say thank you."

"Sorry?"

"Thank you. You were right, in what you said. I've been busy feeling sorry for myself and that's not fair to Fen, because none of this is her fault. I made a decision and it's up to me to take the consequences. I can't have everything I want and that's all there is to it, and I'm jolly lucky that Fen accepted me in the first place. It's time I pulled myself together. And I am *also* jolly lucky to have friends who tell me when I'm being an ass."

"That's all right," Pat said. "I'll do that whenever you like."

Jimmy grinned at her. "Try and stop you, eh? I do appreciate it, old girl. And I hope we'll stay friends once I'm married. You and Fen seem to be getting on like a house on fire."

"Yes." She couldn't manage any more.

"Just don't steal her away from me tomorrow, that's all I ask."

"Sorry?" Pat said. "What do you mean—steal—"

"Well, I'll want some of her time for myself," Jimmy said. "Take advantage of the bad weather to do my duty, show her the house properly, all that. What did you think I meant?"

"Nothing. Nothing at all."

CHAPTER EIGHT

The heavens opened about ten minutes before the party arrived back at Rodington Court—sluicing rain that seemed to come in spears rather than droplets, accompanied by a distant, ominous grumble of approaching thunder, and made the Earl shout back at them all about India and monsoons. By the time Pat finally got inside, she was wet through to her smalls, and the Countess insisted on hot baths for everyone to prevent chills. Pat did not particularly enjoy sitting around in water, but hiding in the bath seemed like a better prospect than facing Fen, or Jimmy, let alone the Haworths. Please God this evening would be better than the one before.

Of course, in one particular respect, no evening could be better than the one before, but Pat had to put that from her mind. Fen had a choice to make about the course of her life, and Pat had no right to distract her. Unless she wanted to be distracted, of course. In which case she could come and find Pat herself.

Pat allowed herself to imagine that for a moment. A soft knock on the door, a rustle of skirts, Fen slipping into the room while Pat reclined naked in the bathtub. A giggling offer to help with the soap, a plump hand, frothy with lather, sliding over her shoulder, down to cup her breast…

This was not helping.

She sat in tepid bathwater a while longer, listening to the rain lash the windows outside, then heaved herself out. Her legs had the pleasant ache of an active day; the persistent ache between them was less welcome. She ignored it and set to dressing, wishing she had more interesting jewellery, or perhaps some face-paint and the experience to apply it, or the sort of hair that looked good in piled ringlets. Anything to make herself less workaday and practical. She settled for a bright Indian shawl that she always brought on visits and virtually never wore, and set off downstairs telling herself that dinner couldn't possibly be more uncomfortable than yesterday.

The raised voices from the drawing-room suggested she was wrong.

Bill was standing outside the open door, looking smart enough in his dinner togs, but wearing the pinched expression of a man with a headache. Inside the room, Preston Keynes was speaking at uncharacteristic volume and without his usual cheerfulness—Pat clearly made out "damned offensive"—while Lady Anna, Miss Singh, and the Countess all seemed to be talking at once.

Pat sidled up on light feet, and whispered, "What on earth is going on?"

"Haworth," Bill said, unnecessarily. "Suggested the Countess order her ayah to fetch her slippers, as a delicate reference to Miss Singh who is second cousin to a Sikh maharajah, and then called her a rather less flattering name, at which point Preston offered to teach him some manners, and Haworth suggested extremely crudely that he had an ulterior motive for doing so. Did you know Preston had an interest there?"

"Mr. Keynes is pursuing Miss Singh?" Pat attempted to picture the intellectual vegetarian and the boisterous hunter as a pair. "Really?"

"So it appears, judging by his reaction: the poor fellow went red as a beetroot. It seems to have come as a surprise to the Countess too. Haworth clearly has a knack for snouting out private matters."

That sounded extremely bad to Pat. She had no idea if her face might give anything away when she saw Fen; she had no desire at all to be mocked as the unattractive spinster with a pash on a pretty girl. "Better stay out here then," she said, half to herself.

"Sorry?" Bill said sharply.

"Until it's died down in there."

"Ah. Indeed."

They stood together in the hall. Pat couldn't help wondering how they'd look to any footman who came by, and then decided she didn't care so long as he carried a tray of drinks. Bill leaned his shoulders against the wall.

"Decent shooting today," she offered, after a moment. In the drawing room, the Earl was speaking in a placatory, almost pleading tone that sat ill on the man who'd been so confident walking his lands.

"I'm hopelessly out of practice."

"You weren't on form, certainly. Are you all right? You look rather worn and this isn't precisely the rest cure you were hoping for."

"You can say that again," Bill muttered. "I'm fine."

He didn't look fine. There were dark circles under his eyes and his face had a tense look, as though keeping composure required an effort.

"Rotten luck about the weather," she said, in lieu of pointing that out. "A few more days in the fresh air would do us all good."

"That's your all-purpose remedy, isn't it? Not that I'm arguing. Suppose you take Haworth for a ten-mile forced march in the rain, there's a good girl."

"Suppose *you* do," Pat said. "Should we…?"

It seemed to have quietened down in the drawing room. Bill straightened with obvious reluctance and offered her his arm, and brother and sister went in together.

Even if she hadn't heard the row, it would have been obvious something was up from the flushed faces and silence. Preston Keynes looked ready to punch someone, and Haworth's smug look made it obvious who. Jimmy was standing by Preston, a restraining hand on his arm. Fen had drawn Victoria Singh over to the side of the room. She flashed a glance over at Pat that held a certain amount of desperation. Outside, the wind howled. Nobody spoke.

"Well," Bill said heartily, into the social void. "Nasty spot of weather we're having, what?"

"Awful rain, yes," Fen returned, voice bright. "Did you get a soaking?"

In true British fashion the weather carried them through the next fifteen minutes or so, with Pat, Fen, Bill, and Jack contributing remarks of varying relevance or interest about weather they had experienced, meteorological patterns at their various homes, and comparative rainfall in different parts of the country. By the time they were seated to dine, Pat felt like a chattering parrot but at least the atmosphere had reduced to a slow simmer. She was quite ready not to open her mouth again all evening, but Fen, who had borne a good half of the conversational burden and whose chirpy tone was starting to ebb, said, "So do tell us all about the shooting!"

Pat repressed a groan and launched into a detailed account of the day, despite Lady Anna's audible sigh of annoyance: if nobody else was going to speak, they all deserved to be bored to death. Bill took over when she ran out of steam, giving an exhaustive account of all his shots and concluding each, "Missed the blighter," with an entirely straight face.

Miss Singh had recovered her composure by then. Once Bill's invention gave out, and as the soup bowls were being removed, she said, voice calm as ever, "Dear me, Mr. Merton, how regrettable. And how was your day, Preston?"

"Good heavens," Haworth said, breaking his silence for the first time. "Do we understand that our principled—"

Miss Singh raised her voice, deliberately speaking over him though her expression and inflection didn't change at all. "I do hope that you had an enjoyable time. I dare say it was somewhat damp in the latter parts but at least you had the sunshine all morning."

Haworth had stopped speaking, apparently startled by the interruption. Clearly he expected to be the only one breaking the rules of good manners. He opened his mouth again as she finished, and Preston said, loudly, "It was a delightful day, thank you. I had a fine bag, but Pat here carried off the honours. She gave a very modest account just now, but the fact is, I've rarely seen such shooting. Privilege to witness."

"Oh, so—" Haworth began, and Fen came in, at a pitch that threatened the glassware and cut right through his deeper voice. "How wonderful, Pat! You showed all the men how it's done. Even Jimmy, and Mr. Merton?"

"I'm rather—"

"Especially me," Bill said. "I'm used to it, of course. Even our eldest brother gives her the laurels, and he's not one to admit himself second best."

"Marvellous." Fen clapped her hands. "Pat was teaching me to shoot yesterday, you know, and she was really wonderful. I learned a great deal. Not that I have any ambitions to be a champion, of course."

"You—"

"You couldn't have a better teacher." Bill was clearly enjoying the game of talking over Haworth as much as Victoria Singh and Preston. Jack looked decidedly wary, and the family did not appear to be enjoying themselves at all. That was their hard luck. Miss Singh had no more volunteered to be Haworth's punchbag than Pat had to be the audience to his nasty little games.

"Fen was remarkable," she said. "Took to it like a duck to water. I think with practice you could be a fine shot."

"I hope so, though of targets," Fen said. "I don't aspire to game, though I am happy to carry on with my wobbly and inconsistent principles and eat what others shoot for me."

"Very reasonable." Miss Singh smiled at her. "I might even join your next lesson, if I may, Miss Merton. I'm fired with a spirit of emulation."

"Oh, yes, do!" Fen cried. "That would be great fun."

"You'd be very welcome, although…" Pat couldn't help glancing at Preston.

Miss Singh's smile widened. "But surely I ought to learn from the best?"

"Argh," Preston said, clutching his heart. "Cut to the quick. Actually, I'd be a rotten teacher—know what to do, but not how one does it, if you follow me—and Pat's a better hand with a gun anyway. I own myself beaten on all points."

"Do you know, I find it thrilling how many men of our party are happy to accept when they've been exceeded by a woman," Fen remarked.

"There comes a point where even a chauvinist like myself has to face the facts," the Earl put in, with a little bow to Pat.

"I should be careful, if I were you, Miss Merton," Lady Anna said. There were red spots on her cheeks, and her voice was shrill. "You might win plaudits by beating men, but you won't win hearts."

It was astonishing how quickly the convivial atmosphere could be destroyed. Miss Singh shut her eyes, and someone gave a just-audible groan. Pat forbore to point out that she wouldn't have taken Lady Anna's advice on men for all the tea in China. "That's all right, thanks. I shan't worry."

"I don't think Miss Merton is interested in men's hearts," Haworth said, finally seizing an opportunity. "Why, she's a man herself in all but the clothing. Give her a pair of trousers and nobody could tell the difference. I can just picture her wooing some pretty girl, can't you?"

"And that will do." Bill's chair scraped in the frozen silence as he stood, tossing his napkin down. "Step outside with me a moment, Haworth."

"Oh God," Jimmy said under his breath.

"Did you not hear me?" Bill enquired, since Haworth hadn't moved. "Get up."

"Don't be absurd, Bill." Pat was pleased at how calm she sounded. "Sit down. I really can't see he's worth bruising your knuckles."

It wasn't a peacemaking comment, but she didn't want to make peace, only to prevent Bill from hauling a fellow guest off the Countess's dining table. All the same, she wished almost immediately that she had temporised, done the little performance of smiling and soothing that women so often used to turn away male wrath, because she could see Haworth's face, and it was pure malevolence.

"Worth," he repeated, spitting out the syllables. "What an interesting word, Miss Merton. Why don't you ask my esteemed father in law about his net worth—"

"Maurice," Jimmy said.

"—or about what his name would be *worth* if the truth about certain arrangements came out? Why don't you ask the *worth* of my wife's chastity, or Jack's honesty, come to that?"

"Maurice!" the Countess and Jimmy said together, and Jimmy went on, "Curse it, man—"

"And tell us, Jimmy, how long do you intend to endure your empty-headed heiress before you return to the lover you keep in London?" Jimmy's mouth dropped open. Haworth bared his teeth in triumph. "Or will your dumpy commoner put up with your illicit trysts as *worth* her coronet?"

Half the room was shouting now. Jimmy had gone chalk white; Fen was scarlet. Maurice Haworth's eyes blazed with unholy pleasure. He leaned forward to see the Countess. "And you, madam—"

Victoria Singh picked up her glass of water and threw it in his face.

Then it was chaos. Haworth lunged for her, shouting a word that Pat wouldn't have expected even from him, sending his wine glass flying. Miss Singh recoiled, but Preston was already on his feet, sprinting round the table. He grabbed the dripping Haworth by the shoulders and dragged him up and backwards, spun him round, and punched him square in the mouth.

The Countess was watching, frozen; the Earl had his eyes shut. Lady Anna and Miss Singh stood, staring, as the men grappled; Bill strode over, speaking in a commanding voice that was entirely ignored; and Fen got up and hurried to the door.

"Fen!" Pat turned, but before she could stand, Jimmy had pushed away his chair and was going after her.

Hell. Hell.

Preston had his hands around Haworth's throat now. Bill was trying to separate them but the purpling of Haworth's face suggested he wasn't having much luck, so Pat took a leaf from Miss Singh's book, picked up the water jug, and tossed the contents over both combatants.

Preston got most of the soaking. He recoiled, spluttering. Haworth, bloody-mouthed and dripping, lunged forward, and found Bill's hand at his chest.

"You'd better get out of here before you get the thrashing you deserve," Bill told him. "No, don't speak. If you open your mouth again, I'll close it for you."

"Mr. Merton," the Countess said. "Please. Stop. Let us deal with this. I would prefer everyone to leave. I— If anyone should like to order sandwiches, please do ring."

Pat looked at her, sat among the ruins of her dinner table and her family, and said, "Come on, Bill. Let's go."

Bill took her arm as they left the room. "Crikey. *Crikey.*"

"I need to find Fen."

"Do you?" Bill said dubiously as she set off for the drawing room. "She might be busy."

Pat hoped she was busy giving Jimmy his marching orders. "We'll see. I imagine Jimmy might need a shoulder to cry on too."

"Jimmy deserves every damned thing he has coming," Bill said, with quiet savagery. "Stupid swine."

"Couldn't agree more."

The drawing room door was open. Pat and Bill came to it together, and stopped.

Jimmy and Fen were in there. They weren't arguing. They were embracing, tightly—not kissing, but holding one another in a desperate grasp, so absorbed that they didn't seem to have heard the Mertons' footsteps.

Bill's fingers clenched hard on Pat's arm, almost spasmodically, then he stepped silently back, pulling her away. "Come on, old thing," he murmured. "Come on. Better leave them to it."

"Christ almighty," Bill said some time later. "Excuse my French."

"Feel free."

They'd settled in Pat's room, since there was nobody in the house either of them wanted to speak to. The room had no chair, so the siblings sat on the bed, backs against the wall, as they had when they were children. The wind howled outside, flinging sheets of rain against the window with heavy splats.

Bill, taking the Countess at her word, had rung for sandwiches and beer. Pat supported that, since she'd done a lot of walking today, although the hollow feeling in her gut had nothing to do with the interrupted meal.

How could Fen forgive him? He'd ignored her, he didn't appreciate her, he was keeping a mistress, for God's sake. Why hadn't she thrown the ring back in his face?

Men keep mistresses, she reminded herself. *Fen's a great deal more worldly than you are, when it comes to society marriages. She'll be a countess. You only met her two days ago.* It didn't help.

She wrapped her arms around her knees, knowing it would probably crumple the dress. She'd put so much effort into looking nice.

"Are you all right, old thing?"

"I feel terrible," Pat said. "I do wish I hadn't said anything. If I hadn't made that remark, given him that opening—"

"He'd have taken another. You heard him. He was going at Miss Singh all evening, and he didn't like being snubbed at all."

"Perhaps we shouldn't have. Although, not provoking him is the Wittons' tactic, and it doesn't work either. One can see why they try not to, of course. I wonder if that sort of outburst happens often."

"I suppose he builds up to it. What a nasty piece of work."

"What do you think is wrong with him?"

"Being a nasty piece of work," Bill said. "He enjoys making people unhappy; I don't see anything more than that need be said."

"Fen thinks he's a drug fiend."

"Does she, now." Bill considered that. "Perhaps. But I'd think the drug-taking is an element of his delightful personality, rather than the root cause. That's a man who enjoys the upper hand, and God help those he has it over."

"Quite. Bill, shall we go home? This is really too awful and I don't know how much more I can bear to watch." She'd be leaving Fen to fend for herself, of course, but Fen wasn't incapable and if she'd chosen Jimmy, with all his faults, as her protector, Pat had to respect that, no matter how much it hurt.

"I think you probably should. We'll get you on a train tomorrow. I don't imagine there'll be shooting for a few days, and being trapped in this house with that swine—no, you should go."

"And you."

"I can't," Bill said. "You don't mind travelling alone, do you?"

"What do you mean, you can't? For heaven's sake, come home. We can ignore Jonty; I dare say he'll be wrapped up in Olivia. Or we could go to the seaside. You really do need a break, and this isn't it."

"It's not that. I've a responsibility."

"To Jimmy?" Pat said. "Really? Because it seems to me—"

"No, not Jimmy. Just a moment, I think that's our dinner."

A harried-looking maid came in bearing a platter of enough sandwiches for six and four bottles of beer, precariously balanced. Bill leapt up to take them with a word of thanks, and shut the door firmly after her. Pat took a sandwich more out of duty than pleasure, but the first bite reminded her that she was hungry, even if she was miserable. It was excellent thick-cut ham, mustard applied with a heavy hand, and she demolished two sandwiches while Bill ate four.

"Goodness, I needed that," he said, taking a swig of beer.

"So did I." Pat sipped hers more cautiously. "You were about to tell me why you can't leave the worst house party since Julius Caesar invited Brutus for dinner."

"Yes," Bill said. "Mmm. Well."

"*Bill.*"

Bill sighed. "All right, you may as well know. Have you heard of Threppel and Swing?"

"It sounds like a gymnastic exercise." She frowned. "Although it does ring a bell. What is it?"

"A stockbrokers' firm that collapsed a few months ago."

"Oh. *Oh.* Is that the place Maurice Haworth used to work?"

Bill nodded. "He was a junior partner, invested all Lady Anna's money in the company, and they were pretty much ruined in the crash. The thing is, there are a number of questions over what happened to the firm. Word was circulating a couple of months before the house of cards came down, you see: questionable practices, paying debts with borrowing."

Pat nodded. "Does this have anything to do with the accusations Haworth was tossing at the Earl?"

"Indeed it does. The Earl was a major investor and on the Board of Directors. That's how Haworth came to his position there in the first place, I believe. He was in some other City firm, rather a shabby outfit, previously."

"And the Earl lost money in the crash?"

"Yes, a great deal," Bill said. "Or so it appears. That's the thing, you see. A lot of money came into the firm, and the question is where it went. Bad investments, of course, but the books are in the sort of muddle at which a clever man would work very hard if he wanted to hide his tracks."

"You think there was something criminal going on?"

"It looks like malpractice, yes. It's a tangle well beyond the Met to unpick—financial wrongdoing is an awfully tricky business—so my office is looking into it."

"Your office is looking into the Earl's affairs," Pat repeated. "And by that you mean, you are?"

Bill made a face. "I declared an interest at once when I was given the job. I assumed they'd take me off it, but our chief thought it might be handy to have an inside track. The upper classes do close ranks, you know, even in this sort of business. I agreed because it never crossed my mind that I could do the old chap anything but good. It was unthinkable that Jimmy's father should be dishonest. Only, you see, it isn't looking terribly bright. His name is on a few papers it oughtn't be on, authorising things that ought not have happened."

"The Earl was embezzling from his own firm?"

"Call it robbing Peter to pay Paul. Using funds unlawfully to prop up the business, and losing people's money." Bill blew out his cheeks. "He was in over his head. I think he was steered to some bad decisions, and to sign things he didn't fully understand, and I'll bet I know who by. But it's his name, in the end, and his responsibility if I can't prove otherwise."

"Oh, hell," Pat said. "Does Jimmy know you're doing this?"

"I told him at the start, and he was happy enough to think they had a friend in the business. We haven't discussed it since."

"But even so, if you believe the Earl is up to his neck in this, whether by accident or design, ought you have accepted an invitation to stay with him?" Pat demanded, and then it clicked. "Oh, no. *Bill*. In his own house?"

"I told them again I wanted to recuse myself when it started to appear that Lord Witton was likely to face charges," Bill said. "I explained I had an invitation to shoot with him. And—well, there was a great deal of discussion, but the conclusion was that I ought to come here and see what I could dig out."

"To spy on your host."

"To see what I could dig out," Bill repeated. "On the clear understanding that if I find anything favourable to the Earl, any evidence of manipulation, that will be taken into account. It's his best hope, Pat. The net's closing around him. He's made a rotten mess of things and lost a lot of people's money, and nobody else will be terribly interested in making excuses. I don't feel marvellous about this, in case you're wondering."

"I'm sure you don't. I can't say I like it much either. Shouldn't you be, I don't know, palling up to Haworth instead of threatening to sock him in the jaw?"

"Probably, but I have *some* standards."

There was a knock at the door. Bill muttered, "Oh God, what now?"

"Come in," Pat called. The door opened, and Fen slipped in.

For a girl who'd just been in her fiancé's passionate embrace, she looked miserable. Her eyes were red, as was her nose, and her hair was something of a mess. She registered Bill as he scrambled to his feet and said, "Oh, I'm sorry."

"Not at all," Bill said, vacating the bed. "I suppose you're come for a word with Pat, Miss Carruth. Let me leave you to it. Pat, about that train—"

"We will speak tomorrow," Pat said. "And I'll decide for myself, thank you. Night night."

"Sleep well, old thing. Miss Carruth." Bill hurried out, nabbing another sandwich and a bottle of beer as he went.

Fen sniffled. "I'm sorry. I interrupted you."

"Don't worry about that. Do you want to sit down? There's only the bed."

"Can I?" Fen heaved herself and her skirts onto the bed with some difficulty, and leaned back against the wall. "It's like being a schoolgirl again. Are those sandwiches?"

"Midnight feast." Pat collected the platter. "Here you go."

Fen gave a laugh that might have been a sob. "Oh goodness. Sitting on a bed in satin and jewels, with beer and sandwiches."

"Better a dinner of ham sandwiches where love is, than a stalled ox and hatred therewith," Pat misquoted.

"I oughtn't even be hungry. I ought to be pouring out my heart about my fiancé or talking about that dreadful man, but it's nearly ten and we only got through the soup course."

"Dig in. I was starved as well." Pat picked up a sandwich to keep her company as she ate, and to stave off whatever revelations were coming. She didn't much want to hear about Fen's fiancé, least of all now when it seemed her brother was investigating Fen's future father-in-law.

Fen polished off her sandwich with evident relief. The maid had only brought two glasses, and Bill had walked off with one of those, so Pat refilled the other and held it out. "We'll have to share."

"I don't mind that." Fen took an unladylike swig and wiped her mouth. "Oh goodness. It's terrible to think about food at a time like this but one simply can't be sensible when one's hungry."

"No, one can't," Pat said. "Are you being sensible?"

"That rather depends what sensible is." Fen took another swig and handed back the bottle. "I've broken off the engagement."

Pat stared. Fen twisted to face her, looking somewhat alarmed. "Pat? Do you think that was a bad idea?"

"No! That is, no, if what that ghastly man said had any truth in it. Is that why?"

"It was lots of things," Fen said. "I asked him point blank if there was someone else, and he said yes. He said he'd broken things off after I agreed to marry him, and he'd thought that would be enough, that he could be a good husband and so on, and then he'd realised it wasn't and he couldn't, and he apologised."

"I should hope he did."

"Oh, Pat, he was a dear. He was awfully sorry, and he said the odd way he's been behaving was never because of me—which I did need to know—but because he'd thought he could forget this affair and he couldn't. He said he simply hadn't realised that he was dreadfully in love until it was too late. It was actually very romantic, you know, although not for me. He's terribly upset."

"Good," Pat said. "I should imagine he's upset this other girl considerably as well."

"I said that too. I said it was a rotten thing to do, breaking off a love affair to marry for money, and he said very nicely that he hadn't just wanted to marry me for my money, with all sorts of complimentary things. It made me remember why I thought I could marry him in the first place. He said he'd had every intention of falling in love with me and that if it wasn't for this other person he thought we'd have been very happy, and he wished he could have been the man for me— You'd better hope the wind doesn't change, pulling a face like that."

"I've never heard anything so sick-making in my life. He's behaved thoroughly badly, and I hope the other girl gives him what-for if he has the nerve to go back to her."

"Oh, so do I," Fen assured her. "I hope she kicks him. But I didn't say so. I stayed on the moral high ground, you know, looking wronged and letting him say nice things to me, and it was such a relief, Pat. To know that he wasn't simply tired of me, that it wasn't about me at all. And to have a really good excuse this time, because Jimmy has said he'll take all the blame for not fulfilling his obligations. But also, to be honest, it's an absolute *joy* to be unengaged again."

"Is it?" Pat asked, with a little flutter in her chest.

"Oh, yes." Fen attempted to twist round a bit more, hampered by her skirts. Pat shifted instead, bringing them closer. "I don't want to go from my father's household to a husband. I want to find out more about what I can do, which is more than who I can persuade to marry me. I want—I don't know if you realise what you look like when you shoot, Pat. Utterly focused, and confident, and your whole body and face and everything caught up in it, and you radiate knowing what you're doing. That's what I want. To find that balance that you have, that certainty. Everyone says a woman has to get married to settle down—to have someone else possess her—but you're *self*-possessed. That's what I want."

"But I'm not balanced or certain most of the time," Pat said. "I'm awfully awkward."

"You aren't, you know. You might feel it, but you don't look it, and honestly, I think everyone feels terribly awkward inside. It's the human condition. But do you see? That I want to have ideas of my own, and believe them myself, and—and have a leg to stand on?"

"Two is better. Good for you, Fen." Pat realised she'd reached for her hand. Fen's fingers curled responsively round hers. "Jolly good for you. I think you're absolutely right. There's not the slightest need for you to rush into marriage. You're far too wonderful to need anyone else telling you how you ought to go on." Fen's smile at that was dazzling. Pat made herself say, "And—and of course it'll be much easier, once you're sure what you really want, to find a husband who'll suit you and listen to you, and—"

"Oh, to hell with husbands," Fen said, and pulled her forward. Her mouth met Pat's, as warm and real as the night before but tasting of beer with a tang of mustard rather than brandy. She wriggled into Pat's arms, and Pat's hands were in her hair, and they kissed with open-mouthed wonder, because Fen was free and wanted to be here with Pat, and it was all right. It was all wonderfully, marvellously *all right*.

Pat could have shouted. Instead she slid a hand up, cupping the edge of Fen's breast, and felt her whimper. Fen's hands were on her now, sliding over what was by comparison a deeply inadequate bosom, but which still did the job because they both quivered at the touch. They were kissing wildly. Fen strained forwards into Pat's grip, and pulled back again with a mumble of annoyance. "Sitting on this miserable dress." She tugged at fabric to no avail.

"Take it off," Pat said, and clapped her hand to her mouth as Fen's eyes widened. "I meant, take it *out*. From under you. I really did mean that."

"How disappointing." Fen's eyes were sparkling bright. "Would *off* be bad?"

Pat reached around her, enjoying the brush of arms against bosom. In an ideal world she would have undone a couple of clasps. As it was, her questing fingers encountered what felt like infinite buttons, and she gave up. "Blast. I need to see."

"Help me up?"

Fen stood, shaking out the sadly crumpled dress and holding up the tendrils of hair. Pat stood behind her, unfastening each in the long row of tiny buttons, one by one, exposing a V of creamy skin and then the lacing of a corset, cinching Fen's flesh. She ran her finger along the top of it, felt Fen shiver.

The dress was unfastened. She wasn't sure what to do—it looked expensive—but Fen pushed it down so it fell to the floor in a rustling silken heap, turned, and stepped out of it. The corset pushed up her bosom, still adorned with sparkling jewels.

"I don't suppose you'd like to take that off too," Pat said. It came out slightly hoarse.

"I'd love to take this off," Fen assured her. "Turn round first, though?"

Pat turned. Fen's fingers slipped nimbly down her back, dealing with buttons, easing her dress over her shoulders. "You don't corset."

"Never started. No mother to insist." She turned back, stepping out of the dress.

"I had governesses. And I've a great deal more that needs lacing in." Fen ran her hands down Pat's sides, eyes crinkling at the edges with concentration. "Have you done this before?"

"It depends what you mean by 'this'." Kissing and stroking, absolutely. She had a feeling that wasn't what Fen meant. "I think you should probably assume I'm a novice. You?"

"Finishing school," Fen said elliptically. "Can I be the instructor now?"

"Please be the instructor."

Fen's eyes brimmed with mischief. "Good. First things first: you're allowed to squeal. In fact, I positively encourage it."

"I'm locking the door, in that case."

She suited the action to the word, and turned to find Fen presenting her back. The white laces that secured her corset were the most delectable things Pat had ever seen. She tugged at the fastening bows, feeling the binding give.

"Oh, that's better," Fen said, easing the corset off. "I can breathe." She did so, a demonstrative filling of the lungs that did remarkable things to her chest. Squealing began to seem a very likely outcome. "Now, that petticoat…"

Pat had never felt both so grateful for and so annoyed by her many layers of clothing. They stripped each other amid kisses and stroking and a certain amount of giggling, and when they were down to combinations—Pat's sensible muslin, Fen's silk—Fen took her hand and tugged her to the bed, pulling her down so they lay face to face, in kissing distance. Pat ran her hand over Fen's flank, glorying that she was permitted this, and thrilling at the delicate trace of Fen's fingers on her own skin.

"Oh Lord," she murmured against Fen's lips. "You are lovely."

Fen leaned in to kiss her, and Pat felt the hand on her bottom give a decided squeeze. She yelped, the sound muffled by Fen's mouth, and wriggled into the touch as though it were quite natural to do so. Bodies pressing together, legs tangling, and an urge for more building between them as Fen's thigh pressed between hers. Fen's hand was on her breast, palm rolling over the nipple, and the movement of cloth against flesh was glorious torture.

Pat whimpered. Fen stilled. "All right?"

"Yes. Oh, yes."

"Could I touch you?"

"Please." Pat wasn't even sure what that meant—surely they were touching now—but the answer was yes anyway, to anything Fen wanted. Fen nudged her so she rolled onto her back, and leaned over her, and Pat gave herself up to the sensation of kisses and strokes, and her own hand on the generous curve of Fen's plump bottom and—

—a hand sliding up her thigh.

She jolted. Fen snatched her hand away. "Sorry! Was that not—"

"Just startled," Pat managed. She could hardly breathe with the thought she'd spoiled this. "Novice, remember?"

"Shall I not do that?"

"No! That is, yes. I mean, please *don't* not do that."

Fen's eyes lit with laughter. "So, just to be sure, you definitely don't want me to not stop continuing?"

"Oh, shut up." Pat swatted her behind.

Fen squeaked, and then narrowed her eyes menacingly. "Excuse me, who's the schoolmistress here? You need to listen to my sage advice."

"I'm sure it's extremely sensible," Pat managed. Fen's hand was roaming again, sliding up over the cloth to the opening of her drawers. Fen was going to touch her *there*, and Pat's heart was thundering with alarm and glory and anticipation. They both inhaled sharply as a finger touched a curl of hair.

"Oh Lord," Pat whispered. Her hand was clenching convulsively on nothing, and Fen's free hand came to hold it, interlacing their fingers. Fen's face was close, with an intently serious look in her pansy-brown eyes, and Pat breathed into the sensation of exploring fingers sliding up and down, touching her, thumb brushing over curls, a finger sliding even more intimately close. Pat didn't even know a name for the place Fen touched that made her gasp, but she was well aware how it worked and she let her legs relax and widen, giving Fen's fingers access to stroke and circle. Tiny circles, a repetitive movement that was just what Pat would have done for herself but a thousand times better because it was Fen's touch, Fen's breath hot on her skin.

Pat realised she was moaning, little mewling noises in her throat. She stopped herself with a stab of self-consciousness, but Fen's finger slid up and down, slick and wet now, and she forgot about anything but the building need, the familiar cresting wave of pleasure.

"Oh, I do want to see you enjoy yourself," Fen whispered. "Please do."

Pat couldn't have spoken if she'd had anything to say. Her whole consciousness was narrowed to the point where Fen's fingers and thumb were working, concentrating on reaching that elusive, glorious peak. She clutched Fen's hand; Fen gave a breathy whimper, and Pat spasmed against her fingers, unthinking and untrammelled, rubbing fiercely up to prolong the pleasure as she reached the peak and her body clenched tight with throbbing joy.

She sank back onto the bed, mouth open. Fen was looking into her face and her expression washed away any nascent second thoughts or fears, because she looked enchanted.

"Oh," she said, and curled to kiss her. Pat kissed her back, brain still slow with the aftershocks of that glorious feeling, and slid her hand over Fen's backside with more confidence now. "Mph. How lovely."

Fen sat up after a moment. They seemed to have disarranged her combinations, somehow, and her bosom was spilling out of the top. Pat reached up and tugged at the fabric, dragging it down, then slid her hand under one warm, heavy breast. Fen said, "Ooh."

"That was awfully good instruction," Pat said. "Could I have a go now?"

"I think you should." Fen lay back, one arm behind her head, one knee invitingly bent, bosom unrestrained.

Pat caught her breath. "You look...I don't know. Like an odalisque."

Fen blinked. "One of those Egyptian stone things?"

"No, *odalisque*. You know." Pat wasn't sure of the definition herself, now she came to think about it. "A voluptuous barely-clad lady in a painting looking no better than she should be. Except you couldn't get any better."

"On the contrary," Fen said with a luxurious stretch. "I could be *dramatically* better. Try it and see. And don't forget, you want me to squeal."

CHAPTER NINE

It was two hours or more before they parted, Fen leaving her with a final kiss and slipping out semi-dressed and with an armful of underthings to return to her room. Pat went to bed in a state of dazed and satiated joy and snuggled into the sheets, enjoyably aware of the damp between her legs, and ready for unconsciousness.

Unfortunately, the weather had other ideas. The wind howled around Rodington Court, banging the shutters and shrieking down the chimney. Rain lashed the walls as if thrown by the bucketful. Pat did sleep, but fitfully, and her dreams were mostly peculiar explanations for the racket. After her brain spun a tale of the house's invasion by a hunt in full cry including horses and several screaming foxes, she gave up trying to sleep, and simply lay and listened to the storm.

It wasn't blowing out. If anything, it was getting worse: there was a deep rumble that sounded like thunder approaching. No shooting today: they would all have a day in Rodington Court, trapped with the others after last night's revelations.

Pat had forgotten the horrors of the previous evening in its glorious ending, but now they returned tenfold. The set-jawed shame with which the Earl and Countess had endured Haworth's accusations said a great deal; Lady Anna had been as good as called an adulteress, and Jimmy's peccadilloes exposed. Haworth was a cancer on the family, eating them out from within and the only thing Pat could do was leave them to their misery.

The day would be awful for Fen in particular, since she would doubtless need an interview with the Earl and Countess, assuming she carried through with her determination to end things with Jimmy.

Surely she wouldn't change her mind, not after last night. Louisa had changed her mind, though, and decided that men and marriage were the only sensible option. *One can't expect these things to last, Pat dear, can one?*

Pat didn't want to think about that now. She would retreat, she decided: find one of the quiet nooks with which Rodington Court was liberally equipped and settle down with a book. If she wanted company there would, God willing, be Fen; perhaps Miss Singh too. She'd avoid Haworth at all costs, sit it out until the storm passed, and then leave. There was nothing else to be done.

She went down early for breakfast, on the grounds that the ghastly man was a late riser. Miss Singh was already there, with a book propped in front of her.

"Good morning," Pat offered, just as a clap of thunder broke almost overhead.

"Not much of one," Miss Singh remarked. "What a shocking day."

"No prospect of improvement, either." Pat hesitated, but it needed to be said. "Are you all right, Miss Singh? You've been having a rotten time of it. I'm sorry for setting off yesterday's explosion."

"If it hadn't been your comment, it would have been someone else's. Believe me, I've seen enough of that man to be sure."

Pat nodded. "I dare say. Good work with the water. It's the only way with a biting dog."

"Quite."

"Are you going to stay?"

"Here?" Miss Singh made a face. "I don't want to leave Aunt Mattie—the Countess, you know. She's my godmother, but I grew up calling her aunt; I lived with the Wittons for a couple of years while

111

my parents travelled. I don't want to abandon her in time of trouble. Unfortunately, my presence makes Haworth worse." She spoke with remarkable calm, considering the amount of insult her words encompassed. "It is hard to know what to do."

"Yes." Pat contemplated the chafing dishes, and helped herself to sausage and mushrooms. "So...will Mr. Keynes stay?"

She tried to ask it casually—delicately, even. Miss Singh sounded equally calm as she replied, "Unless the Earl asks him to leave for attempting to murder his son-in-law."

"Oh, yes, true. Sterling effort. I'm sorry I drenched him."

"It was probably for the best."

Pat caught Miss Singh's eye at that point. They both started laughing at once, Miss Singh's shoulders shaking, Pat forced to put down the toast she was buttering. "Oh goodness," Miss Singh gasped, wiping her eyes. "One shouldn't laugh, but really."

"Laugh or cry. Still, he leapt to your defence in a most impressive way. Or are you a pacifist?"

"Not when it comes to Maurice Haworth," Miss Singh assured her. "And...well. As it happens, Preston asked me to marry him last night."

"Good heavens. Will you?" Miss Singh nodded, the look in her eyes saying everything. "Oh, congratulations. How wonderful."

"I haven't told anyone else. The atmosphere is hardly appropriate, and to be honest, I don't want Haworth's opinion."

"I do understand, and I shan't say anything. But I'm thrilled for you. He seems awfully decent."

"He is. I suppose you must think it's a rather peculiar match."

One couldn't argue with that on the face of it, but Pat shook her head. "Not at all. Nobody could possibly think that when you look so happy."

Miss Singh flushed becomingly. "Thank you, Miss Merton. That's very kind."

"Pat, please."

"Victoria, then. Thank you. Oh, don't let me keep you from your breakfast."

"I can congratulate and eat at the same time," Pat assured her. "Have you known each other long?"

That led Miss Singh—Victoria—into an account of how she had met Preston at a different country house party. She looked about five years younger when she wasn't forced to guard herself, and very pretty. She was speaking with great animation when they both heard a tread on the floorboards. Pat whipped around; Victoria clamped her mouth shut.

Fen came in, looking somewhat wary. "Good morning. I'm sorry, am I interrupting?"

"No! Not at all." Pat glanced at Victoria. "We were just discussing, uh—"

"Really, I can go." Fen had dark rings under her eyes. She smiled with a hint of effort. "I don't want to intrude."

"You aren't, Miss Carruth," Victoria said. "I was just telling Pat, between ourselves, that Preston and I are engaged to be married."

"Oh!" Fen clapped her hands to her mouth, then scurried over to the table, and wrapped Miss Singh in a heartfelt embrace, which she returned, looking startled but pleased. It was the kind of open-hearted reaction Pat was never very good at; she wasn't one for hugs.

Fen was damp-eyed when she released the other woman. "Well, that is wonderful. I suppose you've already told Pat all about it, so…you'll just have to tell me all about it over again."

"I will." Victoria glanced between them. "Thank you both. I didn't expect to have people to share this with."

Fen's eyes rounded. "Does the Countess not approve?"

"I haven't told anyone else." Victoria briefly repeated her situation. "So if you could keep it under your hat for now, just until things calm down?"

"Of course." Fen looked pleased, and a little pink. "Naturally I will. We can find a discreet corner after breakfast—this house is just a lot of discreet corners stuck together, isn't it?—and settle down for a proper talk."

"That sounds like a good idea. We won't be doing much else." Victoria cast a rueful look at the window.

They chatted about possible entertainments for the day while Fen helped herself to breakfast. Victoria was far more voluble than Pat had expected once she'd let her guard down. Pat wondered what it must cost her to keep up the remote, silent facade for fear of unpleasant comment, and sent extra maledictions in Haworth's direction.

Jack and Preston came down as the women were finishing breakfast. Preston beamed when he saw Victoria in a way that Pat suspected would let the cat out of the bag before too long. She took the opportunity to excuse herself, and Fen followed.

"Hello," Fen murmured as they headed upstairs.

"Hello, you." It felt peculiar to walk next to her, demurely clad in a day dress, after last night. The taste of Fen's lips, the weight of her breasts, the way she'd moved under Pat's hands. "Did you sleep well?"

"Oh, well." Fen pulled a face. "Not really. The storm. And the prospect of today."

She hadn't changed her mind about ending the engagement. Pat couldn't help the skip in her heart. "I can see that. You've spent more time in the Court than I have: what's the best discreet corner to lurk in?"

"There's a couple of small sitting rooms on the ground floor of the East Wing that nobody seems to use, and two more on the first floor. All the bedrooms on that side are empty. Apparently the wind catches them dreadfully."

"It's catching the entire house fairly badly. Should we—?"

"I ought to speak to the Earl and Countess first. I can't say I'm much looking forward to that." They'd reached Pat's bedroom. She paused at the door; Fen gave her a gentle shove inside, and quietly closed the door behind them.

"Um," she said.

She's going to say it was a terrible mistake. Or a delightful evening but not to be repeated. She's going to ask me to be discreet. The thoughts buzzed through Pat's head. She made herself stand straight. Whatever Fen wanted, she would be decent and dignified about it.

"Gosh, you look alarming," Fen said. "Are you intending to give me bad news?"

"No!" Pat said hastily. "Not at all. Er, are you?"

Fen shook her head. She looked miserable, and Pat remembered her earlier thoughts and stepped forward, opening her arms. Fen moved into them as though it were entirely usual to do so, resting her head on Pat's chest. "Oh goodness. Sorry."

"That's all right." It would always be all right to hold her. Pat wrapped her arms around Fen's shoulders. "What's up?"

"I feel awful. Leaving Jimmy and the Wittons in the lurch, and I know it's all his fault, but I still *feel* it."

Pat nodded. Fen's hair tickled her face. "I do know, but you aren't obliged to restore the Yoxall family fortunes. Um, Fen?"

"Mmm?"

"About last night."

Fen wriggled. It was a wriggle into Pat, a little happy shimmy that sent remembered pleasure shooting up her nerves. "Ooh. Yes. What?"

"I just wondered—well, how you felt about it."

"Marvellous." Fen tipped her head back. "Quite terrifically marvellous. Which I am a *tiny* bit guilty about, but not really. I shall have to leave, you know, in the circumstances."

"Yes, of course."

"I'll wait until Jimmy's spoken to his parents, and then I shall speak to them, and I imagine they'll have me driven straight to the railway station after that."

115

"Where will you go?"

"Home. I don't really want to go back to London and sit through another scandal." Fen hesitated. "Please don't feel obliged, but I wondered if you'd like to come for a visit? Our place is in King's Norton, outside Birmingham, quite in the countryside."

Hope fluttered in Pat's chest like a trapped bird. "Would you like me to?"

"Very much. You could teach me to shoot. Daddy won't be there so it would be awfully private. Just us. And you need somewhere to stay while you do nothing, and I can't socialise with a third broken engagement, and if it wasn't for this party going horribly wrong we could have had three weeks to get to know one another more and— well, I'd like it awfully if you would."

"*Yes*. When?" Pat probably sounded like a child hoping for a treat, but the prospect felt like Christmas. A private visit, with Fen, just the two of them and countryside to explore...

"As soon as you like. You could say you were keeping me company in my distress. I'm sure I oughtn't be alone with my broken heart." Fen adopted an expression suggestive of a mournful kitten. "It would be only kind."

"You are a menace," Pat said, and kissed her.

Fen extricated herself a few moments later, eyes glowing, and went to check her hair in the mirror. "Goodness. Do I look far too happy for someone who just ended an engagement with a future earl?"

"A little."

"I'll think sad thoughts." She smiled up at Pat, the real, hesitant smile that never failed to stop her breath. "You know, this really ought to count as the worst house party ever given, but I'm so very glad I came."

"Like the curate's egg, good in parts," Pat agreed.

"Exactly." Fen beamed at her. "I'd better go untangle my affairs, hadn't I?"

"Do you want moral support? I wouldn't normally expect the Earl to blame you, in the circumstances, but the way things have gone here, nothing would surprise me." Lord Witton's urgent need for money, so much worse than she'd realised, might well outweigh decency. Pat wondered if she was obliged to mention it. She didn't want to be trapped between Bill's confidence and Fen's well-being.

"No, that's all right. I dare say he'll be disappointed but he's a fine man at heart. I think. Load a gun and come running if I scream. Oh, but one probably oughtn't run with a loaded gun, ought one? Like scissors."

"You are ridiculous."

"I know," Fen said. "It's part of my charm." She sauntered out, looking irresistibly pleased with herself. Pat shook her head, went to the mirror, and discovered she was flushed and grinning like an idiot.

She found her book, which had apparently been knocked under her bed the previous night by some careless person's flailing limb, and headed out. Fen would doubtless need some time to untangle her affairs, so Pat would find herself a nook to sit in where she could wait out the day. She decided to head for the East Wing. She was fairly sure she could reach it by carrying along the corridor from her bedroom; it was worth a try in order to avoid going through the main hall and meeting anyone.

Her room was the last one in use on this floor. The corridor took her past several closed doors, then a turn to the left brought her into the East Wing, past a servants' stair which would lead to the working part of Rodington Court. This looked dusty with disuse, which was reasonable given the house was considerably understaffed. The main stair would be toward the front of the house. She headed in that direction, passing several doors, and indulged herself in a look-around since the area was clearly not anyone's personal quarters.

Most of the rooms were in holland covers. Just two towards the front of the house seemed to be in occasional use: one a book-lined study of the sort that offered absolutely nothing to read, with a wide leather couch and a smell of elderly dogs and disintegrating paper; the other a bare space with a desk against one wall, a chair, and two armchairs by the empty grate, not covered and rather shabby. Neither was an inviting place to sit, though the first floor position on this empty wing would guarantee privacy. Everywhere had a smell of slightly damp dust, although the lashing rain was doubtless partially to blame for that.

She took the staircase down to the main hall once she found it, and realised it brought her back to the room she'd sat in to clean her gun on her first day. She opened the connecting door to the next room to check for blackmailers, and saw a more comfortable area with a deep armchair, which she decided to claim. It still wasn't precisely cosy with the wind and rain thrashing against the window, but that couldn't be helped. She shut the connecting door behind her, and settled down with her book in peace.

That lasted for perhaps an hour before she heard the raised voices from the next room.

"…absolutely shitty thing to do!" That was Jimmy, thick-voiced and furious.

"Shitty?" Bill demanded, explosively. "Me, shitty? Well, it takes one to know one, you bastard. How you have the bloody face to talk to me about deception—"

"For Christ's sake, I had no choice!"

"Nor did I!"

Pat cursed internally, albeit not in the men's appalling language. Did nobody in this house ever take precautions to have a private conversation? Well, she was not going to eavesdrop for a second time, which meant leaving at once or making her presence known. Respect for privacy briefly warred with a combination of curiosity, sisterly protectiveness, and a desire to give Jimmy the telling-off he deserved. Privacy was roundly defeated, so Pat uncurled from her chair, gave the connecting door a perfunctory knock, and opened it.

Bill and Jimmy were facing off on their feet, Bill rather white, Jimmy red. Both had a look Pat couldn't have defined, but which went with the raw notes she'd heard in their voices, and she strode briskly into the room wondering if she'd need a jug of water. "All right, that'll do."

"Would you mind, Pat," Bill said through his teeth.

"If you proclaim your business at the top of your voices, you can take the consequences. We've had enough throttling people."

"I'm not going to throttle anyone. Nor is Jimmy."

"Don't bloody bank on it," Jimmy said. "Sorry, Pat. Sorry. I— hell. Oh *hell*."

He sat abruptly, dropping his face into his hands. Bill looked down at him, then turned away.

"Goodness." Pat shut the door, in case anyone else happened to be wandering around. "Look, I don't know what's going on, but I should say, Fen told me the engagement is off."

"What?" Bill barked.

Pat ignored him. He needed to calm down. "I needn't say how I think you've behaved, Jimmy—"

"I've nobody to blame but myself. You don't need to tell me that." Jimmy's face returned to his hands.

"Well, you seemed to be piling the blame on Bill."

"Ah, no," Bill said. "Jimmy is annoyed with me because I'm here to look into his father's financial affairs."

"Yes, well, that's a rotten thing to be doing," Pat pointed out. "As he well knows, Jimmy, and since he's the only person who's trying to give your father a fair hearing—"

"For God's sake! What do you know about this?"

"Enough to suggest you simmer down," Pat said crisply. "Bill's on your side, you oaf."

"I'm not," Bill said. "Or—God rot it— Look it would have helped a great deal, still would, if you were honest with me. That's all."

"About what?" Jimmy demanded. His eyes were wet. "That I asked Fen to marry me because Father's lost a fortune and Haworth's draining us dry? Well, I did, and I'm sorry, and I couldn't even carry that through, and for all I know your people are planning to gaol my father for his part in the crash so perhaps you could just go away and let me try to face up to this almighty mess with a bit of dignity!"

"It's a bit late for that," Bill muttered.

"Do shut up," Pat told him. There was only one other chair, behind the desk; she pulled it round to sit by Jimmy. "Come on, old thing. We're not going to leave you in trouble. Fen's been awfully good about what you must admit was a damn fool thing to do. Why don't you tell Bill what he needs to know and let him help you?"

"I'm here to do my job," Bill said. "Not help."

"Oh, rubbish. The Earl is patently honest."

"It hardly matters what he is." Jimmy sounded exhausted. "It's his name on the papers. He signed everything Maurice told him to sign. I've no doubt he signed things he shouldn't have, things that are probably inexcusable. He was in well over his head, he really believed for a while that he was some sort of speculator, and—oh, the devil. You have no idea what it's been like for him and Mother with that bloody man in our lives."

"If Haworth fooled your father into signing things he didn't understand, he needs to say so," Bill said. "I am sure we—you—can make his case. This is a complex, clever fraud of which nobody who'd met the Earl could imagine him capable."

"I suppose you mean he's not bright enough to be crooked."

"It runs in the family," Bill said. "Tell him to talk to me."

"I can't. He won't."

"You'd better. The alternative won't be pretty. Other people have lost a lot of money and your father will be the scapegoat."

"Do you think we don't realise that?" Jimmy demanded. "Do you think I *want* to protect that cancerous growth of a man? We cannot act against Maurice!"

"Why the devil not?"

Jimmy flung his hands up, a gesture far more eloquent than any speech. There was a silence.

"Fine," he said at last. "If you want to know... God, where do I start. With Anna, I suppose. She's stuck with him. There's no chance of her obtaining a divorce on the usual grounds because she's played the fool so notoriously—Jack is only the latest of her boy friends. And Maurice isn't physically violent. He lands all his blows on one's nerves, if you see what I mean."

"They could still separate."

"But she won't," Jimmy said. "She's tied to him. I don't understand it. He treats her like dirt and she has her gentlemen friends, but if you say a thing against him she'll defend him to the hilt. And then there's the child, George." Jimmy pushed his hands through his hair. "He's not Maurice's, you know."

"You mean, adopted?" Pat asked.

"No, I mean my sister bedded an American jazz musician," Jimmy snapped. "George takes after his father. Brown as a berry. But in law he's Maurice's, and if Anna left him, Maurice would be entitled to keep the boy."

"Would he want to, given his views?" Bill asked.

"I expect he would like a helpless child to torment, yes," Pat said. "My God, Jimmy."

"Quite. He keeps George from the parents—I told you, didn't I? They barely see him, their only grandchild. He'd be in line for the earldom if anything happened to me, yet he's being brought up God knows how."

"He can inherit through his mother?" Pat asked.

"The earldom is held in fee simple, so it goes to Anna, then George, if I die without issue. Could we not discuss inheritance law now? The point is, Maurice uses the poor scrap as a carrot or stick against the parents, and there's not a damn thing to be done. And then there's this cursed business with the firm. Maurice turned up with things for Pa to sign. Fed him a lot of jargon, switched between treating him as a high financier and shouting that the old chap was trying to get him sacked if he asked questions, held the chance of seeing George over his head—oh, he ran rings round the old man. He claims to have lost everything when the firm crashed, though you'll never persuade me he hasn't squirrelled a good lot of cash away somewhere, and he's been living the high life at our expense ever since. And we're all of us terrified to stand up to him, because God knows what he might do to Father, or Anna, or George. It's like having a family curse."

"Why is Haworth doing this?" Bill asked.

"How the devil should I know?" Jimmy sounded frantic. "I'm sure Anna's a rotten wife, and one can hardly blame him for being upset about George, but it's as if he's set out to despoil all of us as vengeance."

"He doesn't like women," Pat said. "You must have noticed. He's been on at me, at Victoria—at Fen, too, when you might think, if he wanted to carry on living in luxury at your expense, he wouldn't have tried to ruin your engagement to an heiress. And when he was saying things about you and your father, his eyes kept flicking to the Countess. He was trying to hurt her."

"I agree with that," Bill said. "One of those woman-haters who won't leave them alone."

"I wish you had let Preston throttle him," Jimmy said violently. "I wish he was dead. I swear I could stand over his body and laugh. I've never hated anyone so much in my life. It feels as though we're trapped—buried in one of those Egyptian tombs from the pulp novels, you know, with the sand slowly pouring in to suffocate us."

The Mertons exchanged glances. "Steady on," Pat said.

"Less pulp, more planning," Bill added.

"There's no plan to make. There's nothing to be done."

Bill looked down at him, face twisted. "Why did you not tell me this before?"

"Do you think I want to dwell on it? That I'm proud of it?" Jimmy slapped his hand on the desk. "Look at us! My father's at best a damned fool who's helped ruin people, and as for Anna, would you want anyone knowing all that about your sister? The way she's conducted herself—no decent person would receive her again."

"Speaking as the sister in question, I'd be more concerned about finding out why Lady Anna is behaving as she is than complaining about it," Pat said. "She doesn't look like she's living a life of pleasure."

"It's all horribly sordid, I grant you," Bill said. "Did you think I'd care about that, you damned fool?"

"I care," Jimmy said. "It's filthy. You can't know how filthy. And Maurice—any whiff of wrongdoing, of secrets, and he's on it like a ferret down a rathole. I had to keep you away from it. I just wanted it to stop. I *still* want it to stop."

Bill grabbed his hand, caught Pat's eye, and gave a firm jerk of the head. She rose silently, slipping out of the room as Jimmy let out a sob, and returned to the little sitting room next door in thoughtful mood. She closed the door carefully behind her, but it didn't quite muffle the sound of Jimmy weeping.

Bill came to join her perhaps twenty minutes later.

"You look like you've been through the wringer," Pat said. "He's in a bad way."

"It's a bad business." Bill sat, heavily. "I've sent him to beg his father to talk to me. God, Pat, I don't know what to do. I can't cope with this."

"It seems to me you can make a jolly good case to investigate Haworth's dealings."

"While he continues torturing the family, and Jim—" He broke off with a strangled noise.

"Honestly, you ought to leave," Pat said. "You look shocking. You *are* going to have a nerve-storm if this keeps up."

"Jimmy will collapse before I do. He's coming apart at the seams and all I can do is watch." Bill rubbed his face with both hands. "Oh, the devil. It's not your problem, old thing. You ought to go."

"I shall. Fen's invited me to stay at her place for a while. She needs a change of scene herself and she doesn't want to go back to London until the inevitable fuss has died down, and she'd like me to teach her to shoot—" Pat became aware she was explaining too much, and stopped.

"Well, that's good," Bill said, noticing nothing. "Yes, it will be unpleasant for her, I dare say, jilting a third chap."

"Actually, Jimmy ended it."

Bill blinked. "He did?"

"With the admission that he was entirely at fault, of course. He told her Haworth was right and that he's been in love with someone else all along, which is of course dastardly, but at least Fen knows that it isn't anything to do with her. Not that it must be very nice to be sought after for one's money, but—"

"Sorry, sorry," Bill said. "He told Miss Carruth *what*?"

"Oh, a lot of romantic stuff about how he hadn't realised he was dreadfully in love with this other girl until it was too late. You must surely know about her? Or is he keeping this a deep dark secret from everyone?"

Bill cleared his throat. "I'd an idea, yes."

"It seems grossly unfair to her, though I suppose she must be unsuitable in some way." She paused so Bill could fill in the gaps. He did not. Men had no idea how to conduct a conversation. "The main thing is, the fault's all on his side, and he's promised to say as much in public, so hopefully Fen's reputation won't suffer too badly. Even so, there will be a great deal of talk, and I imagine people will blame her anyway. So she intends to lie low a while, and I'm going to lie low with her. Metaphorically, I mean."

"Right. Yes. Good."

"You aren't even listening," Pat said resignedly. "Anyway, I imagine the Wittons will want Fen out of here as quick as they can. She'll head down south today, I should think."

"She'll be lucky," Bill said, returning his attention to the conversation. "In this weather?"

"Motor-cars drive in the rain."

Bill twisted to look at the window, as if he needed visual confirmation of the relentless rain and wind. "I wouldn't bet on it. A storm like this after a long dry spell usually means flooding around here. The roads are regularly cut off in winter. It's one of the things Jimmy wanted to deal with, when..." He made a face. "God damn Haworth. Damn him to hell."

"He's rotten, and all this is rotten, but it's not down to you," Pat said. "Come on, old man, let's think about something else. Tell me about your boxing club."

They chatted for some time, until there was a knock at the door and Fen called, "Pat?"

"In here."

Fen let herself in. She looked as if her morning had been difficult.

"All right?" Pat asked, conscious of Bill's presence.

"It was dreadful, but never mind. The car will take me to the station after lunch."

"I'll come and help you pack."

"Yes, do. I'm sorry to tear your sister away, Mr. Merton."

"Not at all," Bill said. "I don't know if it's appropriate to offer my sympathy?"

"I think you ought to extend that to Jimmy rather than me," Fen said. "I wish him well, but I've made the only possible decision. I hope he will be happy."

She spoke with remarkable dignity. Bill paused a second and then said, "I shall tell him he's a fool, on multiple levels. I'm pleased to have met you, Miss Carruth."

KJ CHARLES

He extended his hand, a strikingly formal gesture. Fen shook it with equal seriousness, and, when they left the room together, whispered to Pat, "What on earth was that about?"

"Goodness knows."

Jimmy was striding down the corridor towards them, face set and grim. He managed a nod to the two women as he passed, no more. They emerged into the main hall just as the grandfather clock chimed its noisy half hour, and saw Maurice Haworth strolling across the hall directly towards them. Fen instantly took Pat's arm and pulled her round so they were walking around the edges of the hall, not towards Haworth. "Yes, do come and help," she said loudly, drowning out any remark that might be made. "I'd like the company."

126

CHAPTER TEN

The luncheon gong was rung at one o'clock, which might as well have been half past midnight for the darkness outside. Maurice Haworth did not join them.

"Where is Maurice?" the Earl enquired of Lady Anna.

She shrugged. She had a higher colour than normal and a self-satisfied look. Pat wondered if one took drugs at midday or waited for the cocktail hour. "I've no idea. He often misses luncheon. We shan't wait."

After that, the meal was conducted mostly in silence, as might be expected given the broken engagement and, Pat thought unkindly, the financial blow it represented to the Wittons. Jack Bouvier-Lynes made some light chat about theatre and night-spots, which Preston did his best to turn into a conversation, with limited support from Victoria. Fen stayed quiet; Jimmy barely ate.

They dutifully trudged to the drawing-room for coffee after the meal. Fen sat with her elbows in and her ankles together, taking up as little space as possible, not meeting anyone's eyes. Pat breathed evenly and wished they were leaving together. She didn't want to be in this wretched house, this poisoned atmosphere, for one more minute.

The clock ticked on; the rain drove down. Jack, Jimmy, Preston, and Bill went off to play cards. Lady Anna announced she had a headache, with no great effort at verisimilitude, and left them to it. At two, Fen asked, with just a hint of desperation, "Might I enquire about the car?"

"I did expect it to be ready before now," the Countess said with a frown. "Ring the bell, please, Victoria."

Victoria did so, walking across the room, then stopped. "Where is the kirpan?"

"On the wall, dear."

"It's not."

Pat followed Victoria's line of sight to the wall, where the beautifully carved, Indian-looking knife had hung. Only the sheath now remained. "Oh, the knife? What did you call it?"

"A kirpan. It's a Sikh weapon."

"Kirpan," Pat repeated, memorising the term. "It had an elaborate metal handle, yes? It was definitely in its sheath when I arrived, I noticed it particularly."

"How odd," the Countess said. "I expect it's being cleaned. We like to keep the decorative weaponry in good order. Oh, Henry," she added as a footman came in. "The car for Miss Carruth to the station, please. Pritchard should have it ready."

"Yes, my lady."

"Do you also keep the firearms in working order?" Pat asked, for something to say. "Including that marvellous old blunderbuss in the hall? Can they be used?"

That made the Earl perk up, and he was enthusiastically describing his experience of trying out various ancient guns and fowling-pieces when the footman Henry returned.

"I beg your pardon, my lord. Unfortunately, Pritchard says it won't be possible to take Miss Carruth to the station."

"Why on earth not?" demanded the Countess.

"Because the rivers have burst, madam," Henry announced, with lugubrious enjoyment. "The man came by from Stonebridge just half an hour back. The line is flooded."

"The railway line?" Fen said with open dismay. "But how will I leave?"

"You can't, miss. It's ankle deep on the roads and Pritchard says he can't answer for the Daimler till it goes down. You could ride down to the village, perhaps, but then you'd just be stuck there instead."

"All right, that will do," the Earl said testily. "Of course you will stay with us, Miss Carruth. We must be informed immediately the situation improves."

Henry shot a glance at the window, which was sluiced by water as though someone was throwing buckets at it. "Yes, my lord."

"Well," the Countess said. "That is…unfortunate."

"Nobody can leave." Pat glanced around the room, seeing her own dismay reflected on every face, guests and family alike. "We'll just have to wait for the rain to pass, then."

The Countess rose. "I think I shall lie down. I hope you will order tea and so on as you please. James?"

The Earl accompanied her out. The three remaining women looked at one another. Victoria summed matters up with a heartfelt, "Bother."

"Quite," Fen said. "Were you hoping to go too?"

"Strongly."

"That man again?"

"I haven't seen him all day, thank goodness, but I should like to keep it that way. Preston offered to escort me back to London."

"I thought you were going to stay, for the Countess."

Victoria made a face. "I concluded it was doing more harm than good. Preston is very keen to get away—he is self-conscious about assaulting his hosts' son-in-law. And we want to tell our families, of course. But it hardly matters what we want if the railway is out of action."

They chatted about Preston's family and Victoria's plans for a while, then as the conversation became more general, about books, mutual acquaintances, almost anything except the fact of being trapped in this house with Maurice Haworth. Victoria rang for tea around three, and had the fire lit. Pat nibbled a scone, letting herself enjoy this:

Victoria's unguarded face, Fen curled up on the sofa, their smiles. This was the aspect of Rodington Court she'd remember and cherish, she decided: a cosy room keeping the weather out, and a new friend, and Fen. It was only everybody else that appalled.

This was underlined a few moments later when Jack Bouvier-Lynes and Lady Anna came in. He was saying, "Well, since the cat's away, the mice may as well play," in such a flirtatious tone that the meaning could not be mistaken. Lady Anna wore a seductive expression that seemed to Pat oddly unreal, as though she had painted it on. It faded almost at once as she took in the scene.

"Good heavens," she said. "Miss Carruth. I thought you'd gone."

"The railway line is flooded," Pat said.

"How unfortunate." Lady Anna's expression didn't allow much room for doubt as to what she found unfortunate. "And how unpleasant for my brother."

Fen rose. "I'm sure you want your tea. I've had mine, so I shall leave you."

"I'll join you," Pat said.

"I think I will find Aunt Mattie," Victoria agreed, and the three of them walked out of the room in an icy mutual silence interrupted only by rustling skirts.

In the hallway, Victoria put a hand to Fen's arm. "Are you all right?"

"I could hardly expect her to take my side," Fen said. "But I might go and hide somewhere now."

"Very wise," Victoria said. "I'll find Preston, I think."

Pat slipped her arm through Fen's as they made their way through the dark corridors. Fen leaned into her with a sigh. "I'm awfully glad you're here. I'm not glad *we're* here, but I'm glad you are."

"I'm glad I am too." Pat could by now have throttled the entire Yoxall family without compunction. Fen deserved so much better. "Do you think we might hide somewhere until dinner?"

"Let's. I honestly don't know how much more I can bear of other people; I was so looking forward to getting away from here."

"At least you know that you haven't done anything wrong," Pat said. "You've nothing to be ashamed of, which is more than one can say for others in this house."

Fen snuggled closer, her fingers seeking Pat's, and Pat held them with a bubble of joy rising despite the circumstances. It was grossly unfair that Fen should be in this rotten place, but at least Pat could be here with her, and if Maurice blasted Haworth had one word to say, she fully intended to drop all convention and let him have it with both barrels. "Let's find somewhere quiet to lurk until the coast is clear."

They headed for the East Wing once more. Pat had intended to try the room she'd sat in earlier, but Fen led the way up the stairs, shooting Pat a glittering look, and Pat followed. She'd have followed her anywhere.

They walked silently, almost tiptoeing. It was so much like playing truant at school that Pat felt a giggle rising. At the top of the stairs she considered her options and decided on the study rather than the empty room she'd seen before. After all, the study had a couch. She tugged Fen in that direction, received an excited nod, and twisted the door handle. It stuck, then clicked, and she threw open the door.

There was someone on the sofa. Someone naked—an expanse of pale skin, far too many limbs for one person, all scrabbling in hurried motion, and then the bewildering image resolved itself and Pat stood and stared at her brother and Jimmy Yoxall, bare and entwined on the sofa, staring back at her with expressions of pure horror.

"Oh," Fen said from beside her.

"Uh," Bill said.

"I'm awfully sorry," Pat said. "We should have knocked."

She shut the door carefully, and stepped away. Fen stared at the door, then up at Pat, then said, "Well. Your room, I think."

She dragged Pat along the corridor, marching along until they reached her bedroom, where she pushed Pat towards the bed, shut the door, put her back against it, and repeated, "*Well.*"

"I had no idea." Pat wasn't entirely sure that was true now she came to consider it. It certainly made sense of a lot of things. "Good God. I suppose that explains Jimmy's behaviour, doesn't it?"

"His mysterious secret unattainable love affair was your brother?" Fen's lips moved silently. "Goodness me. For heaven's *sake.*"

Pat's heart thumped, not pleasantly. "I'm sure you're very annoyed—outraged, even, and you've every reason—but you know I'm awfully fond of Bill."

Fen frowned. "Of course you are. I hope you aren't suggesting that I'm about to rush off and call the police or inform the Wittons."

"No, I didn't mean that—"

"Then you were worried I might casually let it slip at the dinner table?" Fen looked offended, Pat realised with a sinking sensation. "I'm not entirely ignorant, or quite so careless either."

"I really didn't think that," Pat said urgently, and guiltily, because the thought had been there. "Honestly. I know you wouldn't set out to hurt anyone but it's not unreasonable for you to be upset with Jimmy, and people do say things without meaning to."

"If they're silly little feather-heads, yes they do," Fen snapped. "I thought you had a slightly higher opinion of me."

"Of course I do. Fen, please. I didn't mean to imply that at all, but Bill's my brother, and Jimmy's my friend, and what if that had been Haworth who walked in instead of us? I don't want to be afraid for another brother." The truth of that hit her with horrifying force as the words left her mouth. "Oh God, I don't want to. Oh, Bill."

"Of course you're afraid. I didn't think. How silly of me." Fen spoke with quick sympathy, ruffled feathers settling at once. "Come here." She slipped her arms around Pat's waist, and Pat held on, breathing in her scent. "I do see this is a new worry for you, but I promise you needn't worry about me saying anything."

132

"I know. I didn't think you would, really."

"Well, now you have my word for it," Fen said. "And I'm not outraged. I don't think I'm even annoyed. I already knew Jimmy had a tendre for someone else, and it makes no difference to me who that is. Actually, this is probably better than a married woman, which is what I assumed, because at least he isn't betraying someone's vows."

"Adultery isn't criminal," Pat pointed out.

"No, but I don't see why they should be either. We're not," Fen said, with a matter-of-factness that took Pat's breath away. "I can't say I'm *more* impressed by Jimmy's behaviour in the light of this, but it's no worse. Oh, no, but it is though, because your poor brother has been looking like a kicked dog since he got here. Why on earth did he come? This must have been awful for him."

Pat put a finger under Fen's chin, tipped her head up, and kissed her firmly. Fen responded with enthusiasm. "Mmm. What was that for?"

"You are without a doubt the loveliest person I've ever met."

"I know." Fen dimpled. "And I certainly don't—" The flirtatious look dropped away from her face. "Oh. Oh dear. Pat?"

"What?"

"Haworth talked about Jimmy's illicit trysts. I remember because that was what made me think it must be a married woman. You don't suppose he knows, do you?"

"Dear God." Pat remembered—it seemed months ago, somehow—the conversation she'd heard. Haworth threatening someone with exposure. "Oh God, no."

"No wonder Jimmy looked sick."

"I can't have this. I won't. If Haworth threatens my brother I'll shoot him myself."

"Yes, but don't," Fen said firmly. "Not yet, anyway. We need to talk to your brother, to both of them. Preferably when they have some clothes on."

Pat couldn't help a splutter of laughter. Fen cast up a roguish glance and added, "I suppose it would be indelicate to comment—"

"Yes, it would."

"But one sees classical statuary all the time. We're positively encouraged to appreciate naked male bottoms."

"Marble ones. Whereas that was Jimmy's, and I have never aspired to see it, and I wouldn't put it in a museum either," Pat said, and couldn't help but join Fen as she went off into a peal of laughter. Nothing about this was very funny at all, but she'd rather be laughing than crying.

They lurked in Fen's room, alternating quiet talk, comfortable silence, and kisses until the dinner hour, then came down as late as they felt was compatible with good manners. Even so, only Victoria and Preston were in the drawing room, and the rest of the guests didn't make an appearance until the dinner gong had sounded. They filed in silently and sat, with one notable omission.

"Where's Maurice?" Jimmy asked after a few moments.

"I've no idea," his sister replied with glacial disinterest.

"Perhaps he prefers to eat in his room," the Countess said. Nobody chimed in to say they supported his preference, but the sentiment floated around the table like a ghost.

"Is Mr. Haworth eating upstairs?" the Earl enquired of the footman.

"I'm not aware, my lord."

"Well, get someone to find out, and if he isn't, let him know dinner has begun," the Earl said. "And you may start serving now. We won't wait."

The soup was served, an excellent mulligatawny. The footman made a reappearance as they were finishing to say, "Mr. Haworth is not in his bedroom, my lord."

The Earl humphed. "Well, he'll have to fend for himself. There are plenty of clocks in the house if he didn't hear the gong."

Even without Haworth, the gathering was excruciating. Jack Bouvier-Lynes did sterling work to fend off the silence, telling perhaps a dozen clubland stories in a row without flagging. Preston, Victoria, Pat, and Fen made appreciative noises as best they could; the Yoxalls were entirely sunk in gloom. Bill concentrated on his food, but half way through the main course he did look up and catch Pat's eye. She offered him a smile. He didn't smile back.

The women retired after the meal as usual. The Countess looked wrung out as they settled in the drawing room. "Victoria, will you pour the tea? Anna, where is Maurice?"

"I really couldn't say."

"He *is* your husband."

Lady Anna lifted one elegant shoulder. Victoria said, "He wasn't at lunch either."

"Perhaps he went out for a walk?" Pat suggested, a remark which was greeted with the incredulity it deserved. "Yes, I know the weather is vile but he won't melt, and he might have wanted a change of scene. Is there a public house nearby?"

"There's nothing within twelve miles," Victoria said. "I'm not aware he likes to walk."

"Of course he doesn't. Maurice finds the countryside as dull as I do." Lady Anna sounded entirely contemptuous. "I don't know why you're making a fuss. He is a grown man; if he doesn't choose to take dinner, let him be."

"Yes, but has anyone seen him today?" Victoria pressed.

"Fen and I saw him around half past eleven," Pat offered.

The other women shook their heads. The Countess shut her eyes. "Is there no limit— For heaven's sake. Victoria, will you go back to the dining room and ask the gentlemen?"

Pat couldn't help glancing at Lady Anna as Victoria left. It was tiresome to be called upon for every little task, as she well knew, but she wondered how it must feel when one's mother always turned to her goddaughter instead.

Victoria was back a few moments later, frowning. "Nobody has seen him since before luncheon. And he didn't express an intention to go anywhere to any of the men."

The Countess's eyelids drooped. "Ring the bell," she told Victoria, and the footman from dinner duly appeared. "Dennis, thank you. Did you check Mr. Haworth's room?"

"Yes, ma'am. He wasn't there."

"Find out if anyone in the servant's hall has seen him this afternoon," the Countess directed. "Or if anyone knows if he has left the house, or had any plans for the day."

The footman cast a glance at the windows. "Not much of a day to go out, surely. Yes, my lady," he added at her look, and withdrew.

"He can't have gone anywhere," Lady Anna said. "It's pouring. He probably doesn't want to spend time with people he finds uncongenial. You can hardly blame him for that. It's not as though you've tried to make my husband feel welcome in this family."

Fen's eyes opened wide at that analysis of the situation, but nobody replied, and they sat in brittle silence until the men joined them perhaps five minutes later, bearing brandy glasses. "Has anyone discovered Maurice?" the Earl asked.

"I've asked the staff."

"He was around this morning," Jack Bouvier-Lynes said. "Has nobody seen him since?"

"When did you see him?" Bill asked.

Jack gave a gesture too elegant to be called a shrug. "Mid-morning. We had a brief chat about this and that, and then he looked at his watch and left me somewhat abruptly. Perhaps an hour before lunch?"

"Fen and I saw him going into the East Wing at half past eleven," Pat said. "We didn't stop to speak to him. Did he say anything to you about going out?"

"In this weather? Good heavens, no."

"He must be somewhere," Jimmy said. "If he's not in the house he must have gone out. I'm not sure why this is difficult."

The footman returned a moment later. "My lady," he said. "I'm afraid nobody in the servants' hall has seen Mr. Haworth since breakfast or is aware of any plans he may have had. The horses, bicycles, and car are all accounted for."

That fell into silence. The Earl said, "What on earth?"

"If he's gone out in this weather he'll catch his death," Fen said. "Suppose he did and hurt himself, twisted his ankle?"

Lady Anna sighed audibly. The Countess shot her a look of open dislike. "Dennis, see if his coat is there, and if any oilskins or galoshes are missing."

"Yes, ma'am."

"We can't send out a search party," Jimmy said. "It's dark as Hades and blowing a gale, the ground is flooded, and if we don't know when he left, we can't possibly judge how far he might have got."

Pat waited for someone to protest. Nobody did. "But if he's injured...?" she felt compelled to say at last, without enthusiasm.

"Jimmy's right," Bill said. "One couldn't call for him over this wind, and it's far too risky for searchers in the dark. We'd just be inviting more injuries, and that's if he's even hurt at all. He could have hitched a lift and be in the pub."

"I doubt anyone is driving for pleasure today, but you're right about the risk," Jimmy said. "I don't want Rodington Court men put in danger for Maurice. Or for anyone else," he added, rather too late.

Pat didn't argue. If Maurice Haworth had gone out for a walk in a storm without telling anyone, he was a fool and could take the consequences of his folly. She wasn't entirely able to persuade herself he had, and the dropping level of brandy in Jimmy's glass suggested she wasn't the only one to feel unsettled.

Dennis the footman returned at last. He looked distinctly worried now. "We can't see any things missing, ma'am. Mr. Haworth's overcoat is hanging up."

"Good Lord," Preston said. "But—"

"Thank you, Dennis, you may go," the Earl said. "Now, that is good news, surely? He wouldn't have gone out without a coat, so he can't have gone out."

"Then where is he, dear, and why has he missed two meals?" the Countess returned.

Bill said it for all of them. "Ought we search the house?"

"I really don't know why you're all making such a fuss," Lady Anna said. "None of you care for him in the slightest. He's probably fallen asleep on a sofa and he won't thank you for drawing attention to it."

"He's probably stuck a needleful of some garbage into his arm and passed out, is what he's *probably* done," Jimmy said, with sudden savagery. The Countess made a noise of protest. "We all know it, Ma, and someone had to say it. Blast the man. All right, let's go and look. Preston, Jack, you check this wing. Bill and I will go to the East."

They headed out, along with the Earl. Pat would have liked to go with them if only to be doing something, but she didn't want to leave Fen with the Countess and Lady Anna. They sat and waited instead, making whatever pointless conversation they could for some minutes, and then slipping into heavy wordlessness again.

Pat scoured her mind for anything to say but found herself bereft of ideas. There was nothing but the wind and rain and the crackle of the fire, the ticking clock and the sounds of breathing, and as the minutes passed the build-up of hostile silence was excruciating. Would it be rude to go in search of a book?

She shot Fen a look. Fen met her eyes despairingly, took a deep breath, probably to embark on some effort at social lubrication, then swung round. "What's that?"

Someone was running along the hall. The footsteps skidded to a stop, the door opened, and Preston Keynes looked in. His face was an odd shade, pallid and patched with red.

"Excuse me," he said. "Lady Witton—Lady Anna—"

"What on earth is wrong?" the Countess demanded.

"It's, uh—" He looked around desperately. "Perhaps I could speak to you in private?"

Pat, Fen, and Victoria all rose at once. "Preston, what is it?" Victoria demanded. "What's wrong?"

He gave her a ghastly look. "I'm awfully sorry. I'm afraid there's been an accident."

"What do you mean?" Lady Anna sounded shrill. "What do you mean, an accident? Is it Maurice?"

Pat took one look at Preston's face and said, "We'll give you privacy." She had no desire to find herself in the position of comforting a bereaved wife, particularly if that wife was Lady Anna. She hurried out with Fen at her heels. Preston closed the door behind them, and she heard the low sounds of his voice, then Lady Anna's wail.

"Gosh," Fen said. "Should we see if we can help?"

"If you mean, shall we find out what's going on—"

"That was exactly what I meant."

"Let's."

They headed for the main hall and into the East Wing. Jack Bouvier-Lynes stood on the staircase like a sentinel; Jimmy sat on a low step, head bowed.

"What is it?" Pat asked. "What's happened?"

"I don't think you ladies should go up," Jack said, and for once there was no hint of a smile on his face. "There's been an accident. A bad one."

"Is that Pat down there?" Bill's voice came from above. "Thank goodness. Pop up, will you?"

She hurried up the stairs, brushing past Jack's protest, Fen at her heels. The study door was shut, but the door to the bare room next to it stood open. She went in.

The Earl was in the corner, leaning on or possibly holding onto the mantelpiece, trembling visibly. Bill stood by the desk, over which a seated man was slumped, face down. His back was clothed in a dashing grey twill, with a sort of long grey protuberance sticking out of it. The image made no sense at all for a couple of seconds, and then Pat realised it was the carved metal hilt of a knife.

"Oh," she said.

"Miss Carruth, Miss Merton," the Earl panted. "This is not a fit sight for you."

"Not at all," Bill said. "Perhaps you could take Miss Carruth out, sir. I dare say she needs your support." He gave Fen a meaningful glance.

She stared back, then shook herself and leaped into action. "Oh yes, if you would be so kind, Lord Witton. I feel dreadfully faint. The poor man. Oh, the poor man!"

"Don't distress yourself, my dear," the Earl told her, looking more focused now he had a task. Fen took his arm, and a fair bit of his weight, and they proceeded out.

Bill's shoulders relaxed slightly. "Thank God he's gone. Come here, old thing, I need some common sense. How long would you say he's been dead?"

Pat had laid out four bodies in her time: her father, a kitchen-maid who had died of appendicitis, and two neighbours. It was more experience with corpses than she supposed Bill had. She approached, feeling as weirdly slow as a woman in a nightmare.

The knife jutted from Haworth's back, obscene and wrong, surrounded by a small dark stain. He lay over the desk, face down in a litter of playing cards, black and red. The aces were a scattering of blood-drops, lone and garish against their white backgrounds, as if marked by a steady drip, drip, drip.

His hair was still swept back, kept in place by pomade. That was the most horrifying thing of all because he had combed it this morning, made it perfect, and its orderly arrangement had not slipped even when the knife brought fatal disorder to his suit, his back, his life.

"There isn't very much blood," she said, and was pleased to find her voice steady.

"The knife went in deep. I suppose he must have died at once. Or all the bleeding is internal. What about the time, do you think?"

Haworth's neck was cold to Pat's touch, and stiff. She pulled at his arm and felt the resistance. "Rigor has set in solidly. That means he must have been dead at least six hours."

"It's half past nine now. So he was definitely dead by mid-afternoon. But he could presumably have been killed well before then?"

Pat opened her mouth in instinctive revulsion at *been killed*, and shut it again. The knife protruding from his back didn't leave much room for debate. "Yes. He must have died before, let's say four o'clock at the very latest. Fen and I saw him at half past eleven, going into the East Wing—that was just after we left you. So it was between those times. Nobody else saw him after I did."

"Nobody else has admitted to seeing him, you mean," Bill said. "We're going to need the police."

"We're not going to get them tonight."

They looked at one another, then both turned sharply as someone entered. It was Jimmy, with a glass of whisky in each hand.

"Hello," Bill said. "I thought you were keeping out the madding crowds."

"Jack's doing that. I've told everyone to have a stiff drink, thought you might need one. Sorry, Pat, I didn't realise—"

Pat couldn't imagine anything she wanted less than alcohol. She shook her head, and remembered the afternoon as she did so, with the dreamlike dizziness of a fact she couldn't possibly have forgotten. Her brother and Jimmy. She couldn't think about that, not in here.

"I need it urgently," Bill said, taking the glass. "Do you recognise this knife? Rather odd handle."

Jimmy peered closer, with obvious reluctance. "Yes, it's— Oh."
"What?"

"It's the kirpan. Or at least, it looks like the kirpan. Or *a* kirpan, I suppose it could be."

"And a kirpan is…?"

"A Sikh knife," Pat said.

"That's right. All the men wear one. Ours was a gift from Harpal Singh, Victoria's father. It hangs on the drawing-room wall."

"Not any more, I'm afraid," Pat said. "Victoria noticed it had gone just after you went off to play cards."

"Oh," Jimmy said. "Hell."

"When was that?" Bill asked.

"After luncheon. Perhaps two o'clock."

"We'd better go and talk to the others," Bill said grimly. "And we'll need to lock this room while we do it. Is there a key?"

CHAPTER ELEVEN

The Mertons stayed on guard, carefully not talking about anything, until Jimmy returned with a key. Bill locked the room, considered a moment, then slipped the key into his pocket. "You needn't mention I have this to anyone. Let's go down."

They passed a couple of groups of panicky-looking servants whispering in the hall. The house party was gathered in the drawing room, all present except for the obvious omission, in total silence. Victoria sat very straight, with Preston hovering by her; Lady Anna was next to her mother on the sofa but not touching her, dry-eyed and white-faced. Jack stood behind her, as if on guard. The Earl huddled in a chair with Fen crouched next to him in a pool of skirts.

Bill touched Jimmy's arm as they walked in. Jimmy turned to look at the fireplace, a gesture so obvious that everyone followed it. The emptiness of the sheath hanging next to the mantelpiece seemed glaring now.

"The kirpan," Victoria said in a thread of a voice. "It's missing. Was that—"

"I'm afraid so," Jimmy said. "I'm awfully sorry."

"You saw it was gone at two o'clock, is that right? Did anyone notice it was gone earlier?" Bill asked, to a general shaking of heads. "Nobody?"

Victoria's hands were entwined, knuckles standing out. "I didn't observe— It's always been there. That was my father's gift. It is an *insult*."

"Some might say the insult was to my husband," Lady Anna said, in a voice cold and sharp as broken glass.

Victoria turned sharply. Fen rose, putting herself between the two. "May I ask, what is to be done now?"

"We'll need a doctor, and the police," Bill said. The Countess gave a faint cry of protest.

"It's thirty miles to the nearest police station," Jimmy said. "We could 'phone from the village if the lines haven't come down in the storm, and summon Dr. Chorley as well, but we can't send a man there tonight unless we want another—that is, we can't."

"Why do we need a doctor?" Pat asked. "It's a bit late for that, isn't it?"

Fen made a noise that sounded like a giggle, and clapped her hand over her mouth, eyes widening in horror. Pat couldn't blame her. She felt on the edge of hysteria herself.

"Procedure," Bill said. "I dare say the police will have their own man, but someone needs to examine the body as soon as possible."

"And he must be laid out," the Countess said, sitting up. "Anna, you must—"

"No," Lady Anna said. "No, you can't make me do that. You can't!"

"Nobody must do that, madam," Bill said. "It—*he* must be left untouched until the police arrive."

"I beg your pardon, Mr. Merton. My son-in-law will be given the respect that any man, any member of this family is due."

"Rites," the Earl added. "Decencies."

Bill looked between them, then pointedly at Jimmy, who swallowed. "Ma, Pa, you don't understand. It's—well, it's murder."

"No," the Countess said. She was shaking. "No."

"He's got a knife in his *back*." Jimmy's control sounded to be slipping. "The knife from down here, stuck in his back while he was sitting at a desk. He didn't trip and fall on it!"

"Jim," Bill said. "Get another drink. Get me one, while you're at it. I'm afraid he's right. Mr. Haworth has been murdered and this is a police matter."

"But that's not possible," Preston said. "That is, obviously it is, but for heaven's sake. How did the fellow get in?"

"What fellow?" Bill asked.

"The murderer."

"What murderer?"

"The one who put a knife in his back!"

Bill massaged his temple with one hand. "I grasp that, but what do you mean, get in?"

"I think he means that it was a—a passing tramp," Pat said. She could feel a laugh rising again, and dug her nails into her thumb.

"Exactly," Preston said. "Someone who came in to steal. Maurice must have surprised him."

"He was stabbed in the back while sitting at a desk on the first floor." Jimmy spoke with tenuous calm. "He was killed with a knife taken from this room. And how many passing tramps have you seen out there?"

"It's a nice thought," Bill added, more gently. "But it isn't awfully likely."

"But it has to be," Fen said. "Because if it wasn't someone from outside the house, you know, it would have to be someone inside, which— Oh."

"One of you." The bones were stark under Lady Anna's skin. "That's what you mean, isn't it? One of you killed him."

"The servants—" Jack began.

"Have all been with us for years," Jimmy flashed. "And had no reason to kill him."

"And any of us did?" Jack retorted, and then his face changed. The silence spread like spilled oil, rolling and dripping over them all.

"You hated him," Lady Anna said. She was looking straight ahead, not at anyone in particular. Jimmy and Preston both shifted. "You all hated him and one of you killed him."

"One of us did, yes," Bill said. "Would anyone care to confess?"

"*What?*" Jimmy's eyes bulged.

"The police will come tomorrow and the first thing they'll ask is what reason any of us had to dislike Maurice Haworth. As Lady Anna says, there will be a lot to talk about."

A cry of protest came from several throats at that brutal statement. Bill ignored it. "We're all going to have to account for our whereabouts, and our motivations, and each other's motivations. The police do not respect personal feelings, and they will find out the killer in the end. Whoever murdered him could spare us all a great deal by admitting it."

He was carefully not looking at anyone, so Pat scanned every face she could. She saw anger, shock, incomprehension. She couldn't see that anybody looked guilty, whatever *guilty* looked like.

The silence stretched for a moment, then Bill shrugged. "In that case, I suppose there's not much more to be said except, of course, that nobody ought to leave the house."

"Well, there is something else," Fen said. "I'm sorry to labour the point, but either one of the servants is a homicidal maniac or someone in here is a murderer, and I'm a little nervous about going to bed under these circumstances!"

Thunder cracked overhead, with stage-perfect timing. Several of the women jumped and shrieked.

"For heaven's sake," Preston said. "You're not in danger."

"That depends on why somebody killed Maurice," Victoria pointed out.

"We could pair up," Pat said. "Or at least anyone who'd feel safer that way could. Er…" she added, as the flaw in that dawned on her.

"Indeed," Victoria said. "One would need to be sure of one's pair."

The Countess put a hand over her mouth. Preston moved closer to Victoria, a protective sway.

"Anyone who wishes to, should," Bill said. "In fact it might not be a bad idea if we could all vouch for each other's whereabouts from now on."

"What do you mean?" Pat asked.

"Just thinking ahead. I can't see there's much more we can do except batten down the hatches, summon the police tomorrow, and wait."

"*Wait*," Lady Anna said. "Wait for what? She hated him, and her father's knife killed him! What are you waiting for?"

"Anna!" the Countess almost shrieked. Fen gave a sharp gasp, Preston an inarticulate shout.

Victoria looked at her accuser with bafflement. "I'm a *vegetarian*."

"The Sikhs are a fighting people. Didn't you always say that?" Lady Anna swung to her father. "You always said, rely on a Sikh to avenge an insult. Of course she had a grievance against Maurice because he said what he thought."

"If you're going to accuse everyone your husband insulted, the field will be pretty wide," Pat said. It wasn't, perhaps, the kindest remark to a widow, but Lady Anna wasn't being terribly kind herself, and Victoria's look of stunned betrayal was unbearable.

"Quite. What utter nonsense," Preston said. "As though we don't all know who had an actual motive to kill him."

"I don't know who you're directing that at, and I don't care to find out," Jimmy said thinly.

Jack held up both hands. "We all need to stay calm. This won't help anyone. Granted the use of that particular knife is, ah, suggestive—"

"Yes, it is," Pat said. "The blade must be six inches long judging by the sheath, and it was driven in to the hilt. I doubt I could do that and I'm stronger than Victoria. And more used to cutting up carcasses."

There were multiple noises of strong objection. Bill said, "Could have put that better, old girl."

"I'm still right. A man struck that blow. If I don't have the arm strength, none of us women do."

"We've only your word that you don't," Lady Anna said. "And you made your dislike of Maurice very clear."

"Luckily, you don't need Pat's word for anything," Fen told her. "I've been with her almost every minute since we last saw Mr. Haworth alive, so you may keep your nasty insinuations to yourself, and I *would* if I were you before people wonder why you're so awfully keen to assign blame to other people considering that horrible man was your husband!" She took a much-needed gasp of breath.

"How dare you, you impudent slut!"

"Stop it, all of you. This is getting us nowhere," Bill said. "We're all tired and shocked and we all need to sleep. And Miss Carruth made a good point, I fear: someone in this house killed Haworth, and we all need to be conscious of that. I think we fellows should pair up, so we can account for one another's whereabouts. Preston, suppose you and Jack share a room, and so will Jimmy and I." He did not look at Pat as he said that.

Jack and Preston looked warily at one another. Pat said, "Good idea. Victoria, if you want to squash in with Fen and me…?"

"My room has a lock and a key," Victoria said. "And I shall put a chair under the door handle. But thank you."

"Then I think it's probably bedtime," Pat said. "Coming, Fen?"

Fen headed across the room, then took a detour to the drinks table. She poured two hefty whiskies, handed one to Pat, said, "Now I am," and led the way out.

"Cheers," Bill said from behind them.

Fen's maid was waiting in her room, eyes wide. "Miss Fen!"

"I know. Are you doubled up with someone for the night?"

"Yes, miss."

"Good. Get along now. Miss Merton will be in here tonight, so she can unbutton me, if you shouldn't mind, Pat."

"Not at all."

"But, miss—"

"No, go," Fen said. "The sooner we're all in our rooms the better. I don't want you wandering around the corridors."

"Sir Peter would want me to stay with you," Travers said obstinately. "In case anything happens."

"Miss Merton is armed," Fen said. "With a *gun*. And she can shoot it, so off you go."

"I'll get my revolver if you like, but I'm not bringing it to bed," Pat said, once the maid had left.

"I can't think you'd need it. There's no maniac prowling the halls, is there? He wasn't killed at random." Fen handed her a glass, hopped onto the bed, and patted the covers. Pat locked the door—she agreed about the homicidal maniac but there was no point taking risks—and came to sit by her. "I suppose you're right that it had to be a man?"

"Probably," Pat said. "I wouldn't swear to it. I wanted to end that line of conversation, but the truth is, if the knife was sharp enough, I'm pretty sure I could have done it and so could any determined woman."

"Oh. So Victoria could have killed him, theoretically?"

"Probably, but I can't see why she would. She could have just left the house and never seen him again."

"Unless you believe this idea that she would be naturally inclined to avenge an insult."

"That sounds like a lot of nonsense to me," Pat said. "I don't know anything about Sikhs, but it's a silly way to talk about people. I don't feel 'naturally inclined' to behave like every Anglican alive. And Victoria studied at Girton, for heaven's sake. I suppose there may be

Girton women who would avenge an insult in blood, but she doesn't strike me as one of them."

"Indeed. I'm sure she hoped something awful would happen to Haworth; I'm sure we all did. But I can't see why she'd kill him either, so when you said 'any determined woman', you were thinking of Lady Anna?"

Pat supposed she'd get used to Fen's occasional sharpness, peeking out from her lush appearance like a velvet-handled stiletto. "I was, rather."

"She has arms like chicken bones," Fen said unkindly, considering her own delightfully round and dimpled arms. "Then again, the papers say drug fiends are capable of all sorts of unexpected physical feats. Why would she kill him?"

"You don't think being married to him would be a motive for murder?"

"Well, obviously, but I suppose I meant why today. I dare say there may have been something."

"A row in the night, an insult too far. This is an awful conversation." Pat wrapped her arms around her knees.

"It is awful," Fen said. "And it would be nice to believe in the passing tramp, or blame one of the servants, but—"

"But the house is full of motives."

"Is it full? Who else would want him dead?"

Of course. Fen didn't know about Lord Witton's troubles. Pat hesitated a second, then threw caution to the wind. She needed to talk this out. "I'm afraid the Earl is in a tricky situation."

She explained the business as she understood it. Fen looked appalled. "My goodness. Of course I knew they'd lost money, but I had no idea the Earl was to blame. I'm extremely surprised Daddy didn't find this out after Jimmy proposed." She paused. "Unless he did, and didn't tell me."

Pat winced on her behalf. "It's under investigation. He might not have known the Earl is personally implicated."

"With your brother investigating." Fen made a face. "I don't suppose Jimmy likes that. But why would it benefit the Yoxalls to have Haworth dead?"

"I got the impression he was wringing money out of them under the threat of making the financial business look bad for the Earl. And of course he was holding Lady Anna's well-being, and the child's, over their heads."

"So the whole family had every reason to want him to go away," Fen said. "Ugh. Does anyone else apart from the family have a motive? Mr. Keynes?"

"I'd have said no, except that he had a good try at killing the blighter last night."

"He did, didn't he? I suppose he'll have some explaining to do to the police, with the bruises on Haworth's throat."

Pat hadn't thought of that. "Oh, dear. Yes, that won't look good at all. Though that was a hot-blooded response to insult, whereas this was cold-blooded murder. And that particular knife points the finger at Victoria. I can't think Preston would do that."

"If he realised it would be taken that way, of course. But even so, it seems utterly out of character, though murder generally must be, mustn't it? What about Mr. Bouvier-Lynes?"

Pat frowned. "There's his affair with Lady Anna, but wouldn't it be more likely that Haworth would have murdered him?"

"I suppose Jack might be desperate to marry her?" Fen offered dubiously. "A grand passion, no chance of divorce, this is the only way for her to be free?"

"How...newspaperish. People do kill for love, I suppose."

Fen pulled a face. "I wouldn't have guessed that he loved her that much. Not that he could show it in the circumstances, so perhaps I'm wrong, but it doesn't *look* like a great tragic love affair. Which brings us back to the family."

"Yes. Although— Oh Lord, Fen, there's something else. Haworth was a blackmailer. I heard him at it."

Fen's eyes rounded. "*What?* When?"

"My first morning here." Pat explained how she'd come to hear the conversation. "I couldn't tell who he was speaking to, only that it was a man, but he was unquestionably demanding money and threatening to spill the beans about something."

Fen nodded slowly. "Are you going to tell the police what you heard?"

Pat hugged her knees closer. "It would be concealing important evidence not to."

"Does it make a difference, though? I suppose if he were blackmailing Mr. Keynes—but that's awfully hard to imagine. I don't see how he could do much damage to Mr. Bouvier-Lynes either. A scandal might be inconvenient to him, but not in the way it would be to Lady Anna."

"I wasn't really thinking of him."

"No." Fen took a gulp of whisky. "You're thinking of Mr. Merton and Jimmy."

"Oh God, Fen," Pat whispered. "He was a blackmailer, and Jimmy hated him, and we saw Jimmy heading into the East Wing with Haworth coming after him—and if it was Jimmy, if Haworth was blackmailing him over Bill— Oh dear heaven, what will I *do*? I can't tell the police about the blackmail if it risks Bill, but if I don't and someone gets away with murder—"

"Stop it. Come here." Fen held out her arm. Pat hesitated a second and then leaned against her side. Fen pulled her close, and Pat twisted to bury her face in the warm shoulder.

"I can feel your heart beating," Fen murmured. Her hand was moving gently over Pat's hair. "Breathe."

Easier said than done with her nose and mouth pressed against Fen's skin. "I can't," Pat mumbled.

"Of course you can," Fen said, apparently unaware that the mound of her bosom was almost as much an impediment to working lungs as the shadow hanging over Bill. "And don't panic. This is dreadful, I grant you, but we don't know what sort of dreadful. Haworth *might* have been blackmailing Jimmy, but it might just as well have been, uh, someone else." Pat didn't miss that little hesitation: evidently no alternative candidate leapt to mind. "The fact is, Mr. Merton was quite right in what he said, that the police will pry into everyone's private business. So I think we just have to do what he suggested, and everything will be all right."

Pat couldn't remember Bill offering a solution. "Mph?"

"Find out who did it, and have them confess before the police arrive."

Pat sat up as if pulled by a string. "*What?*"

"Well, what else is there?" Fen asked reasonably. "If we're mired in a police investigation, with journalists hanging round and so on, it will be awful. We can't have your brother's private affairs come out at all, Victoria might well be accused because of the knife, and Jimmy could be *arrested* because honestly he is the obvious suspect from about three different directions. And I don't wish to be selfish, but it's bad enough ending my third engagement at all, let alone while my fiancé is under investigation for murder. No, there's no two ways about it. We need this cleared up right away before everyone's dirty linen is washed in public."

"So we're going to clear it up?" Pat asked faintly. "You and me?"

"Why not? You've got more sense than anyone I know, and I can ask the most awful questions because people expect me to be silly. And we were together more or less every minute since we saw him going into the East Wing, so unlike everyone else, *we* didn't do it, if you see what I mean."

"It would be something if everyone else did do it." Pat briefly pictured the guests and hosts of Rodington Court queueing up outside that first-floor room, knives in hand, and had to rub her eyes. "I'm not sure I know how to investigate a murder."

"I've never done it before either, but there's a first time for everything." Fen took her hand. "I'm serious, Pat. Everyone else is afraid or untrusting, and hiding something. You and I are the only people with no—what's the phrase? Motive, means, or opportunity."

"Everyone had the means," Pat pointed out. "Anyone could have taken that knife off the wall."

"But whoever it was stabbed Haworth in the back at the table while he wrote, so it must have been someone he was intimate with, enough to pay them no attention while they stood behind him. He'd have looked round at someone who'd just come in, wouldn't he?"

"They might have crept up on him, I suppose, but I think you're right. He wasn't writing, though. I didn't see paper or a pen, and there were playing cards spilled over the desk." She frowned. "The desk faced the wall so he wasn't playing opposite anyone. I suppose he was playing Patience."

"Why would he go to a room in the East Wing to play Patience? Everyone else was retreating to remote parts of the house to get away from *him*."

"Maybe he wanted a private conversation," Pat said. "Possibly with the chap he was blackmailing. Maybe he was playing Patience while he waited, or even while he talked to him. It's the kind of discourtesy he'd show."

"That's it. He arranged a discussion with his victim, or perhaps it was the other way around. 'I'll get your money but we need to discuss terms.' And then whoever it was took the knife off the wall and—ugh. But someone will have seen them, on their way to or from the East Wing, say. We'll work it out." She must have read Pat's uncertainty in her face because she added, "We can certainly try, at least, and you never know, we might find it was a tramp after all. Please don't fret, darling. Of course you're worried about your brother, but we might be completely wrong, mightn't we? We've no reason to suppose Haworth had any idea about him and Jimmy."

"He was good at snouting out secrets, though" Pat said. "He noticed about Preston and Victoria. And he twice said things to me, which…well."

"That remark about wooing a pretty girl? True. Although he obviously wasn't that good, or he might have noticed the pretty girl wooing you."

Pat felt her cheeks flame. "You were not. Were you?"

"Of course I was. Goodness, Pat." She took Pat's whisky glass, leaned over to put both on the bedside table, then turned back with a look that blended determination, uncertainty, and a definite glint of wickedness. "You do know I like you awfully, don't you?"

"I don't really know what that means." Pat's chest felt constricted. "That is—well, I don't know where it gets us."

"We're here," Fen said. "That's a good start, isn't it?"

Pat nodded. Fen leaned forward, and Pat met her mouth, tasting the whisky, feeling a sense of sudden urgency. She grasped Fen's shoulder, felt a hand on her own hip, and found Fen's soft lips devouring her own, open and greedy, a tongue touching hers, darting and stroking, shockingly intimate.

"Let's go to bed," Fen whispered, the breath warm on Pat's wettened lips. "I want to hold you."

"Can we? That is—" She didn't want to say it wasn't right, but she couldn't forget what was going on outside this room. *There's a dead man in the East Wing. A murder. A hanging to come.*

We're alive.

"We're alive," Fen said, as if she'd read Pat's mind. "I'm sorry for Haworth, but— No, actually, I'm not. I'm *tired* of him. He made too many people miserable, I don't see why he should do it any more, and I want to be with you. That's important. Please?"

Pat nodded, breathless. Fen brushed a kiss over her lips. "Thank you."

They undressed each other mostly in silence, with gentle strokes and touches rather than the giggling excitement of the previous night.

This time, though, Fen took off her combinations instead of leaving them on to be worked around. Pat could barely breathe at the sight of pale skin, unrestrained breasts, soft belly, the dark hair that formed a tangled triangle over her mound. Fen had left her hair up as she undressed; she removed the pins now as Pat watched dry-mouthed, and glinting brown hair spilled over her pale, naked shoulders.

"You're so beautiful," Pat whispered. "I'm not sure how anyone can be so beautiful."

She felt a tiny bit self-conscious shedding her own combinations. Fen had made her feelings clear last night, but one night didn't change a lifetime of being plain and practical, no matter what the eye of the beholder might see. All the same, she stepped out of the heap of muslin and stood unclothed under Fen's gaze.

"*You're* beautiful," Fen said softly, stepping forward. She traced a finger down Pat's arm. "Diana the huntress, strong and lean and...sparse? That's not the word, but you know what I mean. Like the countryside around here. Bare and beautiful."

"Whereas you're more of a lush landscape." Pat stroked the side of one heavy breast, heard Fen inhale. "I prefer curves."

"Then we're both lucky, aren't we?" Fen caught her hand. "Come to bed."

The sheets were cool against Pat's skin. Fen gave a little squeak as she lay down, and Pat winced. "Shh. No squealing. The last thing we need is someone rushing in here thinking there's another murder going on."

"I shall be quiet as a mouse," Fen promised her. "Despite all provocation. I hope you're planning to offer provocation?"

"Lots of it." Pat shifted to lie half over her, and felt Fen move a warm thigh so that their legs were entwined. She rubbed up against Fen's hip, feeling the pleasure build at her centre as Fen pressed back against her, and angled her head so their mouths met again. Kissing, clutching, pushing urgently against one another, the join of Fen's legs wet against her thigh. A moan rose in Pat's throat and she had to clamp her lips shut against the urge to cry out.

She moved instead, pulling away to prop herself on her elbows. Fen looked up. "Mmm?"

"Mmm," Pat agreed, and crawled backwards down the bed to settle herself between Fen's legs.

"*Mmm.*"

Even Fen's private hair was different, Pat reflected, as she stroked with an exploratory finger. Pat's was fairish and thin, Fen's far bushier, the hairs thick though still silky, a dark brown with hints of red in the candlelight. She parted the curls, clumping with damp, to reveal Fen's sex, and wished to goodness she knew what a sophisticated woman might call those parts. The carelessly-speaking men back home said *cunny*, which always made her think of rabbits, but with Fen lying before her, thighs parted, somehow it didn't seem so inappropriate. Maybe one just had to get used to it.

She slid her finger up and down, parting the folds of pink flesh. Fen was breathing hard, restraining her usual volubility. Pat wished she could squeal. She let her fingertip rest a second over Fen's opening, then pushed it in.

Fen gave a tiny gasp. She was impossibly smooth and hot and slick against Pat's skin. She slid her finger in further, astonished at herself and Fen and this glorious dream, saw Fen's thigh muscles twitch.

She'd come down here for a reason. Pat kept her finger where it was, leaned in to the curly hair, and kissed Fen's cunny.

"*Oh.*" That was a pant. "Yes please."

Hair in the way. Pat parted the curls with her free hand, then carefully licked at the little nub of pleasure, and Fen went rigid. "Oh!"

"Shh," Pat breathed against her.

Fen mumbled something under her breath. Her hand came down to Pat's head, and Pat leaned in and ran her tongue up the length of her cunny, then over the nub again, and then set to work. It felt so animal to be licking like this, or at least natural. Unfettered, unrestrained, without concern for any rules except the one that said Fen should have whatever she wanted. The taste of Fen filled her mouth. Her hand was clamped in Pat's hair, her hips rocking to push her cunny against Pat's tongue, and Pat lavished her with all the adoration she could, with finger and tongue and free hand kneading her perfect, plump buttock, until Fen gave a shrill gasp and Pat felt her muscles, inside and out, contract violently. She couldn't help a tiny moan herself, muffled by Fen's skin, as Fen thrashed and clutched her hair, and finally sagged back onto the mattress with a shuddering sigh.

Pat carefully withdrew her hand, wiped her mouth, and crawled up the bed to lie by her. Fen's lips were bee-stung, dark red, her eyelids heavy. She looked wanton, thoroughly pleasured, utterly irresistible. Her dark nipples were peaked too. Pat captured a breast with a hand and ran a thumb very lightly over the tight point. Fen squeaked, and snuggled up into her arms.

"You look wonderful," Pat said. "That was right?"

"It was outstanding," Fen said. "And considering that was, what, only your second time of trying, do you know what that tells us?"

"No?"

"I'm a better teacher than you."

She looked so delightfully smug that Pat was forced to kiss her before pointing out, "Or I'm an apter pupil."

"Pish tosh." She ran a hand down Pat's back, over her bottom. "Goodness, that was lovely. I hope you appreciate my restraint. Left to myself, I should have made enough noise to wake the dead."

"Thank God you didn't."

Fen gave her a raised eyebrow that would have suited a dowager duchess. Pat clapped a hand to her mouth. "I meant, thank God you didn't make noise. Not—"

"Yes, but we wouldn't have wanted that either, in fairness." She pushed Pat gently on to her back. "Your turn to be very, very quiet indeed. Do you think you can manage it?"

"Of course."

Fen's eyes glittered like diamonds in the candlelight. "Would you care to put a wager on that?"

CHAPTER TWELVE

At nine o'clock that night, Pat would have been surprised to hear that she'd sleep a wink. As it was, she passed out somewhere past midnight, Fen curled against her like a cat and purring with satiated pleasure, and was startled to open her eyes to light. Not a lot of light, because the rain was still coming down in sheets outside, but at least it was normal rain, not yesterday's driving torrents. It would pass soon.

It would pass, and the police would come.

There was a tap on the door which, Pat realised, was what had woken her. She swung her feet out of bed, realising she was naked and, frankly, a bit sticky. She donned Fen's dressing gown, unlocked the door, and let Travers in.

"Good morning, Miss Merton." The maid came bearing tea. She put the tray down, casting a reproachful but affectionate look at Fen, still apparently asleep. "Shall I light the fire?"

"No need, I think. It's not cold, just wet. Thank you very much." Pat took the proffered cup. "Did you sleep well?"

"As much as might be expected, thank you, miss, what with murderers roaming the house."

That was fair, but unanswerable. Pat got back on the bed to be out of the way while Travers went about her work. "What are they saying in the servants' hall?"

Travers pursed her lips. "I wouldn't wish to gossip, miss."

"Oh, yes you would," Fen said from under the covers. "You always know everything. You knew Mrs. Mapesborough was going to leave her husband before she did herself. Cough up."

"That's not ladylike, Miss Fen," Travers said severely. "And if I had happened to hear talk, I shouldn't dream of repeating it."

Fen sat up. "What are they saying? Stop fiddling with my hairbrush, pour us both some tea, and tell me at once."

Pat, slightly startled at Fen's high-handed tone, was about to point out that she already had tea, but Travers was already pouring out two more cups. She handed one to her mistress, added an extra spoon of sugar to the other, and settled on the end of the bed with it. "Well. For a start, nobody's sorry to see the back of that man."

"Was he a nuisance to the maids?" Fen asked.

"Not that anybody said. He wasn't liked, to say the least of it, but I don't think he made himself unpleasant to the staff in a particular way. Almost the other. Too friendly, when nobody wants a gentleman being friendly."

"Isn't that what I said?"

"Not like that." Travers waved a hand, groping for meaning. "Insinuating, is what Mr. Keynes's gentleman called him. Sneaking and prying with a smile on his face."

"He was trying to butter up the staff to get information?" Pat demanded.

"Just repeating what I've heard, Miss Merton."

"Oh, don't be stiff," Fen told her. "Pat's one of us. *Is* that what he was doing? Because you may as well know, he was a blackmailer."

Pat opened her mouth to protest that wild indiscretion, and took a mouthful of tea to prevent herself. Putting Travers' back up would be a tactical error of horrendous proportions.

"Was he now? Doesn't surprise me," Travers said with a sniff. "Everyone says he was a brute to the family."

"Is it a loyal house?" Fen asked.

"Very, miss. Lady Anna has always been difficult, as I hear, but, but the Earl and Countess and Mr. Yoxall, well, nobody wants to see ill come to them. Or Miss Singh, either. She's getting on very well with Mr. Keynes," Travers added, superbly casual.

"So well that they're getting married," Fen said, trumping that with a hint of smugness.

"I wish them very happy, I'm sure. A nice gentleman, by all accounts and his man is a decent fellow. Good man, good master, that's what I say."

"What about Mr. Haworth's man?"

"Doesn't have one. Lost everything in the crash. That's why they're hanging on the Earl's sleeve, not but what he's felt the pinch too."

Fen nodded. "So, what about yesterday? Did anyone see anything in the East Wing?"

"Now, why would you ask that? What are you up to, Miss Fen?"

"Asking questions."

The maid pursed her lips. "Curiosity killed the cat."

"Somebody killed Mr. Haworth, and I'd like to know who. Otherwise the police will ask a lot of impertinent questions, and it will be awful because, you know, one might well have done all sorts of things that one wouldn't want to discuss with the world." Travers raised a meaningful brow but didn't comment. "And it might not even be clear who did it, and what then? What if whoever did it gets away with it and the rest of us are suspected forever?"

"I doubt anyone will think it was you, Miss Fen," Travers said. "As for what anyone saw, I couldn't say. All the gentry were moving round and about yesterday, cluttering up the place as usual."

"Could you find out?" Fen asked. "Who went to the East Wing, and when? Really, Travers, it's important. I want to know where I stand."

"Stand indeed. Lounging in bed till all hours, more like." Travers rose on that snub. "I dare say there'll be plenty of people ready to gossip instead of doing their duty."

Fen beamed at her. "Thank you. The movements of staff and the gentry, please, between—what time would you say, Pat?"

"We saw Haworth going into the East Wing at half past eleven. The dagger was missed at two o'clock, but the family and guests were at lunch from one, and of course Haworth wasn't there. I think it must have happened between half past eleven and one o'clock."

Travers nodded briskly. "I see, miss. I suppose I ought to look for cuffs, too."

"Sorry?"

"Shirt cuffs. I understand Mr. Haworth was stabbed, and I dare say that would be a messy business."

Pat's mouth opened. She cast a look at Fen, who beamed smugly back. "I rely on Travers, Pat, you've no idea. Yes, of course shirt cuffs. What a good thought."

"It wasn't *very* messy," Pat temporised. "There wasn't much blood at all. I suppose it would still have..." She sought for a word. "Sprayed."

"Small spots would be all the easier to miss. I'll see what I can do." Travers topped up the teacups, gathered up the tray, and disappeared. Pat said, "Good heavens."

"She's marvellous," Fen said. "I'd say she was wasted as a maid, but she's awfully good at that, too. Come on, let's get dressed."

Everyone else was up early with the exception of the Countess and Lady Anna. Most of them looked as though they hadn't slept, and the party ate breakfast in yet another awkward silence.

"I wonder if you could all come to the drawing room," Jimmy said after breakfast. "We need a conversation."

"We're all here," Preston remarked.

"I'm not discussing this business over black pudding. I'll order coffee. Father, if you'd like to go upstairs and sit with Mother, I'll handle things down here."

The Earl nodded. He looked exhausted, Pat thought, as if his son-in-law's miserable end had been one piece of bad news too many.

The rest of them gathered in the drawing room as requested. Jimmy stood in front of the fireplace, as Bill leaned against the wall. "Well. Thank you, everyone. The first thing I should say is that I sent for the police this morning."

"When will they get here?" Pat asked.

"It's hard to say. The police station is thirty miles away. One of the grooms has gone on horseback rather than risking the motor-car. He'll telephone from the village if he can, which is twelve miles, but it's possible the wires came down in the high winds. I'd be surprised if they're here until the afternoon and perhaps not even then."

"Obviously, none of us is able to leave, given the trains," Bill said. "But I hope you all understand that we mustn't leave even should there be an opportunity to do so."

"What does that mean?" Jack asked.

"Someone in this house killed him, not to dress the matter up. Therefore, everyone remains until the police arrive. That's what it means and there's no point anyone taking offence. We're all in the same boat."

Jack's mouth tightened, but he nodded. "I dare say you're right."

"He is right," Jimmy said. "I know this is all very awful, but the staff are being absolute trojans. There will be meals served as usual. Bill thinks we should stay together."

"Do you think we're in danger?" Victoria demanded.

"It would be best for everyone to be in company," Bill said. "That's all we're saying."

Pat attempted to catch his eye, without success, so had to convey her displeasure verbally instead. "I'm not sure we can sit in here together for the whole day."

"No, we cannot," Victoria agreed. "Preston and I will stay together, and we won't leave the house. I hope that will suffice."

"I'll be with Fen," Pat said.

"Bill, Jack, and I will stick together, then," Jimmy said. "I don't know if Anna will get up. She had a dreadful night, Mother said. Everything sinking in, I suppose."

"Poor thing," Victoria said. "Can I do anything for Aunt Mattie?"

Jimmy opened his hands. "You can try. I'm sure she'd appreciate it."

Victoria and Preston headed out. Jack looked between the remnants of the party. "And now I suppose we simply wait?"

"Actually, while you three are here, I'd like a word," Pat said. "I think it might be useful if we compared notes on what happened yesterday."

"Ought we not leave that to the police?" Jimmy said.

"We don't know when they're going to arrive, and meanwhile we're all in here together. And the fact is, I think Fen and I might have been among the last ones to see him alive, excepting the murderer, so—"

"Really?" Bill said. "When was that?"

"When we left you in the East Wing."

She only realised how her words sounded when they came out. Bill blinked. Jack's well-shaped brows rose steeply.

"We had that chat in the downstairs sitting room of the East Wing," Pat ploughed on. "As Fen and I left, we passed Jimmy heading along the corridor towards us, and then Maurice Haworth coming through the hall behind him." This was sounding worse and worse. Jimmy's cheeks had reddened. "That was at half past eleven, because the clock struck right next to me," she finished desperately. "So of course it would be useful to know who saw him after that."

"You said you spoke to him an hour before dinner, Jack," Bill said. "Where was that?"

Jack frowned in thought. "I don't think it can have been an hour before, you know, now I consider. I was in here with Maurice at some point that morning. We exchanged some talk, about nothing in particular, then he looked at the clock, and went away in a meaningful sort of fashion in the direction of the hall. I assumed he had an appointment of some kind."

"With whom?" Pat demanded.

"I have no idea. I might be wrong about that; it was merely an impression I had because he looked at the clock in such a marked way."

"What time was it?"

Jack exhaled. "That's what I'm trying to remember. The thing is, I had no reason to notice. I had nothing else to do so the time wasn't important. It might well have been around half past eleven, or a little before, but I shouldn't care to say so on oath. I certainly didn't see him again after that, whenever it was, poor fellow. So you saw him, Jimmy?"

"No," Jimmy said shortly. "I spoke to Father in his study, came across the hall, went straight in to the sitting room where Bill was, and shut the door after me. I didn't know Maurice was following me, if he was. I didn't see anyone except Pat and Fen on the way."

"I stayed in the sitting room after you ladies left," Bill added. "The door was open until Jimmy came in. Once he shut it, I don't suppose I'd have noticed anyone walking past unless they made a racket, which nobody did."

"What did you do then?" Pat asked. "Were you both in there until lunch?"

"No," Jimmy said. "I went—"

"Yes," Bill said over him. "Of course we were."

There was a second's silence, in which nobody breathed. Jimmy looked round at Bill, eyes wide. Bill said, "You're thinking of the other day, you fool. You were with me yesterday morning, in the sitting room, until lunch. Weren't you?"

His tone didn't allow for contradiction. Jimmy swallowed. "Uh, yes. I suppose you're right."

"I am right."

"What were you up to?" Jack asked.

Jimmy opened his mouth, then flickered a glance to Bill, who said, "Just talking. We sat and discussed various matters—financial, you'll excuse me from going into detail—until the luncheon gong sounded. Jimmy was with me the entire time."

"Yes," Jimmy said. "That's right. How absurd of me."

Pat opened her mouth with no idea what to say. Fen put in, "But you must have heard something in that time?"

"What do you mean?" Jimmy asked.

"Well, Mr. Haworth didn't come to lunch, which I expect is because he couldn't. And that room, the one he was found in, is right above the one you were in, isn't it?"

Bill shut his eyes. "Great Scott. Are you seriously suggesting he was murdered up there while Jimmy and I were talking downstairs?"

"Wasn't he?"

"All I can say is, we didn't hear it. Not consciously, at least. This is a creaky old place at the best of times and there was that howling wind. I would have thought I'd have heard a scream, still, but I didn't. Given how little blood there was, he may not have had time to cry out."

Fen shuddered. "Would you not have heard someone walking around above you?"

"Well, I didn't," Jimmy said shortly.

"Nor I," Bill said. "Or perhaps I did but it's what Jack said: there was no reason to notice or remember. There are plenty of people in the house, all of whom were entitled to go anywhere they pleased, including upstairs."

"Indeed," Jack said. "So you didn't notice if Maurice went straight up to the room where he was killed? Surely you'd have heard him going up the stairs after Jimmy came in, if he was right behind you?"

"I don't know that he was right behind me," Jimmy snapped. "I'm told he was. I wasn't paying attention."

Jack's brows drew together slightly. "You don't seem to have been paying attention to much that morning. You don't recall where you were, or who was around you—"

"He was with me," Bill said.

"I dare say I was in a flap," Jimmy said. "Forgive me if the end of my engagement and my father's troubles and Maurice's behaviour seemed more important to me than listening to footsteps on the stairs."

"So you did hear footsteps?" Jack asked.

"No!"

"Oh!" That was Fen, hand coming to her mouth.

"What's that, Miss Carruth?" Bill asked.

"Footsteps. I just remembered. When Pat and I left you, Mr. Merton, we went through the hall, where we saw Mr. Haworth, and straight up the west stairs to Pat's room, while my maid packed. But do you recall, Pat, we heard footsteps go past the door? And I *do* remember that because we'd been talking about private matters"—she gave Jimmy a nod to indicate the broken engagement—"and I didn't wish to be overheard. So I stopped, and someone went past, coming from the East Wing and going past our rooms. And I did think they were walking awfully quietly. I remember wondering if they might have been listening and telling myself not to be silly."

"You're right," Pat said. "Someone came past...oh, at perhaps twenty to twelve, would you say? Not much later. Quarter to at most."

Bill frowned. "Along the first floor back corridor, coming *from* the East Wing. Who would come that way? Staff?"

"Can't see why. There's a servants' door on the west side," Jimmy said. "And Ma told them not to trouble with anything in the East Wing while we've a houseful of guests."

"Nobody came along there before," Fen said. "Or, at least, that was the first time I'd noticed someone walking past my room in the whole time I've been here."

"There's no obvious reason for anyone to come that way, is there?" Bill said. "Not unless you were already on the first floor of the East Wing."

Fen's eyes were huge. "Was that the killer, walking past Pat's bedroom?"

"It's a theory," Bill said. "A pretty good one, but still a theory for now. We'll need to pin down who the walker was. Man or woman?"

"I don't know," Pat said. "It was a fairly light tread. If it was a man, he wasn't thumping around like a herd of elephants. Which rules you out," she added to Bill. It was an automatic sisterly jibe, but Jack Bouvier-Lynes raised his brows with a sardonic lift that brought the colour to her cheeks. "That was a joke."

"Of course it was," Jack said. "And of course we all want to be ruled out. May I make an observation? If someone were leaving the room in question yesterday—let us say, with an urgent need to wash their hands—they would have taken the first floor back corridor to reach a bedroom on the first floor. If that person was billeted on the second floor, they would surely have taken the East Wing stairs all the way up, and followed the back corridor from there. No?"

He didn't point out that he, Bill, and Preston were the only people sleeping on the second floor, while Jimmy's room was on the first floor. He didn't have to.

Jimmy's mouth tightened ominously. Pat rushed in before this became personal. "That sounds plausible but as Bill says, it's a theory. We need to know where everyone was still. So where did you spend the rest of the morning, Jack, after Mr. Haworth left you? Were you with anyone between then and lunch?"

Jack opened his mouth, but didn't answer at once. He looked decidedly self-conscious. "Did you stay here alone?" Pat pressed.

"I'm afraid I'm not willing to comment at the moment."

"I beg your pardon?" Bill said.

Jack grimaced. "As you've said, we all have our own concerns. I should like a chance to consider mine before I reply."

"I don't think so," Pat said. "The police won't give you a chance to consider, and they'll be here soon. If you've something to say, you'd better say it."

Fen looked at her with startled admiration. Bill, however, was wincing. "If it's a delicate matter—"

"Oh, I think we're beyond that," Jimmy said roughly. "Murder isn't delicate. I suppose you 'aren't willing to comment' because you were with someone you oughtn't have been with. It's hardly a conundrum, is it? I don't know why you don't come out with it; it's not as though you've had any other care for her reputation."

Jack held up a hand to stop him, paused as if thinking for a moment, and then said deliberately, "I suppose indiscretion is the lesser of two evils. When Maurice left me, I went to Anna's room, and I spent the period until luncheon with her."

"Was anyone else with you?" Bill asked.

"No, dear fellow. That was the point."

Jimmy pushed himself straight, fists clenching. Jack winced. "No, *think*, Jimmy. You may not like this conversation but you must be glad to know Anna has a witness to her whereabouts."

"*What?*" Jimmy almost shouted. "Are you accusing my sister?"

"No, curse it! I'm giving her an alibi."

"Do you think— Shut up, Jim. Do you think it's necessary to do so?" Bill asked.

Jack pushed a hand through his hair, disarranging its sleekness. "There's no point sugar-coating this, is there? When a husband dies, especially an unkind one, the police look first to the wife. Murder is so often a family affair. And perhaps I'm wrong, but I doubt I'd have seen a wall ornament as a weapon. One might well conclude the killer knew the house intimately." Jimmy's cheeks darkened. Jack shook his head. "I'm talking about what an outsider might think, not what *I* think. And I know not to think it, because I bade farewell to Maurice, went straight to Anna's room, and remained with her until luncheon. Disapprove all you like, but I'd rather save her neck than her name. I can only add that I hope this discussion will remain private and I have no intention of repeating it to anyone except, if need be, the police."

"You really are a damned cad," Jimmy remarked, voice shaking. "Conducting this under my father's roof—"

"Does it make a difference if one keeps one's mistress in London?" Jack snapped, his normally smooth tone fracturing at last. Jimmy moved, but Bill grabbed him.

"Steady. *Steady.* Your sister is a grown woman, Jim. You may not like it, but Jack's not wrong about where suspicion might fall. And it's probably best to have this out here instead of in front of your parents, isn't it?"

Jimmy cast Jack a look of loathing. "It ought not have been necessary. What are your intentions now?"

Jack blinked at that. "My what?"

"Your intentions. You can't expect me not to ask, since you've shared your business so generously with us. And given Anna has already brought one damned smirking fortune-hunter into the family—"

"Jimmy!" Bill barked. "For God's sake. This is not the time or the place. In fact it's the least of our worries, would you not say?"

"It isn't yours at all," Jack said. "I know what I want, but it will be Anna's choice. And I hardly think it's right to discuss the matter with Maurice barely cold."

They glared at each other for a moment, then Jimmy threw up his hands and turned on his heel. Jack relaxed visibly, the movement making Pat realise how tense he'd been.

"How did you go to Lady Anna's room?" she asked, keeping her voice calm as though this were a normal question. "What route?"

"Up the west stairs."

"Did anyone see you?"

"Well, I didn't see anyone," Jack said. "Which isn't the same thing of course. The place felt deserted, though."

"And what time was this?"

"Very shortly after Maurice left me. Which, if he went straight to the East Wing, would be around half past eleven."

Pat didn't feel she could press any further questions about the pre-prandial period within decency. "All right. It seems that the, er, period of interest is between half past eleven and one, during which Jack and Lady Anna were together the whole time. So were Fen and I. And so were you?" She hadn't meant to make that a question, but it came out that way.

"Yes," Bill said flatly, for himself and Jimmy.

"That leaves Victoria, Preston, the Earl and the Countess, and if everyone has an alibi for the period before lunch then we'll have demonstrated that none of us was responsible. I'm going to talk to Victoria." She knew it sounded abrupt but she didn't care. She rose, feeling jerky and ungainly, and strode out. Fen followed, and Pat felt a warm hand close over hers.

"Pat?"

"Let's find the others first. I want this over with."

The engaged pair weren't far away: in the West Wing's library, talking quietly. Victoria looked up as Pat entered. "Hello. Is something wrong?"

Pat plunged in, unwilling to hedge. "Sorry to bother you. We're interested in knowing where everyone was before lunchtime yesterday."

Victoria's brows rose. "That is the question of the day, I suppose. Should we not wait for the police to do the asking?"

"I'd prefer to ask now. I'm not terribly happy about waiting."

"All right with me. We were together," Preston said. "Met up at breakfast, went to speak to Lady Witton to let her know our news, and then we rather went and hid, didn't we?"

"Where?"

"In here," Victoria said. "We had tea around eleven; Mary—the housemaid—brought it, and came to clear away when we were finished. I suppose that was around quarter to twelve or so but I couldn't swear to the exact time."

"Did you go to the East Wing at all?"

Preston shook his head. "We stayed in here until luncheon, then decided we ought to make an effort to be sociable in the afternoon, since Haworth wasn't around. I played cards with the other chaps. Jack won, naturally."

"Did you see Haworth at any point yesterday?"

"Glad to say I didn't." Preston reddened. "That is—oh, you know what I mean. It was jolly awkward, having laid hands on the blighter. I felt I'd behaved badly enough the night before."

"Did you think you might hit him again if you saw him?" Fen asked, so wide-eyed and innocently curious that Preston was half way through his answer before Pat realised her meaning.

"I should hope not. Talk about uncivilised. I'd have hopped on the milk train this morning and rid the Wittons of my presence if it hadn't meant leaving Victoria in the lurch. But since I couldn't do that, I felt I'd be best off avoiding the ghastly swine. Not to speak ill of the dead."

"Were you suggesting Preston might have wanted to avenge Maurice's insults?" Victoria enquired.

"Oh, I say," Preston objected. "Hold your horses. I'd gladly have darkened his daylights for him, but there's a difference between giving a man the thrashing he deserves and, well, what happened."

"There certainly is," Pat said. "And you weren't alone in your desire to give him a thrashing. My brother asked him to step outside, if you recall."

"But it's Preston whose finger-marks are on the corpse's throat," Victoria said. "Which is something we'll have to explain to the police." Her face was tense.

"That's the problem," Fen said. "An awful lot of us will have to explain very personal things when they arrive, because Mr. Haworth was an expert in digging up very personal things, wasn't he? Digging them up, sniffing them out, and using them against one."

Victoria frowned. "What do you mean?"

"He liked to make people unhappy. Everyone knows I've been engaged before but nobody else found it necessary to taunt me about it. He liked to make people do what he said, as with the Wittons, sitting there letting him speak monstrously because they were afraid of what he'd do if they crossed him. Or for profit. He made a good thing out of knowing people's secrets, didn't he?"

Preston's mouth dropped open. "Are you suggesting he was a blackmailer?"

"Good heavens," Victoria said. "Really? Although I can't say I'm astonished. Are you sure?"

Pat nodded. Preston made a face. "If he was blackmailing someone, I've every sympathy for the victim. It's a foul thing."

"It is, but one can't take the law into one's own hands," Victoria said. "Especially not if one attempts to cast suspicion on other people."

"I couldn't agree more," Fen said. "Do you think the killer used that particular weapon on purpose?"

Victoria gave her a sardonic look. "It seems likely that someone wished to direct suspicion at me. That said, it was also an easily available weapon, and extremely sharp."

"Yes, the Earl told us the weapons on the walls are kept in good condition."

"Uncle James insists. I dare say we're fortunate the killer didn't use one of the broadswords in the hall."

Pat had an instant mental image of that, which she attempted to forget. Fen said, "That's unusual, isn't it? Who would have known that's his practice?"

Victoria opened her mouth, paused, then gave Fen a look sharp as the kirpan blade. "The family and me, I dare say."

"Mmm," Fen said. "I don't suppose you saw or heard anybody, between half past eleven and luncheon?"

Both shook their heads. "We had the door shut," Victoria said, sounding self-possessed as ever but her cheeks reddening a little. "We really didn't want to encounter Haworth. Is that the period—"

"It seems so. It would be an awful help if everyone could pin down their movements."

"Unfortunately, we can only speak for ourselves. I heard people walking by at various points but I've no idea who or when."

That was all of use the engaged couple had to say. Fen took Pat's hand as they left the library and steered her gently up to her bedroom, which was mercifully free of Travers. She shut the door and said, "Come here."

Pat walked into her open arms, burying her face in Fen's hair and inhaling her scent. Fen pushed up against her, warm and soft and desperately comforting. They held each other for a moment that Pat didn't want to break and then Fen stepped away, sat on the bed, and patted the quilt next to her.

"Sit down. We need to talk about it."

Pat sat. She didn't know what to say; she didn't want to speak.

"I'm inclined to believe Victoria and Preston," Fen said. "They had every reason to hide away together like that, and they sounded truthful. And they both seemed surprised about the blackmail, one could see that."

"Yes. I agree."

"So, unless they're hiding some deep dark motive, I don't see they had a reason to kill him, other than this idea of avenging insult," Fen persisted. "They could just leave and not see him ever again."

"Yes."

"So it probably wasn't them. And it wasn't us. And Jack was with Lady Anna—assuming she supports his story, of course. We still need to know about the Earl and Countess."

"Yes."

Fen took a deep breath. "And your brother was lying."

CHAPTER THIRTEEN

Pat knew it as well as Fen did. She still hated hearing the words aloud. She wanted to clap her hands over her ears and blot them out.

"Now, one mustn't overreact," Fen went on.

"Why not?" Pat demanded. "Jimmy admitted they didn't stay together and Bill talked over him to tell him what to say! When Jimmy went past us, Haworth was on his heels. Jack says he thought Haworth was meeting someone, and everyone else except the old couple is accounted for. And Jimmy hated him like poison."

"Yes, but—"

"You didn't hear him. He was barely rational on the subject. Which is understandable because Haworth destroyed your and Jimmy's engagement, he's ruining the family and sending the Earl to gaol, you only need *look* at Lady Anna, and he might have known about Jimmy and Bill. Jimmy wanted him dead. He said as much."

"He did?"

"Speaking wildly, of course, but he was at the end of his tether."

"And you think he snapped."

"I don't want to think it," Pat said. "I hate thinking it. But Bill gave Jimmy an alibi, even though he must have known how dreadfully unconvincing it sounded. He wouldn't have lied like that if he didn't have to. He's not a fool."

Fen's arms came round her waist. Pat leaned against her, needing all the comfort she could get. "But you know, darling, it might not be as bad as it looks. Suppose Haworth was threatening Jimmy and they had a row that morning. It would look dreadfully suspicious to admit it, even if he left the man alive and well."

"Not as suspicious as Bill telling obvious lies to protect him," Pat said. "Not to mention that if Jimmy had said, *yes I saw Haworth*, we'd have a better idea of the time of death. There's only one person who wants to sow confusion in this situation, and it's the guilty party."

"But it was Mr. Merton who lied," Fen said, very gently. "Not Jimmy."

The drumbeat of fear was echoing through Pat, making it hard to think. Of course Bill wasn't a murderer. She would never believe that. Except that if Haworth had been blackmailing them, he and Jimmy could have faced two years in gaol, hard labour, shame and disgrace and the besmirching of two ancient family names. What would Bill do to protect himself and Jimmy from that? What would she have done to save her brother, if it had been down to her? What might she do for Fen?

She put her face in her hands. Fen's arm tightened. "Darling, stop. You're thinking terrible things and you oughtn't."

"Why not? Everyone else has an alibi!"

"No, they don't," Fen said. "We don't know about the staff yet, or the Earl and Countess. And I don't want to impugn my former in-laws to be, but they had as much motive as anyone could possibly require."

"I don't know if they'd have the strength," Pat said, but she recalled the Earl out on his lands. Elderly, yes, but a hale and hearty countryman all the same.

"I'd find the strength if it were my children he threatened," Fen said. "And if it wasn't them, well, it might be a servant, or someone else might be lying. It might be that famous passing tramp. You're thinking about Jimmy and your brother because things always seem more likely when we don't want them to be true, and the more we fear it, the more inevitable it seems. Don't you find?"

Pat took a deep breath. "Yes."

"So don't panic. I'm sure your brother won't lie to the police."

"But he's already lied to us, and suppose Jack tells the police about that? If I've made everything worse—"

"If he and Jimmy get their stories straight before the police arrive, it would be a jolly good thing," Fen said, with breathtaking disregard for the rule of law. "And I'll tell you something else, too. It's nonsense to say Haworth ended my engagement. You did that."

"I?" Pat said, appalled.

Fen's arm tightened. "Of course you did. Not in an underhand way, I don't mean that. You were bending over backwards to be fair to him. But really, if you go around teaching me to shoot and taking me seriously and listening to me and having such wonderful eyes—"

"I don't have wonderful eyes."

"Of course you do. So kind and hazel." Fen's unquestionably wonderful eyes were locked on Pat's with undoubted sincerity. "I know we've only known each other three days—although another way to put it is that we've known each other for the length of this house party, which has been going on forever. But the fact is, when I compared the way you talk to me, and listen to me, and kiss me, with the way Jimmy or any other fiancé ever did any of those things, there's no comparison. None at all. And I couldn't possibly have married Jimmy once I realised that." She looked up into Pat's face with a soft smile that made Pat's insides twist. "I am absolutely sure that whatever happens, you'll be able to cope with it, and help the people you love. But everyone is allowed to wobble, so I'm here to remind you just how wonderful you are and give you a shoulder if you need one. We're going to do our best, together, and your best is All-England Ladies' Champion. All right?"

"But I'm not wonderful at all," Pat said. "I'm truly not. I'm desperately ordinary."

"You're the least ordinary person I've ever met. *I'm* ordinary, apart from being rich—"

"Nonsense. Absolute rubbish. You're—" Pat groped for a word. "Outstanding. You're beautiful and kind and—champagne, everything about you is champagne. Bubbling and delicious and special."

Fen's eyes sparkled like any glass of Veuve Cliquot. "Perhaps we're both special. In fact, we're both *so* special that we deserve someone equally special who appreciates us." She took Pat's hand. "You oughtn't be sitting around being a companion to an old lady, or a housekeeper to your sister-in-law, or ever feeling unwanted, which is the stupidest thing of all because *I* want you. I know you can't think about what next until this is all cleared up for your brother, but I'm sure it will be cleared up if we put our backs into it, and of course, I shan't leave you until then. I don't suppose I can stay at Rodington Court, under the circumstances, but I dare say the village has an inn, which will be a novelty. We'll manage, is what I'm trying to say. Won't we?"

Pat took a deep breath. "Yes. Thank you."

"And after that, when Mr. Merton is quite safe, you're going to come to King's Norton and teach me to shoot and do absolutely nothing with me for weeks. Which includes sweet nothings." She cocked her head as if wheedling, but her eyes brimmed with light. "You will, won't you?"

"Of course I will."

"Then that's something to hold on to." Fen squeezed her fingers. "Don't worry too much. We've plenty of questions still to ask."

"But goodness knows how long till the police arrive."

"True," Fen said regretfully. "I suppose we *had* to summon the police."

"As opposed to what?"

"Oh, you know. Dropping the body into a marsh, or a mine-shaft."

"Fen!"

"Well, it's not as though anyone would care if he went away forever. We couldn't really do that, I know," she added at Pat's look. "I was just thinking it was a pity. It's surely a good sign that Jimmy sent for the police, isn't it?"

"It would look awfully strange if he didn't."

"I suppose." Fen sagged slightly. "I don't want him to have done it either, you know. I hate thinking he was driven to it. This whole thing is so poisonous, isn't it? Haworth ruined everything he touched, like an opposite Midas, making everything foul and slimy instead of gold. I do wish we knew who he was blackmailing."

"Jimmy, surely."

Fen frowned. "Yes, but he was bleeding the Wittons dry via Lord Witton anyway. I'm sure he'd have enjoyed having Jimmy under his thumb for his personal satisfaction, but was there any more money to be had?"

"I see what you mean. That's a very good point." Pat made herself say it: "Bill is the other obvious candidate."

"But don't you think you'd have recognised his voice, even if you couldn't hear the words? One does, doesn't one, with a family member?"

Pat felt hope leap, and made herself consider the matter dispassionately. "That's possible, actually. Maybe. But we've been over the others. Unless it was a servant after all, but would one really demand money from a footman?"

"I really don't know. The horrid man had an ace of some kind up his sleeve about *someone*, but—"

There was a sharp knock at the door. Fen removed her arm from Pat's waist and called "Come in."

Travers swished in and shut the door. "I hope it's convenient, miss?"

"Yes, of course," Fen said. "Have you got something?"

Pat wanted to shout aloud with frustration. She'd thought of something, had a sudden moment of intuition or memory or realisation that had wisped away again at the interruption. She resisted the temptation to ask the other two women to be quiet and let her think: it would not be politic to offend Fen's henchwoman.

"I don't know about *something*," Travers was saying. "Mostly nothings, which might mean something. Nobody saw anyone going into the East Wing, and nobody rang for attendance there. Mr. Keynes and Miss Singh took tea in the library at eleven and Mary took it away at quarter to. The Earl was in his study with Mr. Yoxall until half past eleven, when Mr. Yoxall left him. The Earl rang the bell at twelve and sent for the Countess. Mary carried that message to her in her room, and she went downstairs. Nobody saw them after that."

"So the Earl and the Countess were both seen at twelve, but not before or afterwards," Fen said. "The Countess was in her room, wasn't she? Alone?"

"That's right, miss."

"And the Earl was in his study alone. That means either of them could have moved around without seeing anyone else except for Jack going upstairs at half past, and Mary with the tea things at quarter to."

"Ugh," Pat said. "I'm not sure I want to ask them probing questions, you know. It would seem so dreadfully ill-mannered."

"Murder is ill-mannered," Fen said. "Gosh, that sounded rather good, didn't it? Like an axiom in an etiquette book."

"What sort of etiquette book—"

Fen flapped a hand at her. "Anything else, Travers? What about Lady Anna?"

"Lady Anna was in her room with her maid all morning, from breakfast onwards, going through her wardrobe. She dismissed the girl at twenty past eleven. After that she remained in her room until the gong." Travers gave a meaningful sniff.

"We've heard about *that*," Fen said.

"I dare say, miss. I didn't find anyone who could swear to Mr. Bouvier-Lynes, Mr. Yoxall, or Mr. Merton until ten minutes to one, when Lady Anna rang for her maid to put her hair straight. Mr. Bouvier-Lynes was leaving her room as the girl arrived."

"Oh dear."

"And the other thing I didn't find is that any of the gentlemen had sent shirt cuffs for washing. Only Mr. Yoxall and Mr. Keynes have gentlemen's gentlemen with them. Mr. Keynes' man says all his linen is accounted for. Mr. Yoxall's man wasn't receptive. Took offence, he did. What I will say, miss, is that it wouldn't be hard to hide a pair of bloodstained cuffs in this great barn of a house if I may be so bold, but they'd be less easy to destroy. Nobody had a fire lit in their bedroom yesterday, nor anywhere in the house except the kitchen."

"So there may be a pair of bloodstained cuffs hidden somewhere," Pat said. "I suppose the police will look. Or perhaps it wasn't a messy job."

"Would that make a difference?" Fen asked, then answered herself: "I suppose it would remove the question of the killer having to wash his hands, as Jack said. Hmph. If you find out anything more about bloodstained things, let us know, Travers. Excellent. Now, could it have been anyone in the servants' hall?"

Travers raised both brows in reproof. "Miss Fen!"

"Well, they have lives and secrets too. Suppose Haworth was blackmailing the butler? And I expect it would be easier for a servant to get around without the guests noticing than vice versa."

"You may think servants spend all day as idle as you, but I can assure you, we are not," Travers said crushingly. "Nobody had the time to sneak off, steal a knife, murder a man, clean up, and get back to work, not with lunch for ten to put on the table and this house understaffed as it is, so that all the visiting staff have to pitch in. I'm sure as I can be that everybody's accounted for between eleven and one. Mary, the parlour-maid, was the only one running around when she went out to collect the tea things for Miss Singh, and then to fetch the Countess later, but she was straight back in no time: I saw her come and go myself."

"All right, then." Fen hopped off the bed. "Thank you, Travers, you're a wonder and that was awfully useful. We'll go down to join the others now and see if we can get anywhere." She nudged Pat. "And you need to have a talk with your brother."

Pat wasn't expecting anywhere in Rodington Court to be a happy environment, but even so, the icy atmosphere in the drawing room was startling. Preston and Victoria were nowhere to be seen. Bill was in the corner hiding behind a three-day-old newspaper; Jimmy stood by the fireplace, and if he'd had a tail it would have been lashing. Lady Anna was seated on the settee with Jack. Pat could not think that remotely appropriate, and her face probably gave away her disapproval because Lady Anna gave her a frozen glare and said, "You do realise I don't have blacks?"

"Sorry?"

"I didn't bring funereal garments." She spat the words out. "Since I didn't expect my husband to die. And I am hardly going to squeeze into my mother's old clothes."

"I really didn't expect you to," Pat said, moving to the tea tray.

"For heaven's sake, nobody cares," Jimmy added. "If I was going to criticise your behaviour—"

Lady Anna's knuckles whitened. "You had better not."

"No, don't," Bill said, putting the newspaper down. "We've enough to deal with as it is."

"Caused by her blasted rotten husband." Jimmy's voice was shaking. "I don't know if you have any idea how ghastly this is going to be for everyone, Anna."

"You can hardly blame me because someone stabbed Maurice. Blame him, blame me, it's never your fault, is it? You're always the golden boy—"

"If you mean *I* didn't ruin the family with my damn fool goings-on—"

"Jim!"

The Yoxall siblings glowered at each other. Fen jumped in. "You may blame Lady Anna for her choice of husband, Jimmy, though I don't think you've much of a leg to stand on when it comes to personal affairs." Bill's eyes widened sharply. "But you can't blame her for what happened to Mr. Haworth, since Lady Anna is one of the few of us to have an alibi."

Lady Anna's nostrils flared. "I beg your pardon. I am not aware you know my movements."

"We all do," Fen said. "You were with Mr. Bouvier-Lynes in your bedroom yesterday morning, before lunch. Isn't that right?"

Lady Anna looked as though she'd been slapped, down to the reddening of her cheeks. "You impertinent, ill-bred *child*. How dare you?"

Fen had gone rather pink herself, but held her ground. "It's what he said. Is that not the case? I'll apologise if I'm misinformed."

"You are not misinformed," Jack said through his teeth. He held up both hands as Lady Anna swung round to him. "My first concern was to establish your innocence."

"Who ever doubted it?" Lady Anna demanded, pitch rising.

"Jack was good enough to say that only someone who knew the house well would have thought to use an ornamental dagger for murder," Jimmy said. "Like you, Anna, or me."

"Or Victoria," Lady Anna flashed.

"I was not making accusations!" Jack almost shouted as the siblings' voices rose again. "The police won't respect your privacy, Anna. They'll look at your marriage and ask all sorts of offensive prying questions, examine your behaviour and probe for guilt. Think about that."

Lady Anna's facial muscles were drawn tight with revulsion. Pat almost felt sorry for her. It was one thing to misbehave in fast society among peers who would understand, quite another to be held up to conventional morality and found wanting.

Jack went on, urgently. "But the fact is, if you and I were together between half past eleven and luncheon, as we were, you *cannot* be suspected. Maurice was last seen at half past eleven. I left his side just at that time and came upstairs to you. From luncheon onwards everyone was in company. The fact that I can swear to your whereabouts for the entire period before lunch makes your private business irrelevant to the investigation, do you see? And if the police understand that from the start, they will be far less likely to waste their time on impertinent enquiries. We have to be frank, darling."

"And will everyone else be subjected to the same intrusion into their affairs?" Lady Anna demanded, voice cracking.

"I should think so," Fen said. "It will be ghastly for all of us. What time exactly did Mr. Bouvier-Lynes join you?"

"I see no reason to respond to these enquiries from anyone except the police," Lady Anna said. "And I shall not stay to be insulted."

She stalked out. Jack followed her. Jimmy moved forward with the obvious intention of stopping him, but Bill took his arm, and after a second, he stepped back.

"Well, that was a delightful interlude," Bill remarked. "Are you ladies determined to render this visit even more hideous than it already was?"

"I'm afraid so, Mr. Merton," Fen said. "Do you mind if I lock the door?" She moved towards it without waiting for agreement. "I think we need a private conversation."

CHAPTER FOURTEEN

The four of them looked at once another once Fen had locked the door. Nobody wanted to begin.

Bill folded his arms. "I suppose we all know what this is about."

"That depends," Pat said. "Haworth was killed between half past eleven and one o'clock. Fen and I were together. So, according to themselves, were Lady Anna and Jack, and Preston and Victoria. That leaves the Earl and Countess, and you two, and you lied—really very obviously—about your whereabouts this morning. No, don't say anything," she went on as Bill opened his mouth. "I don't want you to lie to me again. And by the way, the day after we arrived, I overheard Haworth committing blackmail."

"What?" Bill barked.

"He was in the process of extorting money to keep a secret. I didn't hear his victim's voice clearly, just Haworth's half of the conversation, but it was a man. And if someone in this house was being blackmailed—"

"Now hold on a blasted minute," Bill said furiously. "Nobody is blackmailing me, and you cannot possibly think I had anything to do with Haworth's death!"

"You lied about Jimmy's whereabouts. He said you weren't together and you stopped him and gave him an alibi. Jimmy had as good reason as anyone in the world to hate Haworth, and you were both in the East Wing when he was killed. And—and I don't care about that ghastly man, he had it coming, but I want to know exactly what the devil you're playing at because he's dead and you two *lied*!"

Jimmy was a horrible shade of grey. Bill looked as if he might be sick. "You're wrong. Neither of us laid a hand on Haworth. We were together all that time—" Pat made a strangled noise. "We were," Bill insisted. "For God's sake, Pat, I didn't lie. Jimmy did."

"*Jimmy*? Jimmy made up a lie so as to *not* have an alibi?" Her voice was rising to the kind of pitch Fen could achieve. "How stupid do you think I am? You lie in murder investigations to look *less* guilty, not more!"

"Oh Christ." Jimmy turned away, shoulders hunched, a picture of wretched shame.

Bill shot a glance at the locked door and lowered his voice to a subdued snarl. "He was *trying* to make us look less guilty, curse it. There are other offences as well as murder, and some of them prey on the mind!"

"*What* other—"

"Pat," Fen said, voice warning. "Deep breath, and *think*."

Pat thought. Then she sat down, heavily, and put her face in her hands. After a moment of silence there was a rustle, and Fen's fingers closed on her shoulder.

"Pat." Bill sounded anguished. "You aren't crying, are you? I dare say you're upset, but—"

"I'm not crying and I'm not upset, you fool," Pat said, smacking away a tear. "I'm *relieved*. Do you have any idea what that looked like, telling Jimmy where he was and what to say, with him having so much reason to loathe the ghastly man?"

"I'm sorry, old thing. You must see, I had to shut him up before he talked himself onto the gallows. 'Oh no, I was definitely on my own all that time.' Idiot."

"I'm sorry," Jimmy said, muffled. "I didn't think."

"You never do," Bill said. "You never bloody do."

Fen's hand flexed on Pat's shoulder, the small palm giving her an unmistakable shove. She rose, marched over, and grabbed her brother in an awkward hug. They weren't a family for casual embraces, but it was surely what Fen had meant, and it needed doing.

Bill was rigid for a second, and then his arms came round her. Pat didn't think they'd held each other since the memorial service for Frank and Donald, and the memory made her grip tighter. She couldn't lose another brother. She couldn't lose quiet, solid, wonderful Bill.

"Oh Lord," Bill said into her hair after a moment. His voice was just a little uneven. "It's a bit ripe, my own sister thinking I'm covering up a murder."

"Serves you right."

"Did you imply you weren't going to hand us over to the police even if we had done it?"

"Shut up."

Bill's arms tightened. It felt…comforting, in fact. Perhaps there was something to physical affection, freely given, that loosened the muscles. "Are we all square, old girl?" he asked, voice muffled. "I'm fond of you, you know."

"Same." And that was enough sentiment. Pat stepped back, wiping her irritating eyes, saw Jimmy's rigid back, and said, "You're a bigger idiot than Bill, Jimmy Yoxall. Do try to use what brains you have."

Jimmy made a noise in his throat. Fen went up to him, putting a hand on his arm. "Don't worry. It really is all right."

"It isn't," Jimmy said violently. "If Pat of all people suspected I could have done this thing, what will the police think? What will everyone think? God knows my family has every reason to want him dead, and if nobody else could have done it, and I've made us look guilty with my idiotic efforts—and if the police find out—"

"Steady." Bill went over, taking him by the shoulders. "Come on. It's not that bad."

189

"Yes, it is," Jimmy said. "It's exactly that bad."

"*Was* Mr. Haworth blackmailing you?" Fen asked. "I don't want to pry, of course," she added as both men turned to look at her with identical expressions, "but you see, it makes quite a lot of difference. If he knew, he might have something written down, say, which we'd need to get rid of before the police arrive because there's no point confusing them with irrelevant facts, is there? And more to the point, if he wasn't blackmailing you, he was blackmailing someone else."

Jimmy gave an exasperated sigh, but Bill's expression sharpened. "That's the nub of it, isn't it? You're sure of what you heard, Pat?"

"Absolutely.

"And Haworth didn't speak to you about this, Jim?"

"I would have told you."

"You've omitted several salient facts in recent months," Bill said pointedly. "However. This is a bit odd, you know. Given the Earl was already paying through the nose, a male blackmail victim surely has to be Preston or Jack, each of whom has a lady swearing to his whereabouts. Unless it was one of the servants."

"Fen's maid thinks all their movements are accounted for," Pat said.

"But *everyone's* moves are accounted for."

"Not the Earl and Countess yet. Sorry, Jimmy."

Bill frowned. "The Earl and Countess, or at least one couple is lying. This really is what the police are for, you know, to pin down the fine detail and find the inconsistencies."

"Yes, but what if they can't?" Pat said. "We were all squirrelled away in pairs, actively avoiding one another, and the staff were busy. If nobody saw the murderer moving around, it will remain a case of 'our word against yours'. In which case they'll start looking at motives."

"Which is to say, at me or Anna," Jimmy said.

"Or Bill, because Jack is unlikely to keep quiet about that blunder of yours," Pat said.

"I'm sure we can rely on him to mention it," Jimmy snapped. "He was very ready to sacrifice my sister's reputation to remove himself from suspicion."

"It would be a bit late for him to start pretending their relationship was innocent," Bill said. "And he's absolutely right that she would be suspected, so there's no point getting on your high horse over it."

"Nevertheless," Pat said, before this could develop into an argument. "We need to work this out for ourselves before it gets down to motives, and interrogations about exactly how people passed the time. The blackmail candidates are Preston and Jack. I asked Preston if he was being blackmailed—"

"You *what?*"

"—and he said no. I believe him."

"You really cannot go around asking people if they're being blackmailed," Bill said. "For goodness' sake, Pat. And I doubt you can believe them when they say no. But assuming that's the case, it leaves Jack, and I really don't see how Haworth could blackmail him over an affair with his own wife."

"Well, no. It's hardly a secret," Fen said.

"That, and Jack wouldn't suffer any significant consequences from it becoming public knowledge. A blackmailer needs to hold consequences, immediate unavoidable ones, over his victim's head. The game only works if he has a trump card."

"Lady Anna would have suffered. Might Jack be keen to protect her name rather than his?" Pat offered.

Jimmy snorted. "Then he should have behaved differently for some time. But one couldn't blackmail Jack anyway, because he hasn't *got* anything. Fellow lives off the card table."

Bill frowned. "Whereas Preston is well off, and he went for Haworth's throat as if he loathed him."

Pat rolled her eyes. "Honestly, Bill. He and Victoria are engaged."

"Oh, well, that explains it. I don't really see Preston pulling off a cold-blooded murder in any case." He frowned. "Whereas Miss Singh seems extremely level-headed. Theoretically speaking, would Preston lie to cover for her?"

Jimmy shook his head. "Preston's a good man but he's no actor, and more to the point, it simply can't have been Victoria. I've known her all my life and she is one of the most decent, principled people I've ever met. I'd—oh Lord—I'd put Anna before her in the list, if I had to."

"Yes," Fen said. "Because Lady Anna does have the strongest motive by miles, Jimmy, except for your parents."

"My parents aren't murderers," Jimmy said, then recoiled slightly as the implication of his own words dawned on him. "That is— Look, Anna's had an awful time with Maurice and she hasn't behaved well herself, but…" He visibly searched for something to add to *but*, and didn't find anything. The word hung, empty, in the air.

"She sent her maid away at twenty past," Fen said. "Disregarding Jack's testimony for a moment, we heard footsteps coming past, from the East Wing towards the family's bedrooms, at about twenty to or quarter to. I didn't hear a door open and shut, and I think we would have done if it had been Victoria's room, which was just two doors up, but Lady Anna's is round the corner. And I am very sorry to say it, but it did strike me, when Jack gave their alibi, that he was telling Lady Anna what to say. *You were with me from half past eleven.*"

Jimmy put his face in his hands. Bill said, "Jim…" Pain throbbed in his voice.

"She would have had to come down here after eleven-thirty to get hold of the knife," Pat said. "Unless she took it early, but her maid was with her all morning, and Haworth and Jack were in here until almost half past. Then she would have gone back up the west stairs and round the back—"

"No, because we went up there at half past to your room," Fen said. "She couldn't have walked along the back corridor towards the

East Wing without us hearing, I don't think. She'd have had to come downstairs after half past eleven, collect the knife, and go through the main hall to the East Wing unseen."

"Either way, Jack is lying," Bill said. "He says he went straight up to her when Haworth left him. He's covering for her."

Jimmy made a noise in his throat. Bill shot a flicker of a glance at Pat, then moved over and put a hand on his shoulder.

"I've a question," Fen said. "How did she know where Haworth was? This is a huge house and it's an absolute nuisance to find anyone, but nobody has reported anyone knocking on doors and looking for people. Even if Jack told her that Haworth went to the East Wing, it has all sorts of rooms."

"The appointment Jack mentioned?" Bill said. "Assuming it exists."

"But that doesn't makes sense," Fen said. "He wouldn't make an appointment to meet his own wife. Unless he made it with Jack, who told Lady Anna. But Haworth was *already* with Jack—or so he says— so they'd surely have talked in the drawing room or gone to the East Wing together."

"You're right. It doesn't make sense," Bill said. "What's abundantly clear is that Jack has been less than honest, and I think we need another conversation with him. It seems to me he's holding all the cards here. He so often does."

It felt like having her ears boxed. The impact was sudden, stunning, filling her head with light and sound that blotted out every other consideration. Pat stared at nothing as the others kept talking. Bill said something she didn't hear, but it made Jimmy uncurl from his hunched misery. Fen replied, equally animated. Pat needed them all to be quiet.

"Because he went directly there!" Fen was saying as Pat surfaced. "It's the only thing that makes sense."

"You're right," Jimmy said. "You're exactly right. The only reason—"

"Everyone be quiet. Stop. Good God, shut *up*!" Pat yelped, throwing manners to the wind. "Bill! Do you have that key?"

"To the room? Yes. I thought I'd hang on to it."

"We need to go. Come on, come on, there's no time to sit around!"

"What on earth is it?" Fen demanded.

"Just a minute. Bill, come *on*."

Pat grabbed Bill's arm, dragging him to the door, which was locked. She fumbled with the key.

"Pat!" Fen almost shrieked. "What *is* it?"

"I think I know what's happened, but I have to check."

"But I think I know too!"

"Five minutes, compare notes." Pat shoved the door open, and she and Bill hurried to the East Wing together, Pat setting the pace.

"What on earth are we doing?" Bill asked as they went.

"Checking something I should have realised before."

"But what will looking at Haworth's corpse tell you?"

"Just get on," Pat said. "I don't want the police to turn up while we're mucking about in there."

They half-ran up the stairs. The first-floor corridor felt very cold. Bill unlocked the room in question, opened the door, and made a face. "You might want to reconsider this. Or let me look for whatever it is."

"Nonsense." Pat pushed past him and regretted it almost at once, since the atmosphere was much as one might expect with an unwashed day-old corpse at the table. She stopped breathing through her nose after the first inhalation, but she couldn't close her eyes.

Haworth lay over the desk, knife-handle still jutting obscenely. His hand on the desk was clawlike and livid, though the position of his arms suggested the rigor had passed. She was glad she couldn't see his face.

She approached, legs feeling oddly reluctant. He looked very dead, but still human in his slumped posture, like a thing that slept. If he stood now, if he leapt from the table and turned to her—

What self-indulgent silliness. It was only a body. She clenched her fists and peered over the dead man's shoulder.

"What are we looking at?" Bill asked adenoidally, since he was also breathing through his mouth.

Pat pointed at the playing cards scattered over the table. "Does that look like two packs' worth to you?"

Bill frowned. "Not unless he's lying on most of them. Why would you say— Good Lord!"

Pat nodded. Bill took a pencil from his pocket and used it to lift one card, then another, squinting underneath. "They've all got the same design on the back."

"One pack of cards, but two aces of hearts," Pat said. "I saw it yesterday, you know. The red aces looked like drops of blood on the table, and there were three of them, drip drip drip. I *saw* it but it didn't sink in, somehow, what with the corpse."

"You can be forgiven for that," Bill said. "A spare ace of hearts. An ace in the hole. That would be an opening for blackmail if ever there was one, when one's victim lives entirely by gambling."

"Does he?" Pat asked.

Bill made a face. "He's a clubman with no visible means of support except for that remarkable knack at cards. If Haworth exposed him as a cheat he'd be expelled from his clubs, which would put paid both to his career as a gamester, and to the invitations to house parties. He'd be ruined. I think Lady Anna will need to be more specific about the time he spent with her."

"Footsteps past my bedroom," Pat said. "If Jack took the knife from the wall, and followed Haworth after a few moments, if he killed him and then took the back corridor to Lady Anna's bedroom—that fits, doesn't it?"

Bill winced. "Was there a plan between them, or do you think he acted alone?"

"I'd guess the latter, or they would have had their alibis aligned in advance." Pat imagined what it might feel like to have a lover's tryst and afterwards discover that your lover had just murdered your husband. "This won't be pleasant for her."

"Not awfully, no."

"He took the dagger with him. He planned to do it when he left the drawing room." Pat could picture Jack making his way through the empty hall, moving softly up the stairs. "He came in here, keeping the appointment he pretended Haworth had with someone else. Saw Haworth sitting with his back to the door, building a house of cards with too many aces. Walked up, and—I suppose the man simply wasn't expecting it."

"I'm sure he wasn't. Jack's no Preston, to lose his temper."

"But he is a gambler," Pat said. "He took a chance, and there were a lot of red herrings to fish for. Maybe he thought it would be easy to cast blame on Victoria. Maybe he knows about the family troubles."

"I'm sure he does. Which makes me reflect that Jimmy and Lord Witton will find it a great deal easier to repair their family situation now Haworth's dead, so Lady Anna might make a very attractive widow for a man who isn't a high stickler. Come to that, she'd be the future Countess in her own right if Jimmy swung for the murder, and I'd rather not believe his calculation went that far. My God, old girl, you've cracked it."

"Thank Fen," Pat said. "It was her idea to look into this while I was sitting around panicking about you. Which— Could we have a quick word? Not in here, though. The, uh, the next room?"

Bill flushed, evidently recalling as vividly as Pat what had transpired in the next room, but didn't argue, which was welcome because the presence of the corpse was becoming overwhelming. He locked the door again and led the way to the study.

"Don't bother locking the door," he said drily as they stepped inside. "It's broken. As you discovered."

"Quite. Look, I just wanted a word about—well, personal affairs. Not to pry, but I feel I ought to understand in case I put my foot in it. And also, there's something else."

"I can't imagine what else there could be," Bill muttered. "As for understanding... The fact is, not everyone is cut out for marriage. Some people, ah, *incline* to members of their own sex, and—"

"Like Oscar Wilde," Pat said. "Or Mr. Grisham in the village with his old Navy colleague. I understand that perfectly well."

Bill gaped. "Who the devil told you about Oscar Wilde?"

"Daddy, of course. I asked him. I was reading the papers to him around that time because his eyesight had failed, and I wanted to know what all the veiled allusions were about. What I meant was—well, for pity's sake, Bill, Jimmy got engaged to Fen!"

"We can't all be Mr. Grisham, and retire quietly with nobody asking awkward questions. Jimmy's going to be the next earl; of course he'll marry at some point. One has...diversions, before marriage. That's the way of things."

"Rubbish. Don't tell me you're a casual diversion sort of chap when you've been looking like a chewed piece of string since we got here. Before that, in fact, because you looked dreadful at Jonty's wedding. Is that why you were so unkind about Fen? And angry that he took her to the theatre?"

Bill winced. "Don't. We'd been that same week, Jimmy and I, and it stung. He didn't warn me, and when I found out..." He made a face. "I don't suppose I had any great right to make a fuss. But I did, because it hurt dreadfully."

"Oh, Bill."

"I didn't want to come here at all after that, but it was all arranged, and the office insisted and I couldn't find a good excuse to get out of it. I told myself I could at least tie things up properly, only then I arrived and learned Miss Carruth would be here too, and that made everything worse to a degree I can't tell you. I thought I might go mad watching Jim dance attendance on that—"

"Hoi!"

"I don't mean to be rude to Miss Carruth," Bill said hastily. "None of this situation was her fault, and she's behaved with great good sense, but I wasn't in a frame of mind to appreciate her qualities. And then they ended the engagement, you see, and you told me what Jimmy had said."

"That he was in love with someone else and hadn't realised it."

"Mmm." Bill seemed to be concentrating on the picture above the mantelpiece. His cheeks were red. "And—well, anyway, we've been trying to settle our differences."

Pat suspected that covered a great deal of desire, desperation, love, and pain, none of which she wanted to hear about from her brother. "It seems to me that Jimmy has behaved extremely badly."

"You don't need to tell me," Bill said, with feeling. "He'd worked himself into a rotten state. He does that, you know, for all everyone thinks he's a country squire type without a thought in his head. And in fairness, he was faced with an appalling situation."

"Which he made appalling for you and Fen."

Bill gave a sudden, rueful grin. "He's an oaf. Never thinks before he acts, as with that stupid lie earlier today. He's terrified of being caught for—you know."

"That's fair enough, surely?"

"It's how things are, and one has to cope. And there's no sense living in dread of two years for gross indecency if it means one talks oneself into being the prime suspect for murder."

"There, I agree," Pat said. "Although to be fair, I'm not sure how sensible I'd have been in his shoes."

"Oh, you'd have been perfectly sensible. You aren't at the mercy of the sex feeling, with emotions flying all over the place. It must be marvellous."

"Just a moment," Pat said. "The fact that I don't make a God-awful fuss about everything doesn't mean I don't have a private life. I simply conduct it with a bit more dignity than some people I could mention."

Bill's brows rose sharply. As well they might, she supposed, because she had never mentioned personal affairs to him before, any more than he had to her. She'd wept about Louisa in secret, just as he'd been alone in his misery over Jimmy. She wanted to share her hope and happiness with him now.

She cleared her throat. "Which is to say, you aren't the only person in this house who's getting on well with someone."

"But...did you not say Preston's engaged to Miss Singh?"

"He is. I'm sure they'll be very happy."

"Then..." Bill's lips moved silently. "Ah. I have noticed you've become very thick with Miss Carruth."

"I have, yes." Pat tried to sound as nonchalant as she could. She wasn't sure she'd pulled it off.

Bill stood unmoving for a moment. Then he said, slowly, "So we—brother and sister—came here to visit an engaged couple, and now—"

Pat felt the blood rush to her cheeks. "Must you put it like that?"

"Oh dear God. Dear God almighty. Who the blazes cast a pair of Mertons in a French novel?"

Pat choked. Bill started to laugh as well, doubling over until he had to hold on to the couch for support. "Great Scott. Have you ever known anything so absurd?"

"It's ridiculous, isn't it?" She wiped her eyes. "I really don't know what's in the air at Rodington Court."

"I wonder myself. We'd better get out before anything else happens." Bill hesitated, then came over and gave her a swift hug. It felt slightly easier than the previous one, as though they could get used to this. "Are you happy, old girl?"

"Awfully."

"Good. I hope it goes splendidly. I'd be very pleased to know someone appreciates you as you deserve."

"Same to you." Pat had a sudden, alarming feeling she might cry. She loved her brothers in principle, and was fond of Bill in practice, but this sudden intimacy and connection was something else. New and precious, to be quietly cherished rather than discussed. "Do you know what you—you and Jimmy—are going to do?"

"I honestly don't. We'll have to see how it shakes out, I suppose." He saw her frown and returned a shrug. "With Haworth gone I should be able to unpick the Earl's mess, which will remove a lot of the financial pressure on Jimmy, and a great deal of the nervous tension. As long as he isn't arrested for murder."

Pat stepped back. "Yes. That. We should probably go and deal with it, shouldn't we?"

"I dare say." Bill interlaced his fingers and stretched them. "What do you think, old girl, as a hunter? Corner the blighter now, or keep quiet and drop a word in the police's ear when they arrive?"

Pat considered. "The latter, if we can pull it off. He's clever and rather quick—he hasn't missed an opportunity to tell Lady Anna she's in trouble if she doesn't support his alibi. Would you say he's dangerous?"

"He's a killer, but from behind. That might be cowardly, or it might be cold-blooded. I think we have to assume the latter."

"Then let's keep it to ourselves. Don't give him a chance to prepare a reaction."

Bill nodded. "Sounds good. And means I'm inclined not to tell Jimmy our deduction, he being an oaf, as discussed."

"But I will tell Fen," Pat said, detecting a hint. "She isn't the featherbrain you think."

"My respect for her good sense has increased dramatically, believe me," Bill said. "Shall we go?"

Pat nodded. "You go now and tree the blighter. I'll meet you downstairs."

CHAPTER FIFTEEN

Pat hurried to her room. She had a faint hope Fen might be there waiting for her, based on nothing but wanting it to be true, and was nevertheless a tiny bit disappointed that it wasn't. She would doubtless be downstairs, with Jimmy, probably rather irritated. Pat got her things together, guiltily aware that she hadn't listened earlier. She ought to have stopped and explained her flash of realisation, but she'd been so desperate to know if she was right, if the memory of those three single drops of blood, the tell-tale heart, had been correct. It was the kind of focus she had on the hunt, brushing away all other concerns and distractions. It now, far too late, occurred to her she'd been rude.

She never had to explain herself at Skirmidge House; she did what needed doing and took sole responsibility for her domain. Collaboration was a novelty, and for all the growing joy and hope of—well, of *something* with Fen, she had forgotten about working together the moment it proved inconvenient. She would have to apologise for that, hope Fen understood, and make sure she didn't do it again, because it simply wasn't on. Pat made a firm mental note to herself on the subject of letting other people have a say, and set off down the corridor to the West Wing stairs.

She was half way down when she heard the whistle, a sharp two-note sound.

She knew those notes. It was Bill's whistle, the one the Merton boys had used to summon each other when they'd roamed Stoke St.

Milborough as a pack, and Pat ran without hesitation, clutching her skirts, trying to follow the sound. It had been faint with distance, but it had come from *this* direction—

She swung round a corner and heard voices from the library.

It was a large room, well lit with a good-sized window, and everyone was there. Jimmy and Bill stood together, visibly tense. Preston and Victoria were by the window. Her brows were drawn together; he had a keen look that she'd seen him wear on the shoot. Lady Anna stood against a bookshelf, very pale, eyes darting. Fen sat in a chair in the middle of the room, very stiff and straight. And Jack Bouvier-Lynes was behind her with one hand on her shoulder, the other resting casually in his pocket.

"What's going on? What are you doing, Jack?" Pat's voice sounded odd, almost echoey, in her own ears.

"As I told the others." Jack's smile was a show of teeth; his eyes flickered between her and the men. "I was just having a little chat with Miss Carruth about how very unkind gossip and slander can be."

"Just get away from her," Jimmy said. "Let's talk about this sensibly."

"I know what your *sensible talk* means," Jack said. "It means brushing everything that doesn't suit you under the carpet. Finding a scapegoat. Well, I don't choose to be brushed away, or made a scapegoat because my family doesn't go back to the Domesday Book. The Wittons always wanted Maurice gone because he wasn't the right sort. Not good enough, not up to snuff, not *one of us*. Then Jimmy decided to blame him for the Earl's handing of Threppel and Swing, and now he can't defend himself any more, can he? And they're all closing ranks against me the same way. You can see them doing it, can't you, Anna? Coming up with a tissue of lies to shift the blame and avoid awkward questions. You see I have to defend myself against that, don't you?"

Pat felt a stab of uncertainty. She knew very well that she wasn't fond of Jack as she was the others. Had she let that cloud her judgement?

"That's awfully good." Bill didn't sound beset by doubt in the slightest. "Very effective. But you lied about being with Lady Anna. You weren't with her at half past eleven; you arrived significantly later, and she knows it. And if she sticks to your story she'll be an accessory after the fact. Making her your accomplice is hardly the act of a gentleman."

"I did not lie," Jack said. "I always told you I didn't look at the time; why should I? *You* lied, and we all heard you. Where was Jimmy when Maurice was killed? Why did you lie about that? Because he did, Anna. He lied about where your brother was when your husband was murdered. I want to know why."

Lady Anna had one shaking hand pressed to her mouth. Pat looked from her to Fen, desperate, and their eyes met. Fen's face was oddly set. She stared into Pat's eyes, then she very deliberately, even jerkily, changed the direction of her gaze up to point, as best she could, at Jack.

It was a shout of warning, and Pat let out a long, slow breath. "I have a question too, Jack," she said. "It's about Maurice Haworth blackmailing you."

Jack's mouth opened, and his fingers tightened on Fen's shoulder. She gave a little gasp.

"I overheard him threatening to expose you," Pat went on. "It's as simple as that. Of course you could assert I'm part of this conspiracy against you but the thing is, when he was murdered, he was sitting at a desk with a pack of playing cards that included two aces of hearts. He'd caught you out, and you killed him for it. Didn't you?"

Fen's brows were almost at her hairline. Pat caught her eye, though she couldn't manage a smile. Jack was too close to Fen; she was sitting too rigidly.

"More nonsense," Jack said. "They're lying, Anna. They've picked me as the sacrificial lamb. Merton probably put the extra ace there himself to throw suspicion on me—he's already lied for Jimmy and you heard him threaten you with that talk of being an accessory. I shan't let them blame you or me, don't worry. I won't stand for it."

"But there were cards all over the table when he was found," Preston said. "And if he was blackmailing anyone over card play, it was you. Of course it blasted was: you've taken enough of my money in the last few days. Two aces? You miserable swine."

"That's not his most serious fault," Victoria observed, her voice very nearly under control. "Why did you use my father's kirpan, Jack? Was that directed at me?"

"I did not touch that knife. If someone wanted to cast guilt on you—I don't know why they'd do that. It wasn't me."

"It'll be easy enough to find out," Bill said. "Scotland Yard has a Fingerprint Bureau now, did you know that? Remarkable business. Everyone's fingerprint is different, you see, and we leave them on whatever we touch. They've just convicted a murderer that way in Argentina. All the police have to do is check the hilt of the knife and compare the fingerprints left there to all of ours, and they'll have the answer, with no room for debate. Unless you used gloves, Jack?"

Jack's expression suggested he had not used gloves. "You're lying," he managed. "This is nonsense. Anyone could have touched the hilt. I could have, when I saw him—in fact, I'm sure I did."

"You did not. I found Haworth's body," Bill said. "I was in there continuously until I locked the room, and I have had the key on me since. I will swear on oath that not one single person touched the knife after the body was found. You didn't go near him."

"And what's your word worth when you already lied for Jimmy?" Jack flashed.

"More than yours, old man. I work in Whitehall for a bureau that doesn't recruit idly, and I'm here on business. If your fingerprints are on that knife, you'll have some explaining to do. If they aren't, needless to say, you'll be fine. Will you be fine?"

Jack's mouth worked. He didn't reply, and the silence damned him.

"Oh God," Lady Anna said, high and shrill. "You killed him. You killed him and you came to me— Oh Christ!"

"I suppose we can't give him a thrashing before the police arrive," Jimmy said through his teeth.

"You will not do a damn thing," Jack said, and withdrew his hand from his pocket, flicking out the blade of the straight razor he held. Victoria cried out. Fen took a shuddering intake of breath.

"Put it down," Bill said. "You'll only make things worse for yourself."

"I don't think so," Jack said. "Now, Jimmy will order the motor-car warmed up while Merton goes and fetches me that knife. Miss Carruth and I are going take a trip out together, and none of you will stand in my way."

He lifted the razor as he spoke, letting the blade flash in the sunlight. Fen's eyes widened. And Pat took her hand from the deep pocket of her plain, practical dress, and with it the pearl-handled Harrington top-break revolver she'd carried there.

"Oh, Pat," Fen said. "You are wonderful."

Jack gaped. Pat extended her arm, levelling the gun at him. "Step away from her. If you think I'll hesitate about pulling the trigger, you're wrong."

"She could put a bullet through your eye at twenty times the distance," Bill observed. "All-England Ladies' Champion. I'd advise you to take her very seriously indeed."

"*Move*," Pat said with all the force at her disposal, and Jack let go of Fen's shoulder and stepped back. "To the side."

She meant to get him away so Fen could stand without blocking her sightline. That was all she was focused on: Fen, safe. She didn't expect him to leap sideways, pushing Lady Anna in front of him, and disappear through the room's side door.

"Damn it!" Jimmy took off after him at a run, Preston at his heels. Bill sprinted out through the door they'd entered by, presumably in case the man doubled back. Pat was glad to see London hadn't entirely dulled his instincts.

She lowered her gun, exhaling. Fen rose, came over to her, waited like a sensible young lady for Pat to place the revolver on a table, and only then collapsed into her arms, her head against Pat's bosom, gripping her waist with shaking hands.

"Fen," Pat said. "Oh heavens, Fen. Are you all right?"

"Mph." Fen took a moment of shaky breathing, then looked up with that determined tilt of the chin. "Yes, I am. He didn't hurt me, not really, but it wasn't at all enjoyable. Jimmy and I had realised it must have been him, and I think he must have heard us talking, because when Jimmy went to find Victoria he came down all smiling and told me to come for a chat, and then I saw he had the razor. He dragged me in here and more or less threw me on that chair and was very threatening—asking who had I been talking to, why I was asking questions and so on. He isn't nearly as pleasant as he seemed."

"No," Pat said. "No, he isn't, is he?"

Across the room Lady Anna was sobbing in Victoria's arms. Pat cast her a questioning look and received a tip of the head that did for a shrug. They were family; Victoria could handle this. And the men could handle Jack, and she had Fen safe, and she had just held a murderer at gunpoint.

"Goodness," she said. "Shall we order tea?"

The police arrived two hours later, a sergeant and two wide-eyed constables, just as the sun came out.

Jimmy as family representative and Bill as intellectually competent adult took them off to explain the situation, which was, in effect, that they had a corpse upstairs and a murderer locked in the cellar. Lady Anna had been put to bed, white-faced and near-catatonic, where her mother sat with her; Preston and Victoria had disappeared once more. So Pat and Fen drank tea until they were awash and kicked their heels with varying degrees of ladylike restraint until the police departed with the battered-looking Jack, and Jimmy and Bill returned.

"In heaven's name let's go outside," Pat said, not mincing words. "I want to hear what's going on without ghosts looking over my shoulder."

Jimmy led them all around a winding path to the summerhouse with the view, where Pat and Fen had sat what felt like years ago. The air was sparkling clean, the sun breaking through the remaining clouds and tinting the purple-greys a vivid pink. The roof had leaked so the seats were all wet and they had to stand, which was no hardship; Pat never wanted to sit down again.

"Well," Bill said. "The main thing is, Jack's been taken off."

"Was he sticking to his line that we'd all made him the scapegoat?"

"That was jolly good, wasn't it?" Bill said, with what sounded like professional respect. Pat made a mental note to ask a few more probing questions about what his job actually was. "Ingenious, and might well have worked under other circumstances. But the fingerprint business knocked the stuffing out of him, figuratively speaking, and then Jimmy did the same in a more literal way, and he spilled the beans when the sergeant picked him out of the cellar."

"He confessed?"

"His line is now that he had to do it because Haworth had learned about his adultery with Lady Anna and was threatening to kill her and their son. Nobly protecting the woman he loves."

"There will be the most dreadful scandal if he argues that in court," Jimmy said. "Anna won't be able to show her face in Society for years."

"That might not be a bad thing, you know," Fen said. "There are doctors who might be able to help her, rest cures and so on."

"I know. Now the swine is dead, she might even agree to see one."

"I don't suppose he's telling the truth?" Pat asked. "I'd feel dreadful if we were wrong about the gambling and he *was* acting on Lady Anna's behalf."

"You needn't worry," Bill said. "There was a letter in Haworth's pocket, one he'd drafted for Jack to sign admitting he was a cheat. Evidently he hadn't turned the screws that far when he was killed. If we'd searched the body, we'd have known who did it immediately."

"Really?" Fen said. "How utterly exasperating."

"That'll teach us to do the right thing," Pat said. "Talking of knowing things immediately, Bill Merton, why on earth did you not say about the fingerprints before? There we were, fretting and puzzling and running around to find the killer—"

"Because I was talking rubbish," Bill said. "The hilt is intricately worked steel and you need a smooth surface to take a fingerprint. I was hoping Jack didn't know that."

"In that case, well played."

"So what now?" Fen asked. "That is, of course Jack will stand trial, but will the rest of us have to answer questions?"

"Probably, but they won't be difficult ones. They have a murderer and a confession. Where anybody else was or what we were doing is neither here nor there."

Fen beamed. "That's a relief. And what about your father, Jimmy? The Threppel and Swing business?"

"The Earl has agreed to cooperate fully with me," Bill said. "Now he's not obliged to protect Haworth, and considering the scandal couldn't really be any worse, the whole thing should become a great deal easier to unpick. I'm going to stick around a while longer and get things sorted out."

"I'm blasted grateful," Jimmy said. "For that, and to all of you. Fen, you've been a brick about everything, and I'm awfully sorry to have played the fool. Pat, you really are the best pal a chap could have. If you hadn't dug into this business instead of waiting for the police, Jack might have got away with it."

"For pity's sake, Jimmy, it was Fen's idea! Not mine. She came up with the idea and led it, and did every bit as much as me." Pat realised she'd raised her voice, and modulated it slightly. "Do stop underestimating her, for goodness' sake. You've done quite enough of that."

"It's really all right," Fen assured her, although her cheeks were pink with pleasure. "Anyway we shouldn't have got anywhere without you being so frightfully clever about noticing the cards, not to mention holding Jack up like a bank robber. It was marvellous."

"Yes, it was," Jimmy said. "Aged me about ten years. Very well: you're both wonderful and I don't deserve either of you, let alone Bill."

"Never mind, old man." Bill was looking out across the vista of the rain-cleansed moors, yellow and green and gently steaming, but Pat could see the smile twitching at his lips. "That's all right."

"I hope it is," Pat said, which was as close as she could reasonably come to *You had better love my brother and cherish him, James Yoxall, or the next person I hold at gunpoint will be you.* "What about that poor boy, your nephew?"

"Well, Maurice is dead, so things are already looking up, and Ma has sent for him. We'll have to see what Anna wants to do, of course, but Ma and Pa would love to have the little chap make his home here. He ought to get to know his people, and it's a good place for a boy to grow up."

"It is," Bill agreed. "Now the worm's been got out of the apple, or the snake out of Eden, or whatever it is. Not that one should feel glad about a murder."

"Perhaps not, but there's no point being sentimental." Pat gave him a nod.

"Oh, I don't know, old thing. I think a spot of sentiment has its place, now and again. Do I understand you two are off to Miss Carruth's house?"

"As soon as we're allowed to leave, yes. The Sergeant asked us to stay tomorrow in case the Detective Inspector they've called in has any questions. The day after, perhaps."

"That's all right," Bill said. "I don't suppose we can take guns out tomorrow, as a matter of respect, but we can certainly go for a decent walk. I'd like a chance to get better acquainted with Miss Carruth in less dramatic conditions."

"Fen, please," said that young lady, dimpling. "That would be lovely."

"And I'm Bill. Excellent. All right, Jim, shall we leave the ladies to their fresh air?"

The two strolled off together. Pat thought she could detect a looseness to Jimmy's shoulders that hadn't been there in the early part of their visit. "It is a jolly good thing," she said aloud.

"Being rid of Haworth?" Fen asked. "Yes, it is. I'm sorry to say it, but he can't complain if people don't miss him. Well, obviously he can't in the circumstances, but you know what I mean. It's all rather lowering from a human nature point of view, isn't it? Haworth himself, of course, but also Jack trying to blame Victoria and incriminate Jimmy and involve Lady Anna. The Earl and Jimmy getting into worse and worse tangles instead of facing up to things. Lady Anna, because *really*."

"Preston and Victoria are a very nice pair."

"Yes, they are," Fen said. "And they were right to step away as much as possible from all the unpleasantness, because it was not in their power to mend it. And then there was you, Pat Merton, teaching a silly, unhappy girl how to shoot and standing up for me in the face of that vile man, and setting out to solve a murder because you were worried about your brother—"

"It was your idea."

"Yes, and you made sure to tell Jimmy so," Fen said. "Don't think I didn't notice that. And as for bringing a gun, like Annie Oakley coming to my rescue—goodness. Would you have shot him?"

"Of course. I shouldn't have killed him unless it had been necessary, but I'd have happily shot him."

Fen wriggled. "You have no idea how extraordinary that is. Not that I want you to shoot anybody for me, but it's something to know you *would*. I shall definitely learn to use a gun. For all we know, I might have to return the favour one day."

"How many country-house murders do you think we're likely to encounter?"

"It's as well to be prepared," Fen said. "When is your birthday?"

"October. Why?"

"Because I'm going to buy you earrings. If you're going to take me seriously, the least I can do is treat you fluffily in return. You deserve a bit of fluffiness."

"You are an entire armful of fluffiness," Pat said, placing her own arms as demonstration. "And I don't know about deserving you but I'd certainly like a chance to try. I didn't ever imagine I'd meet anybody special; I didn't think I was the kind of person who had that kind of thing. Maybe you're special enough for two."

"You know my views on this," Fen said. "We'll go to King's Norton." She rested her head lightly on Pat's shoulder, hair and breath sending a light tickle of pleasure over her chest. "We both need to relax, after all this. You can give some thought to what you want to do with your life, and I can think about what *I* want to do, and we can do all sorts of wonderful nothing together, and perhaps we might even come to some decisions eventually, between us. Mightn't we, darling?"

Pat looked out over the view, the fresh new world opening up in front of her, as bright with promise and possibility and as bursting with life as the glorious woman in her arms. "Yes. I dare say we might."

ACKNOWLEDGEMENTS

With huge thanks to Paul for gun-reading, and Alicia for putting up with it.

Deep gratitude to my invaluable early readers Moog Florin, May Peterson, and Talia Hibbert, without whom...

Thank you to Veronica Vega for editing, and Lennan Adams at Lexiconic Design for the glorious cover, as inspired by the *Think of England* cover by Erin Dameron-Hill.

A big shout out to the KJ Charles Chat group for their support, particularly to the tag team of Zee and Bren who came up with the title!

For more Edwardian country-house plottery, and to see how Pat and Fen got on...

THINK OF ENGLAND

England, 1904. Two years ago, Captain Archie Curtis lost his friends, fingers, and future to a terrible military accident. Alone, purposeless and angry, Curtis is determined to discover if he and his comrades were the victims of fate, or of sabotage.

Curtis's search takes him to an isolated, ultra-modern country house, where he meets and instantly clashes with fellow guest Daniel da Silva. Effete, decadent, foreign, and all-too-obviously queer, the sophisticated poet is everything the straightforward British officer fears and distrusts.

As events unfold, Curtis realizes that Daniel has his own secret intentions. And there's something else they share—a mounting sexual tension that leaves Curtis reeling.

As the house party's elegant facade cracks to reveal treachery, blackmail and murder, Curtis finds himself needing clever, dark-eyed Daniel as he has never needed a man before...

"Downton Abbey meets M/M romance ~ an absolutely brilliant historical novel with industrial espionage, murder, blackmail and two unlikely heroes up against the odds. What more could I wish for?"— *Sinfully Sexy Book Reviews*

And some late Victorian shenanigans here...

ANY OLD DIAMONDS

Lord Alexander Pyne-ffoulkes is the younger son of the Duke of Ilvar, with a bitter grudge against his wealthy father. The Duke intends to give his Duchess a priceless diamond parure on their wedding anniversary—so Alec hires a pair of jewel thieves to steal it.

The Duke's remote castle is a difficult target, and Alec needs a way to get the thieves in. Soldier-turned-criminal Jerry Crozier has the answer: he'll pose as a Society gentleman and become Alec's new best friend.

But Jerry is a dangerous man: controlling, remote, and devastating. He effortlessly teases out the lonely young nobleman's most secret desires, and soon he's got Alec in his bed—and the palm of his hand.

Or maybe not. Because as the plot thickens, betrayals, secrets, new loves, and old evils come to light. Now the jewel thief and the aristocrat must keep up the pretence, find their way through a maze of privilege and deceit, and confront the truth of what's between them...all without getting caught.

"The sparkly heist qualities of this book hide some sharp, painful edges, and Charles' brutally gorgeous prose offers up gem after gem after gem to make the reader laugh and gasp and weep and swoon."—Seattle Review of Books

"Superbly written, evocative, intellectually stimulating, risky in the way it presents two flawed main characters, and, last but not least, sexy as all heck."—Smart Bitches, Trashy Books

ABOUT THE AUTHOR

KJ Charles is a writer and freelance editor. She lives in London with her husband, two kids, an out-of-control garden, and a cat with murder management issues.

KJ writes mostly historical romance, mostly queer, sometimes with fantasy or horror in there. She is represented by Courtney Miller-Callihan at Handspun Literary.

For all the KJC news and occasional freebies, visit kjcharleswriter.com/newsletter.

Find me on Twitter @kj_charles

CPSIA information can be obtained
at www.ICGtesting.com
Printed in the USA
BVHW031828240223
659186BV00002B/105